Angel of Adversity

by

Judy MacPherson

ISBN: 1-4140-7474-3 (e-book)
ISBN: 1-4140-7473-5 (Paperback)

Printed in the United States of America
Bloomington, IN

This book is printed on acid free paper.

1st Books - rev. 02/16/04

In celebration of my cherished friend's life,

Rebecca Stone-Purcer

Who even in death…believes in my ambition to put my thoughts to paper.

With love & admiration for my husband

Gerald

Who has encouraged and assisted in all of my lifelong dreams.

To honor my treasured friends,
Who have inspired my endeavors and guided my footsteps
through my own personal adversities & challenges,

Suzie Pontarini
Caroline DeRoost-Duffy
Karen Loney
Bonnie Handley
Kathy Stamp
Susan Ruhe

My gratitude is eternal!

To My Beloved Reader,

At times, life seems to deal us far more challenge than we think we are ever capable of managing. At times it may seem easier just to give up! Though the adversities we face during our lifetime seem to make us falter, what they actually do…is make us stronger!

Live each day as if it was your last,
Take risks,
Expand your horizons
&
Experience the endless opportunities we have available to us.

**Believe in yourself,
Follow your dreams
&
Make your life extraordinary!**

Chapter One

On that damp, lonely Friday afternoon, Claire stood silently pressing her tear-drenched face against the massive stained glass opening. She felt a sensation of coolness on her cheek as the torrential rain pounded down upon the foggy glass. The elegant parlor in which she stood had been gracefully darkened by the magnificent red floor-length velvet drapes that hung with dignity throughout the long narrow room. The antique furnishings that surrounded her whispered of the haunting grief and sadness they had witnessed time and time again over the past century within the thick brick laden walls. The silence of the room was deafening.

The wallowing depth of despair that Claire held within her heavy heart was nothing she had ever known before. Throughout the ongoing struggles of her young life she had never acknowledged such pain. Enduring one adversity upon another, she had climbed each agonizing mountain of challenge and each time she had survived. But standing alone that dreary afternoon, staring misty eyed through her bleak veil of sorrow, Claire knew that this time she had been given a monumental chore filled with more anguish than she was ever capable of managing.

Closing her red swollen eyes, she lost herself searching through the memories of her past life… her life of fear and torment.

"Thirty-two years of running… always running," she confessed weakly as fearsome visions of her husband and father flashed repeatedly through her mind's eye. "Why did they hate me so?" Claire spoke into the stillness of the room. "I tried so hard to please them. I lived to please them! But somehow I knew I never would," she assumed in defeat, feeling her tightly sealed eyes sting with pain. "And now… once again…I am lonely…I am so very lonely. And once again…I am on my own!"

Claire was a stunningly beautiful woman with penetrating green eyes and a cascade of straight cocoa brown hair flowing around her shoulders and down her spine. Her tall lean frame naturally projected the confident elegance of her nearly two decades of intense ballet training. Leaning gracefully against the soggy windowpane, she stared dazedly out through the cold misty glass. The study of dance had been her saving grace as a child in which she had willingly engulfed herself into hours of training each day of her adolescence. As a child reared in a dysfunctional abusive household, Claire sought comfort, losing herself in the symphonic music that she rehearsed tirelessly to hour after hour, year upon year.

The ballet was also a gift of love that she had shared with her beautiful daughter Amelia. Together they'd arabesque, stretching their long graceful limbs outward, dancing with the shadows cast upon the walls in the living room of their luxurious rented condo. Amelia projected the natural presence of grace and beauty as her mother did, showing unmistakable promise in the art of dance.

"My little ballerina," she whispered with a weak grin as she envisioned her young child wearing pink tights and a tutu. "You were so beautiful," she added sadly, bathing her mind in the loving memory of her daughter.

Claire ran her long willowy fingers down through the fog of the chilled glass as if trying to reach out and seize the cherished image of the past.

"Mommy… mommy! Watch me!" she recalled Amelia's young voice squealing with excitement, commanding her mother's attention as she danced and swirled across the living room floor. Claire vanished into the earthly vision of her daughter, recalling how Amelia's arms gracefully arched with technical perfection upward above her head of blond curls. With her tiny feet enveloped in soft pink ballet slippers, the delighted child would repeatedly pirouette about the room as a broad, beaming smile stretched across her angel wing lips. To Claire, the memory was an absolute treasure.

With a raucous crack of thunder from just beyond the stained glass, Claire was rawly torn from her collective works of precious memories and abruptly brought back to the painful reality of the present. Startled by the storming command from the heavens, she heaved a despairing sigh from her lungs and returned her defeated eyes to stare sorrowfully at the long still frame of her gorgeous ten year old daughter lying at rest in the polished white coffin next to her.

Claire's stunning young child lay motionless in her white satin dress after silently slipping into the valley of death. Her soft, unmarked, peach skin was delicately framed by rolling waves of long golden hair of silk. Her beautiful ballet legs were hidden beneath white lace tights. A delicate bouquet of cream-colored roses wrapped in baby's breath was clenched tightly within her still graceful fingers. Claire's loving child had gracefully departed this life.

It was the day the anguished woman would bury her cherished daughter Amelia. Standing before her sleeping babe, she rested her warm cheek against Amelia's smooth silent lips as if to answer her child's calling. Clutching the soft pink satin that delicately lined the interior of the coffin, Claire pleaded to the silence of the room. Her tears of anguish flowed in torrential waves down her cheeks and onto the silence of her daughter. Emotionally distraught, she felt her heart being torn from her chest.

Alone, the distressed mother would bury her only child. No family members stood by her. No friends knew to attend. No flowers, letters or cards of condolences had been sent. Only a single flowing cascade of pink roses could be seen in the room positioned at the foot of the coffin above her daughter's enclosed black shoes.

At the darkest time in her life, Claire had absolutely no one to hold her. She had not told a soul that her child had passed away as she had been living the life of a fugitive with her daughter for over six years. Together they had fled from city to city in protection of Amelia…her child that she loved more than life itself. She lived in hiding so she would not lose her daughter and yet she lost her anyway.

With trembling fingers Claire lovingly swept a long wave of blond hair back behind Amelia's ear as the distraught mother bent down to kiss her child good-bye.

"Farewell my darling," she spoke tearfully. "Until we meet again, I love you."

Claire slowly backed away from the stillness of her child as the lid to the white coffin was closed gently before her. She stared dazedly as two distinguished gray haired gentlemen prepared the coffin for its final journey. She then knew that she had seen Amelia's beautiful face for the last time.

Alone, Claire hesitantly stepped into the rear seat of the awaiting black Cadillac that would follow her young angel's body to the cemetery. The city blocks blurred past her searching tear soaked eyes as she found herself drowning in a sea of self-pity and loneliness.

Gracefully the car came to a halt, the door slowly opened and a supportive hand reached inside. Claire had chosen a lovely resting ground for Amelia under a magnificent oak tree freshly blooming with a fragrant spring showing of life. Surrounding the coffin was a lush carpet of vibrant green grass. God's promised gift of nature's annual rebirth surrounded her as the vicious storm clouds began to depart the sky.

After collecting his thoughts in prayer, the minister opened his eyes and began to speak to the grieving woman struggling to stand before him. He preached of God. He gave homily to the innocence of children and then finally he spoke of Amelia's wonderful contribution to this life. Fraught with grief, Claire wrestled to remain on her feet. She felt the fragrant wet grass crush beneath her shoes as the sun began to peek out from behind the passing dark clouds. Thin beams of sunlight then embraced her shoulders as though Amelia was reaching down from her new home in the heavens and giving her grief stricken mother a loving embrace.

Closing his bible, the minister raised his wise old eyes to meet with Claire's. He extended a sympathetic hand toward her.

"God will be with you my child," he reassured. "Hold fast to your faith Claire and live on. Amelia is now with God. She is well and whole once again."

"Thank you," she replied humbly through her tears. "Thank you for everything."

The minister nodded graciously in return. He paused for a private moment of spiritual reflection then turned and ambled leisurely back toward his awaiting vehicle. Claire reached out and ran her trembling fingers along Amelia's coffin searching for the touch of her child's flesh.

"Be good now Amelia. I'll love you always," she whispered to her child's lurking spirit.

Then reaching forward a second time, she placed a single long stem red rose upon the breast of the coffin.

"I love you my darling," she sighed in defeat. "I love you."

With what remaining strength she had, Claire turned to leave her child's side. With tears streaming down her vanquished face she trudged toward the patiently waiting funeral director, Ken McDonald. She bid her sincere thanks to Ken and his staff then advised him that she preferred to walk back to the funeral home to pick up her car. As his benevolent eyes searched her blank stare, the sympathetic gray haired gentleman paused then reached to press his hands firmly against her shoulders as if telepathically encouraging her to live on. Claire responded to Ken's heartfelt compassion by forcing out a feeble nod of acceptance. He returned her silent stare and released her shoulders.

"Take care of yourself Claire," he bid her farewell. "Remember…come and see me in my office at anytime. My prayers will be with you."

Claire watched as Ken returned to the awaiting vehicle and then drove from the cemetery casting her a supportive wave from the side window of the car. The two elegant stately vehicles paraded their way back through the cemetery gates. After pausing for oncoming traffic, they turned onto the busy street and disappeared from her view.

4

The storm clouds had completely departed the sky as full beams of sunlight shone down upon her. Standing in the stillness of the cemetery, Claire gazed up into the heavens as if her attention was deliberately being drawn aloft. In astonishment she stared at a magnificent rainbow that had strewn itself high above her in the clear blue sky. Radiant tints intertwined as the extensive band of color danced over the cemetery. Gazing at the breathtaking array of tones, Claire smiled to herself knowing that it was a spiritual gift from above sent expressly for her.

With an inconsolable sigh, Claire hesitantly glanced back over her shoulder to catch a final glimpse of Amelia's coffin waiting in tranquility beneath the magnificent oak tree. Then forcing herself, she turned back toward the cemetery gates. Literally dragging one foot in front of the other, she knew she had to escape the haunting reality of what had so recently occurred. She knew she had to leave that place of misery.

Emotionally drained, Claire clumsily walked through the majestic front gates and down the narrow, lush green pathway that led to the cemetery.

It was finally over! Life had confronted her with the worst fate imaginable and she had no choice but to face it...the loss of her child.

As Claire trudged despairingly along the shaded corridor and out onto the main street her pace quickened. She mentally searched for an escape from the agony that had consumed her in the hours leading up to that moment. Her volcanic anxiety was rupturing as she quickly broke into a frantic run trying desperately to flee the terror of the past three days. A final burst of grief stricken hysteria overtook her strides as she dashed through the manicured streets of Westfield, Massachusetts. Her high heels tapped out an accelerated rhythm as they hit the concrete sidewalk, her long, thin legs swinging rapidly through the slit in her sleek black skirt. She ran for blocks in a furious state of madness as those she passed curiously stared at the frenzied woman. Her brain pounded with stabbing bolts of lightning as her awareness wavered in and out.

Then finally, after her residual strength had been spent, barely able to breath, Claire passed through a set of black iron gates and fell hopelessly against an enormous willow tree that stood just inside the entrance of the city park. She collapsed onto the majestic roots that protruded from the ground where she plunged her head into her hands and wept aloud her immense sorrow.

Hours passed that afternoon as Claire endeavored to calm herself. Leaning back against the billowing tree she dazed in and out of restless consciousness. With her eyes closed, she felt the intense sunlight beam down through the branches and warm her weary face and body. She had cried until she could cry no more.

"What exactly does a person do next after her heart has been cut out?" she feebly questioned. "What is next? Where do I go now?"

As her body relaxed, Claire watched a group of children romp gleefully in the nearby playground. Inaudibly she reflected upon her only personal goal in life. As a young mother, upon Amelia's birth ten years prior, Claire had committed to herself that no matter what hardships life threw at her, she would strive to be a more openly loving parent than her own father had been.

To the outside world, Claire's father was a well-respected super lawyer who based his highly successful legal practice in the heart of New York City. James Hamilton Morgan was the man who was all too often called upon to represent the senior management criminals swindling their way to the top of the vicious corporate web of New York. He represented the CEO's of major business conglomerates whose primary focus was to line their own pockets with gold rather than manage successful, honest corporations.

James H. Morgan was a superior lawyer. He was the best! But his skill set lacked significantly when it came to being a loving father. His workaholic lifestyle and vicious temper left little time and patience for his young daughter Claire and his wife Elizabeth. James Morgan had set the high bar when it came to the expectations of his family. He had worked tediously to attain his stature in society and nothing was going to shame him. In the end nothing did shame him... nothing except his own vicious temper and destructive lifestyle.

Drifting further into silent reflection, Claire recalled the years of her father's cruel abusive behavior. Somehow he was able to be the best lawyer New York City could ask for. But he fell harshly short when it came to the emotional needs of his family.

Claire brought to mind her earliest childhood memory of her father before his drinking became so obsessive. She remembered standing out on the front lawn of their middle class home on a warm sunny afternoon. Her image was that of herself at only three years. Her infant eyes gawked up at her father as his tall stature towered over her tiny body. He stood meticulously dressed in his three-piece suit. He looked so handsome in her youthful eyes. She sweetly gleamed up at him as all three feet of her stood beside him in his radiant glory. She remembered the blue and white cotton sundress she had been wearing along with matching white lace socks and new summer shoes. Her head was strewn with sandy brown ringlet curls pulled neatly back in a soft blue bow.

"He's my dad!" she thought to herself gazing up at his magnificence.

Claire remembered feeling so special that day. Her father then picked her up, hugged her endearingly and for a short moment in time she felt as though she was the apple of his eye. She felt precious to him. She felt he was proud of her and glad that she was his. Claire smiled at the warm image she envisioned in her mind. But as she lost herself in her past searching for more warmth she could only recall the sadness and fear that had succumbed her during the balance of her childhood.

In all her memory Claire had always wanted to be close to her father. She simply wanted him to love her and maybe even approve of her. But James

Hamilton Morgan lacked the emotional competence to outwardly love. He was a man who simply never should've had children.

Claire's mother, Elizabeth Lynn Morgan had always been her best friend and mentor. She was a strikingly well manicured woman who was naturally optimistic in spirit. She was a loving soul who always seemed to bring out the best qualities in other people. Elizabeth was bravura yet a sensitive woman who adored her only daughter and who made every attempt to compensate for the shortcomings of her husband. She was also the person responsible for encouraging Claire's gift of dance. In spite of her husband's vicious temper, Elizabeth was a picture of elegance who had the innate ability to somehow love her insensitive husband.

As James Morgan's legal practice successfully escalated, so did his wealth, alcoholism and verbal abusive. Though Claire never lacked for material things, she was severely deprived of the affection, nurturing and encouragement that every child instinctively craves.

As the years passed and his alcoholism progressed, James Morgan became nothing short of a cruel bastard who heartlessly tantalized his wife and only child. It became increasingly difficult to conceal the mistreatment that both Claire and her mother endured endlessly. On a daily basis he would arrive home, consume a sizable amount of alcohol and repeatedly degrade his wife and daughter within the private confines of their luxurious mansion. He verbally stripped his loved ones of their self-worth and meaning. Confusedly unleashing his frustrations of the day, he besmirched their beauty, talent and dignity. While living in such a destructive environment, he viciously chomped away at their spirits leaving them both feeling belittled and worthless.

In her early teenage years, Claire pleaded with her mother to leave James Morgan.

"Why do you stay with him mommy? Why do you stay? Why don't we run away from this place? We don't need this fancy house!" Claire frequently begged.

Elizabeth tried in earnest to explain the situation without terrifying her young daughter.

"If we stay together here then there are ballet lessons for you, food on our table and a roof over our heads."

But more importantly, Elizabeth knew that if she stayed with her husband then he would remain in front of her where she could see what he was doing. If she took her daughter and fled, there was an intensely looming danger that he would seek them out and kill them both as he had so often threatened to do.

"God Damn-it… I will take out of this world everything I brought into it!" Morgan would often boast with a sick sense of pride, referring to his daughter.

Elizabeth heeded her husband's threat.

"If you ever leave me… Bi-Jesus I'll spend the rest of my life looking for you then I'll kill you!"

His bitter anger with the world spiraled as did his alcoholism and Elizabeth clearly understood his foul threat. A marriage breakdown was unacceptable to James Morgan. He had a "front" to keep up in society.

Intimidation, fear and mind control are what kept Claire's parents together as her home life persistently deteriorated. So goes the co-dependency upon the diseased alcoholic as both Claire and her mother were emotionally trodden and stripped of their poise and self-respect.

As Claire reflected still further upon the horror of her childhood, she recalled the glimmer of hope that her mother clung to so desperately.

"Don't worry about me Claire. I'll be fine! The best thing that you can do for me is to take care of yourself. Once you are out of this house and on your own… I'll be gone as well."

At the time, Claire had no idea just how right her mother would be.

Claire survived a childhood of acrid seclusion. She had no siblings to share the terror with and shamefully vowed not to tell a soul. The two beautiful Morgan women kept the family secret within and maintained outward appearances as they were expected to. Their swelling co-dependency ate away at them as the abuse grew increasingly more intense.

The heavenly shaft of light beamed down upon Claire as she sat motionless beneath the sprawling willow tree. Children's voices wafted through the air carried by the gentle breeze that filled the park late that afternoon. Hours had passed as Claire followed her memory path, dazing in and out of wakefulness. Slowly she tilted her head upward as if to respond to the sun that warmed her face through the branches. Opening her red swollen eyes, she returned a second time to her primary goal in life. With a sluggish bob of her head she awarded herself weak approval.

"Well… I guess I've succeeded. I may have only had Amelia for a short time… but I sure as hell did a better job as a parent than my father did!"

Claire gazed into the bluing firmament searching for her child's visage in the heavens.

"I love you Amelia," she affectionately assured her daughter's spirit. "You have always been my sunshine. The rainbow you sent was beautiful. Thank you my darling," she added sorrowfully.

Unraveling the sodden tissue that remained clutched in the palm of her right hand, she dabbed at a single tear that oozed over her pale flesh. Focusing on the neighboring playground, she smiled at the youthful innocence she observed there.

"Are you alright my dear?" an elderly woman in a tan colored trench coat bashfully inquired.

Startled by the voice that had approached from behind, Claire pivoted her head abruptly. Her body jolted uneasily at the unexpected infringement on her thoughts.

"My dear," the old woman persisted. "I've been sitting here in the park resting for quite some time. I've been watching you. You are obviously troubled. Can I help or call someone for you dear... your mother perhaps?"

Claire grinned at the gray haired woman and at the notion of her calling her mother to assist.

"No thank you... I'm okay," she responded, issuing a fake smile to the fretful intruder. "But thank you for your kindness. It is very thoughtful of you to offer."

The old woman's eyes twinkled with a life span of immeasurable experience. They were prudent yet compassionate. But Claire lacked interest in sharing further information about her whitewashed state. The aged woman nodded in response, understanding that she was not about to receive further explanation relating to the distraught woman sitting on the ground before her.

"Yes I have been sitting here for quite some time now haven't I?" Claire broke the barrier of questioning silence that had fallen between them as the old woman puzzled. "I guess I should get going. Thank you again for your concern," she stated hoping to satisfy the kindhearted trespasser and discourage her from supplementary conversation.

The old woman closed her eyes attempting to mentally organize the thoughts she felt it vital to articulate.

"My dear, please remember... that God never gives us anything we can't handle."

Claire stared at the grandmother figure with wonder as she graciously bowed forward and placed her trembling aged hand down upon her shoulder. She found it astonishing how the astute visitor recognized her splintered casing of internalized sorrow.

"Well... if you're sure you're okay now dear," the old woman regressed. "I'll be going on home to my cat now. It's about time for his dinner and he gets quite ornery if I'm late with his food."

Claire smirked at the notion of the cat waiting patiently for his beloved granny to return and serve him his evening meal. With that, the enchanting mature woman straightened her hunched back, turned away and hobbled back across the grass to the cart of groceries she had abandoned on the gravel pathway. Claire watched the woman totter on her painful overweight legs as she scuffled down the footpath and out of sight.

After four hours of reflection beneath the enormous willow tree, Claire unhurriedly pushed herself to her feet. Wrapping her arms around her torso as if to give herself a supportive embrace, she realized the time had come to leave. Her fragile legs were narrowly able to sustain the slight weight of her body. Feeling her swollen feet throb, she reached down and pulled off her sleek black high-heels and slid her nude toes into the fresh carpet of grass. Wavering with unsteadiness, Claire sauntered back through the iron gates and out onto the sidewalk. Dangling her shoes from her fingertips, she started her journey barefoot back to the funeral home to pick-up her car.

In no particular hurry, Claire meandered through the winding streets of Westfield. Even at the lowest point in her life she was still a strikingly beautiful woman. Her years of ballet training were evident as she carried her shoulders erectly set upon her straight spine. With her silky brown hair fluttering in the soft breeze, she was swept back into reflection of her past.

In spite of her wicked upbringing, Claire was an eternal optimist. As an adult child of an alcoholic parent she was a true survivor. Losing Amelia was certainly the most painful experience she had ever known, but as the old woman had recently affirmed, she knew deep down that she would survive it.

Having received the gift of her mother's loving disposition, Claire lived without spite or thirst for revenge. She generally believed there was good to be found in all people. She was a naturally vibrant young woman with a forgiving will and a spontaneous zest for life. But most importantly, though she had been repeatedly faced with trauma over her thirty-two years, she refused to quit. She declined to give up! The challenge of living in an alcoholic household gave her a unique determination in life to beat the odds of all that challenged her. She had an everlasting spirit.

Claire resided with her parents for the first fifteen years of her life where money was plentiful. She had been sent to the finest schools in the area. But as her father's alcoholism worsened, so did the abuse in the home. Making an anxious attempt to remove Claire from the violence, Elizabeth eventually suggested to her husband that it would be most beneficial for their daughter to finish her high school education in a place where she could seek further opportunity for her love of dance. Knowing how to "work" her husband's mind, Elizabeth assured him that it would "look" very good to his peers and associates if his child attained such magnificence in the study of the arts. Amazingly, James Morgan agreed and shortly thereafter Claire auditioned and was accepted at the National Ballet of Canada.

At only fifteen years of age, Claire packed her suitcases and relocated to Toronto, Canada. Though Elizabeth missed her daughter terribly, she knew in her heart that it was the only way to spare her child's youthful spirit from further violence and destruction.

Claire moved to Toronto and adapted to her new environment with ease. She studied and thrived in the large Canadian city. Engulfing herself in her dance classes and schoolwork, Claire had little time to worry about the life she had left behind. Her dance ability further developed, opening many doors for prestigious performance opportunities throughout Canada.

Contacting her mother regularly by telephone, Claire was reassured with each call that everything was fine at home and that her father was behaving himself. Though Claire knew it was doubtful, she took her mother's supportive words at face value and put it all from her mind the best that she could. Aside from missing her mother, Claire was genuinely happy with her new life of dance and circle of friends.

It was in the second year of her studies in Canada that Claire received an urgent telephone call in the headmaster's office. On a snowy January morning an alarmed straight-laced woman entered Claire's dorm room unannounced at 2:00 a.m.

"Claire! You need to come with me immediately!" the headmaster sharply directed the sleeping girl.

Ringing her eyes with her fists, Claire obediently pulled herself from her bed, grabbed her robe and slippers and followed the highly respected woman down the darkened hallway of her dorm. As she trailed the headmaster into her office, she was instantly alerted to the unmistakable air of tension in the room, taking note that the entire staff of principle directors was sitting solemnly in the high-backed chairs that aligned the wall.

"Am I in some sort of trouble?" Claire inquired with concern.

The headmaster rounded her desk and placed herself gracefully in the chair. Miss Natasha, Claire's primary ballet instructor, then arose from her seated position and while resting her hands upon Claire's shoulders from behind she gently encouraged her student to sit down.

"No Claire my darling. You're not in trouble," Natasha responded softly as she fought back her own tears.

Not knowing how to deliver the message she hesitated for a moment and then forced herself to speak.

"You're not in trouble Claire… but unfortunately… I have some very bad news to give you."

Claire's eyes widened, anxiously searching her instructor's face for an explanation.

"What then!" Claire demanded.

"Well Claire," Miss Natasha continued in a hesitant tone. "I don't know how to tell you this, other than to just tell you. I'm afraid dear…that your mother Elizabeth passed away late yesterday evening back at your home in New York City."

"What! What are you saying Miss Natas… What do you mean?" Claire jumped from her seat as she covered her mouth with her hands.

"Well… I'm afraid we received a telephone call from your father about an hour ago. He explained on the phone to us that your mother had been suffering with cancer for a short while now," Miss Natasha continued as she reached out to hold Claire's quivering hands.

"No!" Claire screeched in disbelief. "She never told me she had cancer!"

"Yes," Miss Natasha continued sadly lowering her eyes to the floor. "I understand that she never told you Claire. But I believe she held it from you because she didn't want you to concern yourself about her. She wanted you to mind your studies here and not be distracted by her illness back at home. She deliberately kept it a secret because she loved you so very much Claire. She did it because she loved you!"

"But now she's gone!" Claire snapped angrily as her eyes filled with tears. "Now she's gone! Oh my God Miss Natasha! Oh my God!"

Natasha took the shaken child into her arms as she openly wept. The usually supercilious group of instructors sat silently along the wall of the school headquarters as tears streamed down their faces. They had all grown very fond of Claire and they shared her sorrow intensely.

After several minutes of silence scarred only by the sound of Claire's grief, Miss Natasha bent down and murmured into the weeping child's ear, "Claire my darling… I will see that you get home tomorrow. I'm so sorry about your loss…so very sorry."

The next morning at 7:00 a.m. as promised, Miss Natasha helped Claire gather a few items of clothing and then drove the traumatized teenager to the airport. She arranged for Claire's flight then hugged her supportively as they stood at the departure gate.

"God bless you Claire," Miss Natasha spoke. "We do hope that in time you will return to us here."

Blindly Claire turned away from her trainer and commenced her journey back to New York City to bury her dearly loved mother.

In the week that followed, Claire assumed her position along side her mother's shimmering silver casket. Internalizing her grief, she stood impassively shaking hands with the infinite rivulet of guests paying their respects to her mother at the funeral home.

Shortly thereafter they lowered her mother's dormant body into the ground. It was perchance the first instance that Claire had ever seen her father break down and cry. Like a pathetic misplaced child he wept openly having lost the only woman he secretly loved but had outwardly abused for decades.

It was the first death that Claire had experienced and she felt it personally devastating. Her mentor, her friend, her beautiful mother was gone. But more so, she had departed her existence without bidding a final farewell to her daughter.

"My darling Claire, when you are off and on your own in this world… I'll be gone also," she recalled her mother saying frequently.

"How right she was!" Claire contemplated. "How right she was!"

For the two weeks that followed her mother's interment, Claire wandered through the deadened corridors of the mansion she had called home for so many years. The rooms that once danced vivaciously with the sound of her mother's cheerful voice then reeked of solitude. Claire felt hollow inside. She felt guilty and deserted.

The man who had manipulated their lives for nearly two decades, sat soberly alone in the parlor. Blinded by realism, James Morgan remained immobile in his reclined chair staring into the raging fireplace hour upon hour. He said little to Claire during those weeks of lingering isolation. But his eyes spoke volumes as he internalized his misery and remorse.

Claire watched her father from the corner of the room wondering what was flowing through his mind. Perhaps he was reflecting upon his past and the terror he had bestowed upon the beautiful woman that was no longer his wife. But James Morgan was a complex individual and she could only guess where his thoughts had drifted off to. During those weeks of grieving, Claire found herself feeling pity for her father. She hated what he had done to her mother but she also despised seeing him sitting in the dark corner looking so very lost.

Claire also observed that during her stay at home, James Morgan had not consumed a drop of alcohol.

"Perhaps he has hit his bottom," the teenager wondered. "What a shame that it took the death of his wife to shock him into realizing what he once had."

Two weeks passed and Claire began packing her suitcase in preparation for her flight back to Toronto that evening. Sitting upon her imposing canopy bed, she reached for the photo of her mother that had always rest on the nightstand. Claire looked deeply into her mother's eyes as she held the oak framed image before her. One would never know the torture that woman had endured judging by the gorgeous smile that arched gracefully over her lips. A tear ran down Claire's colorless skin as she carefully wrapped the photo in her mother's favorite silk scarf then placed it lovingly in her suitcase.

"Claire," her father's voice startled her from the doorway.

"Yes dad?" she responded with surprise.

"Before you leave… I would like it very much if you would go to your mother's jewel box and choose something special to keep."

She stared at the grief stricken man dawning her doorway as he stood hunched over, defeated, with his hands hidden in his back pockets.

"I know your mother would like it if you took something special back with you."

"Thank you dad. I'll do that before I go," she replied as a lump formed in her throat.

She felt incredible grief at that moment. But not only for the loss of her mother, she also felt for the struggling tortured soul that stood before her. Claire shrugged her shoulders in question then turned to finish her packing.

"Claire..." the man forlornly interrupted her a second time.

"Yes dad?" she responded curiously.

"I... I love you very... much," he admitted submissively as if saying the very words made him ache.

Startled by his genuine confession, Claire emptied her hands of the clothes she was packing and walked hesitantly toward him.

With a shy smile she responded, "I love you too dad. I've always loved you...and so did mom. I just know she did."

For the first time in her memory, Claire reached out her arms and tightly embraced her father. The grieving man broke down and openly wept into Claire's shoulder.

Through his sobs he choked out, "I'm so sorry for ever hurting you and your mother. I never meant to hurt you... either of you. I love you Claire! I've just had a lot of trouble being able to tell you that."

Claire had never heard the words spoken from her father's lips. His truthful, honest admission was foreign to her. She had never been privileged to such integrity from him before. Renewed by his confessions, Claire realized instantly that for the moment, she had become the adult and the man weeping into her shoulder was a lost child struggling to liberate himself from the sadistic fiend he had become.

"I know dad," she responded softly in his ear. "And mom knows it too."

Claire held her weeping father for a long moment. Then pulling back she caught both of his hands in hers.

"We're going to be okay dad. We're both going to be just fine."

"I'm so proud of you Claire... and the confident young woman that you've become. Remember now... if you need any money...you just let me know."

Claire smiled at his words and his classic offer for money.

"Yes dad, thank you. I'll be fine and I promise that I'll call you often."

Claire released his hands as he turned from her doorway. Stunned by her father's confession of adoration, Claire hesitated for a moment then called out to him.

"Dad!"

"Yes?" he turned back to her in question.

"Please know...that I've always loved you," she volunteered.

Wiping tears from his melancholy eyes, he threw her a compelling smile, tapped his fingertips lightly on the doorframe and disappeared from her sight.

14

Claire finished packing then solemnly walked down the hall to choose an item from her mother's jewel box. Hesitantly entering the extensive walk-in closet, she could smell the sweet fragrance of her mother's favorite cologne wafting through the air. Gently running her fingers along the row of neatly hung blouses, Claire noticed the jewel case that sheltered her mother's precious gems. As she unfastened the lid to the antique box, the magnificent jewels illuminated their radiance. Claire gazed over the vast selection of earrings, necklaces and stones visually recalling how stunning her mother looked when they each dawned her tiny ear lobes and long slender neck. Without hesitation, Claire reached for a familiar ring that she knew her mother had worn often... a single protruding opal resting upon a plain gold band. It was nothing fancy, nothing complicated, but it had always been Claire's favorite. She recalled the ring embellishing her mother's slender fingers and attractively manicured nails. Claire lifted the ring from the case and slowly slid it upon her own finger.

"I love you mom," she spilled into the silence.

Feeling Elizabeth's presence in the small room, Claire smiled as she imagined her mother's new spiritual home.

"You're free now mom. I'm so happy that you're free." Closing her eyes as tears began to tumble down her cheeks she added, "Please stay close to me mom. Please guide me and give me courage. I need you mummy. I'm happy for you... but I miss you."

Admiring the ring that gleamed with luster upon her finger, Claire gently closed the box. She then pulled a royal blue silk blouse from the hanger feeling the quality texture slide between her fingers. Holding it to her nostrils she filled her lungs with the familiar fragrance of her mother. Then pressing the blouse tightly against her chest, Claire wept brokenhearted.

"How right you were mom," she sounded vague through her emotion. "I'm on my own... and now you're gone! Mom, I always wanted you to be free from your life of torture... but dying wasn't exactly what I had in mind."

Overcome with grief Claire returned the blouse to the hanger and left the room.

That evening James Morgan drove his daughter to the airport in silence. He slipped five hundred dollars cash into the palm of her left hand and closed her fingers securely over it. Without any words spoken they embraced each other one last time. Only upon hearing the final boarding call for her flight did Claire release herself from her father's aching arms. Wiping a tear from the corner of her eye, she kissed him lightly on the cheek then turned to pass through the gate geared for her departure.

Claire returned to the National Ballet of Canada immersing herself in her studies more deeply than ever. Through tragedy, she quickly matured into an adult. She knew her father was alone and heartbroken back in New York. But she also knew that he was a very strong man and quite capable of caring for himself if he had to. She acknowledged the fact that he needed time alone to reflect on his life and the actions he had taken for so many years. Claire wondered if somehow through devastation he might become a better person.

Three months after her mother's death, Claire was comforted to hear her father proclaim that he realized he had a serious problem with alcohol and that he was seeking counseling for it. He had a new tone of humbleness in his voice. It was an attitude that Claire was unfamiliar with but liked the sound of.

Chapter Two

Two years quickly passed as Claire danced her way to the top of the National Ballet. She completed her high school studies with honors then made the extremely difficult decision to leave the school of arts. She decided to venture on into higher education heading toward a profession that she had become distantly familiar with.

As time passed, fences were mended and her relationship with her father bloomed into one of love and admiration. Claire felt it pitiful that it took her mother's death for her father to raise his head from his alcoholic windstorm and cleanse his life.

Claire returned to New York City and began her university education to become a lawyer. She had come to believe that there was a lot of credible work to be done in the vocation of law and so she chose the field as her future career path.

During her post secondary education, Claire naively avoided the campus parties, drugs and mischief that was typical for many young adults.

It wasn't until her fourth year of university that she found herself falling in love with a handsomely slick, yet demanding young man that was also looking to the legal field to become his profession. Claire Morgan and Jacob Redkin dated for over a year. The relationship remained light and uncommitted until Claire revealed herself to be a twenty-two year old, unmarried, "pregnant" university student.

She warily notified her father of her pregnancy to be met with his stern reaction, "Well, certainly I am right to assume that you are going to get married without delay!"

Still taken back by the confirmation of her pregnancy, Claire submissively nodded in agreement and a small private wedding took place within a month. The father of her child, Jacob Redkin therein became her wedded husband.

Claire knew in her heart that marriage was likely not the right answer at that point as she felt she hardly knew Jacob enough to commit herself to him for the rest of her life. Never the less, she was still sensitive to her father's assumptions and she performed as he expected.

The two newlyweds moved into an apartment together and continued their studies throughout the pregnancy. Then after nine months, Claire was rushed to the hospital in advanced labor where she gave birth to a healthy baby girl whom she named Amelia, Elizabeth.

James Morgan was elated with his new granddaughter. He eagerly anticipated her filling the silent void he had been living with since the death of his wife. He showered his precious grandchild with gifts and passed along as much money as the couple could spend. He saw to it that finances were never a burden.

In the four years that followed Amelia's birth, the newlyweds struggled to complete their studies and manage the growing needs of their young daughter.

As time passed and tensions grew between them, Claire found herself faced with the brutal reality that she had wedded a perilous villain. She had unknowingly promised herself to a man that she had become remarkably familiar with as a child.

Jacob's alcohol consumption rocketed, as did his cruelty. Before long he began physically striking at Claire. During his recurrent drunken tirades, he verbally degraded his wife, envious of her promising legal career within her father's law firm.

The concluding battle transpired on Amelia's fourth birthday. Claire arrived home from the office to discover Jacob entirely annihilated. He was stone drunk and had passed out on the sofa. Swiftly Claire ran in to check on Amelia who was supposed to have been taking her afternoon nap. Upon entering her child's bedroom, she found her daughter cowering in the corner behind her dresser sniveling softly to herself. Pressing her much-loved blanket into her four-year old tear stained face, Claire ran to comfort the sobbing child. Hugging her securely, the concerned mother gently pulled the blanket from her eyes and was instantly faced with the horror she had secretly dreaded. Amelia's tiny face was covered with red welts from where she had been repeatedly struck by the hand of her drunken father.

"Oh my God!" Claire shrieked as she rocked the traumatized girl on her knee. "Oh my God Amelia, I'm so sorry!"

Enraged, yet terrified for her daughter's safety, Claire anxiously searched her mind for a solution. But in her heart, she knew there was only one answer and that was to get her toddler out of there immediately. Clutching her confused daughter against her chest, Claire waited only but a moment before she wrapped a warm quilt around her quivering four-year-old. Then after snatching her handbag from the table, she quietly snuck from the apartment.

As Jacob Redkin lay drunk and motionless in front of the blaring television set, Claire and Amelia fled from his life. They did not leave a note. They left no evidence of where they had gone. They simply vanished.

After loading her bewildered youngster into the car Claire reached for her cell phone. While screeching her vehicle from the parking lot, she frantically dialed her father's office. Her call was immediately connected to his answering machine.

"Dad it's me!" she shouted in the receiver. "I've got a real problem here that I'm not sure you'll understand. You've got to help me and help me now! I'm going to need about ten thousand dollars deposited into my bank account today! Please don't ask any questions... just do it! And please do it right away...this afternoon if possible! I'll call you and explain when I can! I love you dad and thanks! Oh and dad..." Claire persisted with a last minute thought, "Please don't tell Jacob that I left you this message!"

With that, Claire folded her cell phone, pitched it onto the passenger seat, jammed her foot down on the accelerator and ramped onto the highway. The car sped as fast as the wheels could carry them. The two frightened young women then left New York City forever.

Claire headed west anxiously anticipating the state boarder. She drove on for hours in debate of what she had just done, where she would go and what consequences she would face in the future. She realized that her marriage to Jacob was not only a mistake but it was an error that would likely haunt her for years to come as she fled with her husband's only child.

As dusk approached Claire glanced at her sleeping four year old through the rear view mirror.

"Don't worry my little sweetheart. Mommy will take care of you. You have been struck for the last time," she spoke softly, smiling at the innocence she saw in the back seat.

Late that evening Claire pulled into a roadside hotel where she checked in for the night. She carried her confused daughter into the hotel room, tucked her warmly beneath the blankets then lay down beside her. Draping her arm over her child, she did her best to respond to her daughter's questions about where they were and why.

"Daddy drinks to much beer doesn't he mommy?" Amelia quizzed.

"Yes he does darling," she responded honestly pulling the child closer to her.

"He scares me sometimes when he hits us mommy. Does he scare you?" the child continued to probe in an overtly mature fashion.

"Yes he does scare me Amelia and that's why you and I are going to find a new home together. You see my darling; daddy has some serious problems that he needs to work out. Although I know you love him and I know he really does love you very much, we can't live in a place that could be harmful to us... now can we?"

Amelia seemed satisfied with her mother's uncomplicated elucidation. She smiled as she rubbed her favorite blanket under her nose. Then pulling from the security of her mother's arms, she reached up and placed a wet kiss upon Claire's cheek.

"I love you mommy. Please don't cry cause you and I are going to be just fine!" Amelia assured her worried mother with a confident smile.

With that, Amelia slid back down beneath the bed covers, nuzzled herself into her mother's arms and peacefully drifted off to sleep.

The next morning as Amelia sat on the bed in their hotel room watching cartoons and munching on cereal, Claire closed herself in the bathroom to make a private call to her father. After connecting with the alarmed voice of James Morgan, she gave him a brief clarification of what had happened.

"Well, well, well, now I understand why I got a frantic call from Jacob late last night," her father stated.

"Dad, I've got to do what's right for Amelia and me! Yes I know Jacob is her father, but he's also the son-of-a-bitch that beat the daylights out of her yesterday," Claire defended. "Now either you're going to help me or you're not!"

"Of course I'm going to help you however I can Claire, so just calm down," her father surrendered. "There is plenty of money in your bank account right now and I will continue to see that you're both provided for. I told Jacob on the phone last night that I had no idea where his family was. I told him that was his damn business, not mine! I must say though he was pretty hostile. But never mind that! I can take of Jacob at my end."

"Thanks for covering for me dad," Claire replied with gratitude. "Listen now, I don't know where we're going but I promise you we won't lose touch. Now I've got to go so you take care of yourself and I'll call you soon."

Without further debate Claire hung up the phone, bundled Amelia back into the car and set out to find a brighter future for them both.

Over the course of the six years that followed, Claire and Amelia moved from city to city fleeing in fear of their lives from Jacob Redkin.

Jacob's bitterness over the disappearance of his daughter spiraled, as did his alcoholism and threats. Each time Claire settled Amelia into a new home and school, evidence would present itself that Jacob was closing in on them.

On six occasions, Claire changed her cell phone number after receiving menacing calls from her husband. Twice Jacob attempted to abduct Amelia from her school. Claire was also aware that Jacob had hired private detectives who were working in hot pursuit of her, providing her husband with leads of their whereabouts as they became available.

Each time the crazed madman reared his ugly head, either by a sighting or a telephone call, Claire instantly abandoned her position with the local law firm she was working for, packed up their belongings and vanished into the night with her daughter.

Jacob became obsessed with the self-fulfilling prophecy of finding his estranged wife and daughter. For six years he used every resource he had available to seek out his lost family. With each near miss he got increasingly irritated. Jacob Redkin was a vicious beast that had no interest in fighting for his daughter's return through legal channels. He thrived on revenge and as time passed, it became his personal vendetta to find his wife, kill her and seek full custody of his daughter.

Claire sheltered Amelia from as much turmoil as she could as together they lived a life of nurturing love and closeness. True to his word, James Morgan made regular deposits of large sums of money into Claire's bank account and continued to fend off her husband's inquiries back in New York. Over the years Claire stayed in regular contact with her father by telephone. She kept him informed of their whereabouts and gave him habitual updates about his beloved granddaughter.

When Amelia turned nine years old her health began to fail. Shortly thereafter Claire was advised that her daughter had a rapidly aggressive form of Leukemia.

"Cancer?" the distraught mother shouted at the doctor. "Oh my God…my mother died of cancer! There must be something you can do for her!"

There were a few treatments that they could try though her prognosis was not good. Nine desperate months later it was concluded that Amelia was failing to respond to all treatment. Doctors advised Claire that the end was near and that she should try to live life as normally as possible for the time that was left.

Then early one Saturday morning as she approached the door of her daughter's bedroom, Claire was met with her child's passing. Amelia lay motionless in her canopy bed. Still clutching her beloved rag doll Anna, her skin was drawn and pale. Her beautiful young lips were arched in a familiar grin of peace. It was the same grin that Claire recalled seeing on her mother's lips after her passing. Amelia had died in her sleep.

After a long stroll through the winding city streets of Westfield and another full hour of reflection, Claire walked barefoot across the parking lot of the funeral home. With a heavy sigh she entered the security code on the door of her car and the locks released. Still somewhat dazed, she opened the door and pitched her shoes inside the car. Her body fell into the driver's seat as she sighed despairingly in defeat.

"I have now officially lost everything in my life that I have ever loved," Claire stated aloud resting her hands on the steering wheel, "my mother, my home and now my child! My God, what do I do now? Where do I go? I don't have to run from Jacob as there is no longer a child for him to steal from me. But God knows I can't stay here. It just hurts too much."

Claire mumbled to herself uninterrupted as she stared through the front windshield. In a state of complete exhaustion her confused thoughts bashed through her brain like a battery of missiles. Being able to avoid the inevitable no longer, she started the car engine and drove back to the lingering stillness of her rented condo.

The house was dark and silent. No longer was there a youthful voice belting out her favorite rock tunes in the living room or dancing a balletic arabesque down the hallway to Mozart. The dwelling was miserably calm.

Claire changed her clothes, grabbed a bottle of wine from the refrigerator and curled up in the comfort of her favorite chair.

Staring into the eyes of her daughter's portrait that hung on the wall beside her, the tears flowed as sinuously as the wine. That evening, Claire cried herself into a helpless drunken stupor of self-pity. She missed Amelia more desperately than one could ever imagine.

As the morning sun peeked through the drawn vertical blinds, Claire awoke in the same chair she had plunged into the night before. Her forehead cracked with the pain of too much wine and her body was still painfully exhausted.

"Well," she ventured, "what the hell do I do now? Where do I go?" she whispered staring up at Amelia's portrait. "Well one thing is for sure... I can't stay here."

Having no particular plan in mind, Claire arose from her chair, showered and dressed in the comfort of her favorite blue jeans and white t-shirt. She packed a few suitcases with clothing, photographs of Amelia and the porcelain ballerina that sat in stillness on her daughter's bureau. The statue had been a gift from Elizabeth to her as a child, which in turn Claire had given to her own daughter. Amelia had always adored the delicate ornament.

Less than an hour later, with suitcases in hand, Claire stood in the front entrance of her condo taking one concluding glance around the apartment that she and her daughter had called home for over a year. They had lived in the condo since they discovered Amelia was ill. It was in a quiet neighborhood with an excellent school and was in close proximity to the local hospital.

"Well?" Claire proposed to the silent apartment. "I guess I've got everything I need to move on. The rest will just have to take care of itself."

Claire had no concern for the furnishings and other personal items she was leaving behind. She was indifferent to it all at that point. After locking the apartment door she walked briskly down the corridor and into the elevator as if she was being chased. With her sunglasses shielding her gaunt bloodshot eyes and her lustrous brown hair wafting through the air, she loaded the suitcases in the trunk of her polished black BMW and backed out of the parking lot. Claire sped her tires as she peeled out into the main street traffic. Spiritually weary and psychologically defeated she left the city. Without a plan or a destination she was moving on.

Westfield, Massachusetts had been their home for the past year but it was home no longer. In fact, Claire couldn't leave the city fast enough. She drove through the well-manicured community and past the cemetery at which she had so recently left her daughter. As her eyes welled up with tears, she adjusted herself in the driver's seat and ramped onto Highway #90. She gunned the gas pedal of her BMW flying past other motorists without concern. Oblivious to everything around her, she turned the stereo on and focused her eyes directly on the road lines losing herself in her thoughts.

Visions of her daughter's smiling face flashed before her. Reminiscences of their loving relationship flooded her heart until Claire found herself actually smiling.

The miles went blurring by as the hours of the day ticked quickly past. She was heading north. She had no idea why. But the Canadian border seemed to be a suitable escape. She had found comfort in Canada before and longed for it's expansive welcoming views once again. Claire drove on through the day and then seemingly regained consciousness of her surroundings as the evening dusk approached.

Arriving in Buffalo, New York she wheeled her BMW into the waiting line at the Peace Bridge border into Canada. After several interrogating questions by the customs officer, Claire was once again on her way. She was back in Canada, the country in which she had found healing solace during the difficult years of her adolescence.

With accelerating speed she ramped onto the Queen Elizabeth Highway heading north toward Toronto. She took no notice of the breathtaking Niagara gardens in full spring bloom as she blew past the tourist exits to Niagara Falls.

Evening had fallen and darkness surrounded her as she journeyed on. Heavy threatening clouds were rolling in over her head as she cornered the rounding edge of Lake Ontario. The reflective road lines flashed beneath her tires in a blur as she was once again caught in the web of analyzing her past.

Claire found it simply astonishing that she herself had plummeted into the precise trap that her mother had years prior. After living with an abusive alcoholic father her entire adolescence, Claire unknowingly wed a mortifying replica of the man she had loathed for nearly the first two decades of her life. It seemed as though she had subconsciously attracted Jacob. She didn't go deliberately looking for an abuser to marry. But that seemed to be exactly what she ended up with regardless. Generation after generation, the deadly cyclone of alcoholism stalks its victims, traps them, chews them up and spits them out for dead.

"Somewhere," she rationalized, "the cycle has to stop! But how?"

Being the natural optimist that she was, Claire seemed incapable of lingering in a negative state for very long. In spite of her atrocious childhood and abusive matrimony, she had been given the heavenly endowment of her beautiful daughter. She had shared ten years of wonder with her little ballerina. Though she only had Amelia for a short time, they were years that she would not trade for anything. Amelia and Claire spent a full decade, loving, laughing, dancing and sharing with each other. They both treasured every precious moment bonding closer and closer together.

The Toronto skyline flashed with brilliant forks of lightning in the distance over Lake Ontario followed by the thunderous echo of authority as the rain began to fall. Claire ramped onto the colossal 401 Highway jetting across Toronto then veered north on Highway 400.

With heart wrenching ballads of love vibrating through the stereo speakers and the windshield wipers tapping out their synchronized rhythm, the anxious tension that held Claire's tired body captive began to release. The sky was vastly dark as the rain pelted down upon her windshield. Heading north, Claire obliviously departed the blinding lights of Toronto, the city she loved and had called home years prior. As the evening wore on into the night she found herself one of the few remaining vehicles speeding along the slick wet roadway.

As she sped onward through the darkness fleeing from her all-consuming torment, Elton John sang out the lyrics to his hit song, "Tiny Dancer." Instantly Claire was caught up in the beautiful tune that echoed through the car. Quietly lip-syncing the familiar words, her somnolent eyes welled up with thick undulating tears as she was again reminded of her own little ballerina.

How different her life was only a week ago. How quickly it had all changed. She missed her daughter terribly. Only a few shorts days before, Amelia was staring up into her mother's dark worried eyes from where she lay snuggled beneath her pale pink blankets. Amelia was a loving, optimistic child who always did her best to convince her mother that everything was going to be all right.

"I'm fine mommy!" Amelia chanted with a grin from her pillow. For the first evening in weeks, Claire felt that her child actually looked vibrant and well though she couldn't keep herself from worrying. "Mommy…. try to relax and go to sleep! I love you…good night!" her daughter assertively closed the conversation.

Amelia winked at her mother as she sleepily pulled her covers beneath her chin.

"I love you too my darling," Claire confessed.

The fretful mother then kissed her treasure on the cheek, dimmed the light in her bedroom and closed the door. Then only a few hours later as the evening darkened into the depths of the night… Amelia went to sleep… never to awaken.

The next morning Claire entered her child's bedroom bidding her ten-year-old a cheerful greeting, "Good morning Amelia!"

She was then met with the horrendous sight of her daughter's lifeless body still tranquilly cuddled beneath the blankets just as she had left her the night before.

Tears surged from Claire's eyes rolling in rivers down her face as she recalled that dreaded morning. Overcome with recurring grief, Claire's knuckles whitened as she tightly gripped the steering wheel. With self-pity plaguing her on that murky night, her hands began to tremble and her eyes glazed over from the ceaseless flow of water.

"Oh my God Amelia! I miss you so much! How will I ever go on without you?"

Faced with the permanency of her daughter's absence, Claire broke down completely. Blinded by the sorrow that discharged from her eyes as heavily as the fierce rainstorm outside her car, she lost all sight of the road. Then mistakenly, she jammed her foot down heavily on the gas pedal, which caused her BMW to rapidly hydroplane across the waterlogged highway. Instantly realizing her loss of control, she tried to compose herself as she unintentionally veered her speeding vehicle to the right where the front wheel grabbed at the edge of the gravel shoulder. Claire was hastily reminded that she had been traveling at an excessive rate of speed. She tried to pull the car back onto the slick highway as the gravel snarled angrily beneath her speeding tires, shooting the pebbles out like bullets from the rear of her vehicle. Yanking the steering wheel to the left, the car fishtailed back and forth across the highway, narrowly escaping a head-on collision with two oncoming vehicles. Shear panic kicked in as Claire slammed her foot down upon the sensitive brake pedal sending her vehicle furiously whirling in a three-sixty spin in the center of the quadruple lane highway. As if it was all happening in slow motion, the distraught female wrenched the BMW from its cyclone twist and narrowly out of the passage of an oncoming truck. With the back end leading, the extravagant black vehicle flew recklessly into a massive ditch on the right, angrily smashing the rear bumper into a concrete drainage culvert.

Moments of stillness passed as Claire's bleeding head remained fully plunged forward into the exploded airbag. Pain throbbed irritably across her skull as she struggled to pull her head back and open her eyes in recollection of what had just occurred. While trying to regain her focus, the radio continued to play, the engine purred on and the windshield wipers tapped out an uninterrupted tempo as the heavy rain pelted down upon the shattered glass.

Claire pulled her twisted arm from beneath the airbag and lightly dabbed at the agonizing gash on her forehead. She felt warm blood trickle over her cheekbone as her entire body throbbed, having been shaken to its very core. Her face and hands were burnt from the abrasion of the airbag and her chest heaved from the bolting constraint of the seatbelt.

After several moments, Claire reached up and wiped the fog from the driver's side window. Peering through the droplets of rain she could see only darkness. There was not another vehicle in sight. There were no buildings, no houses or streetlights anywhere in the distance.

"God Damn it!" she yelled in anger pounding her fist on the console. "God Damn it! I just can't get a break!" she hollered into the ceiling as if venting her anger at God himself. "Don't you understand? I'm doing my very best here! I've lost everything that I've ever cared about…and…and I don't want to cry anymore!"

Lowering her eyes from the ceiling, Claire punched miserably at the power button on the radio then covered her face with her hands in utter defeat. She sat alone in the hush of the night for what seemed an eternity.

Still stunned by the accident, the blood from the gaping wound in her forehead began to spurt out furiously. Her head throbbed as she freed herself from the tangled airbag and fumbled around on the floor for her disheveled purse. Yanking a tissue from her handbag she sat upright and pressed the Kleenex firmly against her thrashing forehead. With a vanquished sigh, she leaned back feeling as though she had just made her way through the passage of hell.

Momentarily startled by the sound of a passing motorist, Claire raised her head and peered through the foggy windshield in time to see that an enormous transport truck had pulled off the road directly in front of her and was slowly backing up toward her partially ditched vehicle. The rain struck the pavement in torrents as the blazing red taillights of the trailer drew dangerously close to the front bumper of her car.

"Jesus Christ…now what?" she screamed irritably into the shattered windshield tossing the blood soaked tissue to the floor. "That guy doesn't even know I'm here! He's going to back right over me!"

Panic overtook her as the fluorescent taillights drew intimately close to the hood of her car. Claire jostled with the airbag frantically searching for the door handle preparing to dive onto the ground and out of the way of the massive tires that were about to crush her BMW. The hammering rain and driving winds swirled through the air pounding against her windows leaving visibility nearly zero. As her fingers fumbled over the door release the rear lights of the truck instantly dimmed and the massive vehicle drew to a whining halt.

The disgruntled woman glared anxiously at the cab of the truck wondering what was about to happen. She then saw the driver's door open slightly and the interior light cast a dim glow in the distance. The wind swung wildly at the truck door forcing it angrily against its hinges. Claire watched as a tall, dark figure made his way from the truck and down into the storm. He struggled to wrap himself in a long dark coat and then lumbered against the wind toward her vehicle. His face was darkly shadowed hidden beneath his rain soaked Stetson with water pouring from the curled brim. Claire watched as he approached her mangled vehicle with one hand clasping his coat together and the other bracing his hat. Arriving at the car, he cautiously tapped his abrasive knuckles on the driver side window.

"You okay in there?" his deep, raspy voice questioned loudly being drowned out by the wild elements of nature.

Feeling partially afraid of the stranger yet at the same time relieved, Claire lowered her window.

"Yes I'm okay... I think," she confirmed.

As the window opened before him, the stranger noticed the blood pouring down Claire's features and his tone immediately changed to that of concern.

"Looks like you need a doctor lady. Are you hurt anywhere else? Can you move your legs?" the stranger questioned shielding his eyes from the storm.

"I think everything else is okay," she responded still stupefied by the accident.

"Come-on, lets get you out of there and find a doctor," he directed with intention.

With a heavy reef on the handle, the stranger opened the wedged door of the BMW and reached in to support the shaken woman as she struggled free of the airbag. Claire hoisted her body from the ditched vehicle defending her bleeding face from the blinding rain. The stranger removed his full-length canvas overcoat and bound it tightly around her quivering shoulders. The torrential downpour showered them both as the stranger thumped the car door shut. Enveloping his long, muscular arm around Claire's upper body he supportively directed her footsteps toward the passenger door of his enormous rig.

Claire slopped through the gushing water that brimmed over the ditch and gravel shoulder. The stranger reached ahead and yanked the weighty door of the tractor open. Straining her arm upward, she took hold of the protruding chrome handle and hauled herself up into the truck collapsing onto the passenger seat. The warmth of the cab was a welcome comfort as she drew the collar of the raincoat securely in around her neck.

"You stay here, I'll be right back!"

Claire nodded as he swung the heavy door closed and vanished from her sight.

The stranger ventured back to the stranded BMW, turned the hazards lights on, lit a roadside flare to warn oncoming motorists and returned to the truck.

"Okay now!" he announced as he pulled his tall, sodden body from the ground and into the driver's seat.

But as he turned toward Claire to inquire further about the accident, he found her limp body slumped forward against the dashboard, still and unconscious.

"Oh Christ!" he panicked reaching over to pull her back into the seat.

As blood poured from the gash in her forehead the trucker instinctively reached behind him and pulled his first aid kit out from behind his seat. Quickly he bandaged the woman's hemorrhaging wound, wrapping a thick band of gauze firmly around her skull. The stranger then held his trembling fingers against her throat in search of a pulse. Satisfied for the moment, he tightly bound the unconscious woman in a large quilt that was pulled from his bunk.

Snatching at the microphone from his CB radio, he questioned loudly into the small hand piece, "Hey there friends... I need some help here fast! I'm traveling on highway 400 about 50 minutes north of Orillia. I need to know where the nearest hospital is? I've got an emergency here!" he pleaded aggressively over the bantering squelch of the radio.

Breathing heavily he waited until an obliging voice responded through the squealing static in the speakers, "Huntsville friend! There's a hospital in Huntsville. You've got about a ten-minute journey from there. Good luck friend," the voice signed off.

"Thanks big guy. I owe you one!" the stranger responded then tossed the microphone back onto the dash of his truck.

Reaching over, he swept Claire's frail body into his arms. After maneuvering her between the seats in the cab, he caringly placed her on the bed in his bunk. Positioning her blood soaked head upon his trodden pillow; he sheltered her trembling, wet body with a second cover then returned to the front.

The air brakes released as the transport vehicle groaned forward, the stranger quickly ramping the massive rig back onto the highway. Forcefully he geared the eighteen-wheeler into high as the enormous engine roared onward in its mission to hastily seek medical attention for the mysterious young woman he had rescued from the roadside.

Within minutes the hospital was in sight and the stranger's rig roared directly up to the emergency room doors. Insistently he yanked downward on the raucous air horn warning others to unarguably clear from his route. Pulling at his seatbelt, the trucker leapt from his chair and bundled Claire's unconscious body into his arms. Carefully he lifted the woman from the cab and boldly barged through the hospital doors.

"Help! I need some help here right now!" he demanded as he watchfully positioned the woman's thin frame on a vacant bed in the vestibule. Attendants scurried to his side and began pulling at the blankets that enclosed Claire's body. The stranger presented the doctors with what little information he had about the woman he'd rescued from the ditch in the dark, torrential downpour.

With his heart pounding in his chest, he wedged his leather hands into the stiff front pockets of his faded blue jeans and paced across the foyer as he watched the woman being wheeled from his sight.

Five hours later Claire awoke from the depth of her unconscious slumber. Numbly perplexed she had no recollection of where she was or how she had gotten there. Elevating her arm weakly into the air, she felt the sting of the intervenos needle pierce the back of her right hand. The room was dimly lit as she struggled to focus on her surroundings hearing the nearby heart monitor beep away its steady tone of blips and bleeps. She reminded herself of the slick, wet roadway. She recalled swerving out of control. She remembered the riotous crash as she slammed her BMW against the drainage culvert. As she induced the accident in her mind, her heart rate accelerated envisioning the shadowed man who approached her car in the storm. But that was the last memory she had.

Reaching up with her left hand, she ran her fingers over her bandaged forehead, her brain feeling as if it was about to explode with painful jabs shrieking across her skull.

"Hello my dear," a voice chirped from across the room. "I'm glad to see you're awake. Now you just lay right there for a while," the sympathetic nurse instructed as she rushed to pull the window blinds closed shielding her patient from the glare of the rising sun. "It's almost morning dear but I want you to try and get some more rest. Sounds like you've had quite a night! My name is Rosie," the tiny, round nurse introduced herself in a thick Scottish accent. "Now dear, I've given you something for pain as well as something else to help you relax and sleep. Sleep is the best thing for you right now! I'll be close by if you need anything," Rosy chattered as she busied herself about the room.

Claire's eyes chased the nurse as she completed her routine duties and hastily rushed from her patient's bedside. Slowly raising her head in the air, Claire noticed that her hands had been treated and wrapped to ease the burning abrasions she received from the airbag. Fatigued, she then replaced her head upon the spongy pillow and closed her eyes as she searched for a memory of what had happened after the crash. Trying to relax her tense anxious body, her thoughts raced as a huge tear escaped from the corner of her eye.

"Just when I thought I had no tears left," she mumbled wiping the tear with the back of her scorched hand.

A short moment later, the jubilant nurse hurried back through the doorway and over to Claire's bedside.

"My dear," Rosie whispered into her patient's distressed eyes. "Are you up to having a short visit with your friend? He has been waiting patiently all this time and is very concerned about you," she continued as she gently swept a damp lock of hair from her patient's forehead.

Claire turned her eyes to meet with Rosie's.

"My friend?" she questioned feebly.

"Why yes," the nurse replied slightly puzzled. "The man who brought you in here last night?"

"But I don't know who brought me in here…" Claire initiated her response just as pain shot fiercely across her head. "Sure… I guess," Claire conceded as she closed her eyes scrunching her forehead in response to the agony she was feeling.

"Well that's great then dear…I'll tell him that he can pay you a short visit," the nurse replied in her thick Scottish tone.

Still perplexed but without further question Rosie abandoned her patient. The suffering woman then rotated her strained features to visibly explore the room noticing that the two suitcases from the trunk of her car had been placed neatly against the wall.

"Well how did they get here?" Claire remarked in question.

"I brought them in for you," a deep masculine voice replied from the doorway. "I thought you might need some clean clothes when you get out of here."

The voice drew hesitantly closer as the door swung closed behind it. The sound of cowboy boots ruggedly tapped along the floor as the footsteps approached her bedside. Claire's eyes tried to focus on the man towering over her having only a flash of recognition as she spotted the well-worn Stetson cowboy hat that he held clenched beneath his arm.

"How are you feeling little lady?" the man inquired shyly. "You didn't look so good last night let me tell ya."

Claire searched his shadowed face in the darkness of the room.

"I'm really sorry but… I just don't remember much about what happened last night."

She studied the man drawing her eyes upward from his lean muscular legs hidden beneath tight stone washed jeans, then up to his plaid flannel shirt, his tanned unshaven face, finally meeting with his stunning royal blue eyes.

Trying to recall the details of the previous night, she closed her eyes as tears welled up, tightly wriggling her forehead as the stabbing pain returned.

"I'm so sorry," Claire apologized. "I just don't remember… much."

"There's no need to remember," the raspy voice reassured her. "Hey," he laughed with a shrug of his shoulders, "actually it's probably better that you don't remember."

Claire's eyes drooped closed and then open again as the sleeping pill began to take effect.

"Say now," the handsome voice continued, "Not meaning to intrude mam'... but ...is there someone I should call for you? You know... to let them know that you're here."

Forcing her eyes open a second time wanting to learn more about the sexy deep voice, Claire sighed with exhaustion.

"No... you don't have to call anyone for me...But...hey... thanks. Thanks for everything. I'll be okay," she responded sleepily.

Feeling the need to reassure the stunning young woman before him, the dark stranger struggled with his own shyness.

"I...I had your car towed to a garage near here. So...so there's no need to worry about that."

"Thank you," she yawned, barely able to keep her eyes open. "Thank you for everything."

She cast a drowsy smile up to the man who had rescued her and dazedly fell in defeat of the medication. Claire's eyes groggily closed as she floated off in the distance.

Gazing down upon the woman with no name, the stranger reached out his tanned, thickly callused hand and brushed a wave of brown hair across Claire's cheek and out of her sleeping eyes.

"You gave me quite a scare last night little lady," he whispered persistently to the sleeping woman. "Quite a scare!"

Not wanting to leave her side but knowing his intrusion should end, the stranger stood quietly for a moment breathing in the sight of the beautiful woman that lay before him.

Then bowing forward he whispered softly in her ear, "You take care of yourself now little one... you take care."

He paused longingly at her side admiring her loveliness. With her head bandaged and her eyes swollen with redness, she was still absolutely beautiful. External scars could not hide the exquisiteness of Claire with her silky peach skin framed by her flowing cocoa hair. Goodness of the heart radiated from this woman. Though she had managed a painful journey throughout her life, Claire's spirit remained undefeated. Her soul was embedded in that of an ardently loving person. The stranger had quickly realized that her beauty radiated from her soul.

Only then, after an extended moment of hushed admiration did the stranger straighten his body but leave his magnetic royal blue eyes still locked upon her. A smile of adoration snuck across his lips as he struggled to break his gaze. Then reaching up to position his Stetson lightly upon his tasseled sandy blond hair, he tapped his fingers nervously on the bedrails.

"You take care of yourself now," he whispered.

With a swaggering turn of his broad well-built shoulders he quietly left the room.

A full six hours later, Claire groggily awoke a second time prying her eyes apart as Rosie entered the room.

"Well dear, how are we feeling now?" she inquired reaching to draw the window blinds open.

"Well… to tell you the truth…I'm not really sure," the patient replied sleepily, quickly closing her eyes again as the blinding sunshine beamed in through the large window.

"Now I've left you some clean towels dear so you can have a shower if you're up to it. They're on the sink in the bathroom when you're ready. In a few minutes the doctor will be in to check you over once again and then I'll put a fresh dressing on your head," the busy nurse advised. "You should be able to go home today if you promise to take it easy and get some rest. That's quite a nasty bump you gave yourself last night. A fairly severe concussion is what the doctor said."

Claire watched Rosie rush about the room chattering on in the changing pitches of her accent. "My shift is almost over for today dear. But I'd like to see you off before I go home."

"What time is it?" Claire questioned in a lethargic slur.

"Almost noon my dear! You've slept half the day away!"

Claire listened to Rosie's words then watched her pull the door open with her elbow. She hastily departed the room with her hands full of sterile utensils and an empty water jug tucked securely beneath her arm. Claire proceeded to raise her body from the bed as each muscle in her torso ached.

"Oh Christ!" she groaned aloud. "What the hell have I done to myself now?"

Painfully sliding her throbbing body from the bed, she paused noticing that a single, long stem red rose had been placed neatly on the nightstand beside her. Picking up the beautiful flower, she admired its perfection as she held it to her nose inhaling the romantic fragrance. Holding the flower in question, she stared out the window as the sun beamed brightly and the birds chirped their delightful tune in the trees just beyond the wall that separated them. Slowly she shook her head trying to recall who may have left the rose. Still in wonder, Claire replaced it on the bedside table and continued her painful journey to the shower.

Within an hour, Claire had refreshed herself and dressed. Rosie replaced the bandages on her forehead and did her best to get Claire packed and back on her feet. The doctor advised her to take it easy for a couple of days and to be sure and see her family doctor as soon as she got home.

"Sure," she agreed with the physician thinking to herself that home did not exist.

After receiving her final discharge, Claire shuffled to the admitting desk with her suitcases in hand and requested that the attendant call her a taxi.

"I'll be waiting just outside the door," she advised the clerk.

Trudging along the corridor and out the emergency doors, Claire dropped her baggage heavily as she reached the front steps of the hospital. Parking herself on a nearby bench she searched through her handbag for cash to pay the taxi driver.

In frustration as she fumbled through her purse she was startled as the roar of a huge engine started up in the distance. Shaken by the far-off racket, she raised her eyes noticing the tractor of a transport truck parked about two hundred feet away at the rear of the hospital parking lot. The massive hood of the rig was tipped up as if it was under repair while a man busied himself in among the roaring motor parts. As she studied the enormous red vehicle from the distance, the man repairing the engine suddenly stopped his work and turned to look in her direction as if he could feel her gaze acutely penetrating his shoulder blades. With his eyes staring into hers, he hesitated for only a moment. After calming the roaring engine he turned and climbed down from the massive truck. Pulling a grease rag from his back pocket, he wiped his hands then tossed it back over his shoulder onto the hood of the rig. Slowly the man began to wander over to the bench on which Claire was sitting waiting for her taxi. He sauntered across the parking lot with long swaggering strides never removing his eyes from hers. He had changed his red plaid shirt from earlier that morning and was dressed in tight fitting blue jeans, a white t-shirt and matching denim jacket. She recognized the worn Stetson hat and cowboy boots as he drew nearer to the bench. Claire couldn't help but focus on his handsome unshaven face and stunning blue eyes. With his hands shyly pressed into the front pockets of his jeans he approached.

"Hey there," he greeted her informally.

"Hi," Claire replied struggling to release her vulnerable gaze from his penetrating stare.

"How you feeling now?" the man inquired softening his tone.

"It's you! You're still here?" Claire cut him off in mid sentence as she started to vaguely remember his visit earlier that morning.

"Yeah... well... I thought you might need a ride somewhere once you got out of the hospital. You're car isn't going to be ready until tomorrow," he responded. "So you being without wheels, I just wanted to make sure you were settled somewhere before I moved on."

"Thank you... that's very considerate," Claire replied with surprise. "But don't you have some place to be?" the embarrassed woman questioned.

"No... I'm good for time now. I dropped my load at a local yard earlier this morning. A buddy of mine is going to take it the rest of the way for me," he answered in his slow retiring drawl, unsure if the woman would take him up on his offer to assist.

"I'm not sure where you were heading last night but I heard that there is a real nice resort down the road a piece. I figured you might want to spend the night there and get some rest until your car is ready. I can give you a ride over there if you like," the stranger offered with hesitation.

"Wow…" she replied taken back by his hospitality. "I don't know what to say."

"Then say yes!" the man grinned urging her timidly. Claire smiled sweetly at the man standing before her. She smiled for what seemed to be the first time in weeks.

"Yes… that would be great," she agreed as the stranger broke into a wide grin. His stunning face caught her attention as she reached down to pick up her cases.

"Have you ever had a ride in a big rig before?" he joked taking the suitcase handles from her grip.

"No… this will definitely be the first time!" she laughed.

"Well then, you're in for a real treat," he stated, pleased that she was taking him up on his offer to help.

The two walked across the parking lot in the warm sunshine of the early afternoon. The stranger loaded her cases into the cab of the truck then extended a large callused hand to assist her up the steps and into the passenger seat.

"Thank you," she giggled at the thought of her own image.

The stranger closed the door behind her and quickly walked around the front of the truck where he pushed the massive hood down and latched it securely back into place. Smiling broadly, he climbed into the driver's seat and turned the key as the mighty engine purred beneath them. As the air breaks released, the truck slowly pushed forward as it moved from the parking lot and turned onto the busy main street of the quaint cottage town.

Claire stared out the window in silence reflecting upon what the past twenty-four hours had brought to her.

"So… after all we've been through together, could you possibly tell me your name?" the stranger timidly broke the silence, inquiring with a hint of sarcasm.

His passenger giggled to herself, "Yes," she replied, "My name is Claire… Claire Morgan."

The man smiled at her reaction, repeating her name aloud, "Claire…Claire Morgan…Yep that suits you!"

Drumming his fingers nervously on the massive steering wheel he tried to disguise the attraction he instantly felt for her. Then in the same teasing manner Claire cocked her head slightly to the right, smiled and mocking his shy, yet inquisitive tone she inquired back to him, "So… do you happen to have a name or should I just refer to you as my hero?"

"Your hero?" the stranger laughed heartily. "Hey… I've never been anyone's hero before. That has kind of a nice ring to it now don't you think?"

Claire laughed sweetly awaiting his answer.

He paused for a moment then responded, "Yeah… people call me Luke… Luke Johnston."

Hearing his response Claire tore her gaze away from his handsomely tanned profile to stare back out the front window.

"Luke…Luke Johnston… Yep… that suits," she mocked.

Claire found the magnetic attraction between the two embarrassing as she struggled each time to pull her gaze from his face.

"Well Luke," she spoke into the front windshield, "It's very nice to finally meet you… while I'm awake that is!"

They both laughed as the rig purred onward out of the city and along the fresh rolling green hills of northern Ontario. As the miles passed beneath the mighty eighteen wheels that carried them, Claire unrolled her window as the welcome sunshine beamed in against her delicate skin. The afternoon breeze fluttered through her long brown hair as she pressed her head against the backrest relaxing with a silent sigh of relief.

Claire closed her eyes as moments of escaping relaxation swept over her. Then, breaking the silence, Claire turned to Luke and smiled into his ruggedly handsome profile.

"Thank you for the beautiful rose Luke," she spoke with heartfelt gratitude.

Without a verbal response he turned to his lovely passenger, smiled and winked a sparkling blue eye into her grateful face.

"Actually Luke…" Claire continued as she reached out to softly touch the muscular arm that gripped the massive steering wheel, "Thank you for everything you've done for me. I don't know what would've happened if you hadn't stopped to help me last night."

Her soft feminine touch sent a shiver through Luke's body as he blushed with timidity.

Turning again to meet with the gaze of his indebted passenger he responded, "Well Claire, I don't usually have the good fortune of assisting beautiful damsels in distress stranded on the side of the highway," he joked as his lips arched across his face. "Believe me when I say… it was my sincere pleasure! Hey, I'm just real happy that you're okay."

Embarrassed by the flattery, Claire turned her head back to stare out the front window longing to know more about the man in which she had entrusted herself. She wondered about him but was relieved that he asked very few questions of her. Claire simply didn't want to think about the sadness of the past week. She didn't want to talk about it and for a while longer she didn't want to cry. Luke was a welcome surprise. He did not press or probe her with questions. He seemed satisfied just to be able to help a woman who had obviously been through a lot. He hadn't been told about her past or of the recent traumatic loss of her daughter. He did however recognize the unhidden sorrow across her brow, but still he asked nothing further.

The truck rounded a wide bend on the country road then slowed as it approached the entrance to the magnificent grounds of Deerhurst Resort.

"I guess this is the place!" Luke supposed as the engine groaned. "I stopped for a coffee in a little café earlier this morning," he explained, "and someone told me about this place. I hope it's okay for you Claire. It sounded like just the kind of place you might want to relax in for the night. Your car should be back on the road by the morning."

The huge tractor tires hummed along the winding roadway as the luxurious country inn came into sight. A rush of panic crept over Claire as it suddenly dawned on her that her new friend would soon be leaving.

"You're going to stay the night as well, right Luke?" she blurted with urgency failing to monitor how she sounded and what she was implying. "I mean… I mean the least I can do is get you a room and buy you some dinner," she sheepishly regressed worried that her approach was overly boisterous.

Surprised by her generous invitation, Luke found himself equally relieved not wanting to remove himself from the beautiful woman he was aiding.

"Well I usually sleep in the truck at night, but hey… the thought of a clean shower and a comfortable bed sounds rather nice."

"That's great! Then it's settled!" she confirmed, slightly embarrassed by her own aggression.

Luke easily maneuvered the truck up to the magnificent front doors of the grand resort. The glass entranceway sprawled outward as the exquisite antique furnishings displayed themselves through the sparkling windows. After activating the air brakes, Luke jumped from the truck and scurried around to assist Claire to the ground. The cherry red transport truck appeared oddly out of place where it remained squeezed into the prestigious entranceway of the ostentatious resort. With the massive rig parked immediately outside the front doors, Luke supported Claire's arm as the two ventured through the doorway.

"Welcome to Deerhurst," a friendly voice beckoned to them.

Claire smiled graciously as she stepped toward the reception desk to make arrangements for two rooms for the night. Then a short moment later, she returned to the truck where Luke had retreated and was waiting with her luggage. With a wink of her eye, she tossed him the key card to his room and bent forward to pick up her suitcases.

"All set?" she inquired.

"Lead the way!" he responded taking the heavy baggage from her hands once again. "We'll get you settled first then I'll come back out and move the truck."

The two laughed at the vision of the massive tractor parked among the upper crust cars of the wealthy.

Claire sauntered down the tastefully decorated corridors with Luke close behind, eventually stopping to unlock the door of her assigned room. She swiped her key card then pushed the door open. As she entered her eyes quickly scanned the attractively adorned suite in which she would spend the night. Feeling slightly awkward, Luke stepped in behind her still burdened with luggage.

"Wow!" he commented, noticeably taken back by the luxurious splendor of the room. "This is really something isn't it?"

Claire was intrigued with his reaction as she turned to open the door to his adjoining suite.

Luke laughed at the arrangement then nervously blurted, "Hey now… we're going to be neighbors." His discomfort was evident as his eyes explored the lavish splendor. "But Claire… I'm afraid I'm likely to be a bit out of my element in a place like this." He motioned at his worn blue jeans.

"No you're not!" she quickly affirmed, not allowing the trucker the opportunity to change his mind about staying the night. "It's just a simple room to sleep in. Okay… it's a very nice room to sleep in. But since neither of us have had much luxury lately, we both deserve it and I really hope you'll stay."

Luke stared at Claire as she motioned toward the walls of the suite. Stimulated by the magnetism he felt for the mysterious woman he had only just met, he carefully placed her luggage down on the racks just inside the entrance and quickly stepped through the open door of his own room.

"Well," he informed her, "I think…I'll go out and move the truck then grab a shower. Why don't you lay down for a while and get some rest?"

"Yes… that sounds great!" she nodded in agreement recalling the tenderness in her neck and back.

"I'll swing back and check up on you in a couple of hours… sound okay?"

"Sounds great!" Claire approved feeling tired. "Then perhaps we can get some dinner?" she probed, seeking confirmation that they would be spending more time together. Luke winked and passed through the adjoining door between their rooms.

As the door latched closed, Claire reached up and passed her fingers over her bandaged forehead noticing that the pain had subsided. After walking over to draw the attractive floral curtains adorning her massive window, she paused to admire the finely manicured grounds surrounding the resort. The thick carpet of grass sprawled outward where it eventually met with the placidly flowing waves drifting in from the private lake.

Satisfied with the serenity to be found in such a magnificent country setting, Claire reached down, unzipped her jeans and slipped them off onto the floor. Feeling slightly groggy from the medication, she pulled back the floral spread on her majestic king size bed. The two enormous down-filled pillows found hidden under the floral bedcover lured her thin, shapely body beneath the fresh linen sheets where within seconds she drifted into a comforting slumber.

Four hours later Claire awoke from a sound, restful sleep. She felt better than she had in days. Sliding out from the crumpled sheets she yawned and stretched her arms upward as she walked toward the huge window. Sweeping the curtains aside, she found the sun slowing its glow preparing to set for the evening. The glistening fireball beamed a brim of blazing orange light above the tall row of pine trees at the far edge of the property. Pleasantly surprised, she noticed Luke standing on the shore skipping stones across the rolling waves clapping in rhythm upon the sand. Admiring his tall, muscular stature from the distance, she thought how strange it was that she felt such an irresistible attraction to this man. She knew nothing about him, not whom he was nor where he had come from. Though strangely enough, she felt as though she had known him forever. Never before had she experienced such an instantaneous draw. Only the day before, Claire felt as though she had fallen into a smoldering black pit of despair with no hope of climbing back out. Yet how quickly she had developed a curious, magnetism to a man she knew nothing about. It was as if divine intervention had put this stranger in her path to help her back onto her feet. Closing her eyes, tipping her chin up toward the ceiling, she gently rolled her head from side to side feeling her shoulders blades ache with tenderness. The jarring impact of the accident had shaken her being to the very core. With an admiring smile for the man she watched in the distance, she left the window and walked to the bathroom where she drew a hot soothing bubble bath. Slipping her sensitive body into the swirling jets of the expansive whirlpool tub, she relaxed into meditation as the fragrant bubbles foamed up around her chest.

Thirty minutes into her bath, Claire was abruptly brought back to the present as she heard a fist pounding furiously on the adjoining door of her suite. Startled by the aggressive thumping, she quickly sat up and reached to turn off the humming whirlpool jets that had entranced her aura. Leaping from the tub, she grabbed a fluffy white towel from the rack and wrapped it around her dripping body. She hurried through the large washroom to be instantly stunned by Luke's frantic voice hollering as he barged through the door of her suite.

"Claire! Claire! It's Luke! Are you alright in here?" his concerned tone questioned as he pushed forcefully into the room.

After quickly hooking the towel around her dripping body she met him only a few steps into the suite.

"Hey… hey… I'm fine," she responded reaching out to gently touch his arm and calm him.

As his eyes adjusted to the dim light in the room he focused upon her freshly dampened skin.

"Oh God! I'm so sorry Claire!" he immediately turned his blushing face to the side.

Laughing heartily at the unexpected assembly she brushed her wet hair back behind her ear.

"It's been four hours and… and I knocked and knocked… and I was worried you hadn't… well that you hadn't woken up yet. A nasty bump on the head can do that to a person you know," he chattered nervously, embarrassed over his impetuous invasion of her privacy.

"Luke… it's okay! Don't worry about it!" she continued to laugh at the sudden meeting. "But as you can clearly see, I'm fine... just fine."

"Yeah!" Luke closed his eyes at the vision of natural beauty he saw standing before him dripping wet. "Yeah, I can see, you're just fine!"

Hypnotized by the state of her nude splendor, Luke seemed unable to move his feet that were firmly planted on the rich beige carpeting. The two stared into each other's eyes for a long silent moment with an obvious hunger to draw closer.

Then becoming self-consciousness, Claire spoke first, "So hey! Give me ten minutes to get dressed and we'll grab some dinner together… sound good?"

"Sounds great!" Luke repeated rolling his eyes away from her loveliness as he turned and made a quick attempt to exit the room. "I'll wait for you in the bar on the patio," he shyly regressed, careful to direct his eyes out into the corridor through the open door. Claire caught the door three inches before it closed and peered out as Luke hurried to make himself scarce.

"Hey!" she jokingly shouted after him.

"Yeah?" he turned back to lock his eyes with hers.

"A glass of white wine would be just great!"

"You've got it!" he responded with his sexy deep voice.

Tearing his eyes from hers he forced himself to turn his head. Then mentally recalling the abrupt encounter with the woman he admired, Luke smiled and disappeared down the marble corridor.

Still chuckling at the intrusion and at Luke's embarrassed expression, Claire carefully dressed herself in a gray sleeveless turtleneck and cream woolen pants. Hooking pearl earrings through her delicate lobes and draping a matching string of beads around her neck, she stared at her reflection in the steamy mirror.

"Well girl!" she spoke into her likeness. "Life certainly is an adventure isn't it?"

She dried her silky brown hair then swept it up into a loose bun at the base of her graceful neck. Removing the bandage from her forehead she lightly brushed a few wisps of hair down in front to cover the wound. After a quick dusting of make-up and a spray of fresh cologne, she left the suite and ventured to find her new friend.

As she entered the patio, the male patrons on the deck were instantly imprisoned as her radiant beauty overtook the air. Claire visually scanned the cluster of tables in an anxious search for her cowboy. Luke was sitting alone at a small candle lit table in the far corner of the deck. His sandy blond hair tossed gently in the warm evening breeze as he held a tall cool glass of dark beer in his right hand. The handsome man stared out into the beautiful sunset. Claire quietly approached him from behind and placed both slender hands on his broad masculine shoulders.

"Hey there stranger," she whispered into his right ear.

Startled by her approach, Luke nervously jumped from his seat, placed his beer down on the table and bashfully jammed his hands down into the front pockets of his jeans.

"Claire… I'm really sorry. I've… I've never barged in on a woman quite like that before," he apologized.

Claire laughed again at the thought of her sopping wet body draped in a towel standing in front of this gorgeous stranger.

"Well… hey, I've never been approached quite like that before either," she assured him with a giggle as her eyes reflected the glow of the candle. Wrapping her long graceful fingers around his biceps in an effort to relax him she continued, "Don't worry about it! And thank you for your concern."

Stretching up onto the toes of her sandals she placed a soft, grateful kiss upon his darkly tanned cheek. With a pleasurable smile, he then stepped around the table and pulled out her chair as Claire gingerly placed herself within its welcoming frame.

"My muscles are still pretty sore from the accident," she stated, trying to lighten the magnetism felt between them.

"I'm not surprised about that," he responded uncomfortably, making an effort to hide his attraction for her. "That was quite a bad hit you took last night!"

Nodding in agreement Claire reached for her glass of wine and tapped it gently against Luke's beer.

"Cheers," she spoke with contentment. "Here's to a lovely evening with a new friend and an even better tomorrow."

"Cheers," Luke agreed. "Luck finally seems to be on my side."

The evening progressed and the conversation remained fun and light. Both had quickly realized that the other was hiding a painful past of loneliness but neither pried for information. The evening breeze flicked the candle on the table while relaxing jazz music hummed through the patio speakers.

As the glorious gourmet dinner arrived at the table, Claire was reminded by her hunger that she hadn't eaten in several days. The two new friends laughed and conversed over simple stories of their lives as they indulged in sumptuous crab legs and fresh vegetables. The dinner wine flowed in a current as the evening turned into darkness on the patio.

"So, where do you call home?" Claire probed timidly as they both entered a relaxed state from the Canadian grape vintage.

"Actually I'm just your basic cowboy from Western Canada," he replied. "I'm afraid I'm a bit of a down-home country boy. I... I really don't know much about big city life but I do know wheat fields and cattle ranching. I drive a truck through the Canadian winter months to appease the wanderer in me, which also helps me out with my mortgage payments. Tomorrow I aim to start my last run for the season. Then I'll park the truck and go back to farming for the summer," Luke explained.

Claire smiled serenely as Luke hinted about his personal life.

"And you?" he prodded feeling the door of information crack open slightly.

"I guess...I guess I could say," Claire thought carefully how to answer his question. "New York City is where my roots are. But I've also been wandering quite a lot these last few years," she answered dropping her eyes down to the table. "I'm a lawyer... and...I guess it all just got to me. I needed to get away from it... so here I am." Claire selectively worded her response not intending to lie about her past but also not wanting to relive the pain of it either. For a few hours she didn't want to feel grief or sadness. She wanted to feel alive again and for a short time she was selfishly allowing the strikingly handsome cowboy to help her escape from it. She was enjoying the hours of casual light freedom with Luke and did not want to spoil the serenity of the evening by getting into the heavy despair of what she had so recently experienced.

The light-hearted conversation slowed to a gradual halt as midnight approached. The two sat back in their chairs staring off in the distance. As the music humming from the speakers changed to a varied mix of enchanting love songs, Claire turned to openly stare at Luke. She admired his tanned weathered face and blond hair as he focused off into the shadows. Wanting desperately to be held by his luring rugged arms but not wanting to seem too forward, she mused as to how to approach him. Then as a familiar country voice began serenading the remaining patrons on the patio, Claire finally spoke up.

"Well now... here's a nice country boy song! Would you like to dance?" she inquired.

41

With a broad sexy smile sweeping across his highly set cheekbones, he responded with embarrassment, "Unfortunately Claire, I drive a truck better than I dance."

Unwilling to let the golden opportunity pass idly by, Claire lifted her serviette from her lap and placed it neatly on the table. She then arose from her chair and reached out a long graceful arm in his direction.

"Well…why don't you let me be the judge of that?" she urged a second time.

After a short pause, Luke conceded as a self-conscious expression extended across his brow. He stood, pushed his chair backward and reached out to join in on the stunning woman's invitation.

Hand in hand they walked to the dance floor as the country music droned through the air. With a formal distance between them, the two joined hands and gently swayed from side to side. The sorrowful melody overtook the romantic atmosphere as Claire's eyes began to well up with tears. Though she tried to push the memories from her mind, she couldn't help but rethink the pain of the past few days. Feeling a slight quiver in her body, Luke glanced down into her face noticing the crystal droplets that were beginning to roll over her cheeks. Not understanding the depths of her sorrow but wanting to comfort her, he cast the formality aside and pulled her thin shapely body in to meet with his. Towering a full eight inches above her, he enveloped his strong arms around her tiny sculpture, pulling her in closely, soothing her beaten, bruised body with his strong masculine frame. The warmth of his aura consumed Claire as she responded to his physical invitation for comfort and safety within his arms. Nestling his chin into her shimmering brown hair, he closed his eyes overtaken by the floral fragrance of the brown locks that were gently swept up into a knot at the back of her head. The two swayed amorously to the soft music without comment and without probing questions. The mood was intimate as was the music that seemed to flow on for hours. Neither had realized such an enchanting attraction for another. In silence they both knew they had a swelling need for the other.

As her desire surged, Claire released her embrace and looked up into his amazing blues eyes.

"Do you want to go for a walk?"

Wanting the moment to go on forever, Luke pulled her in tightly, embracing the ravishing beauty as if time was standing still.

"Sure," he conceded quietly as he released her and let the warmth they shared slip from between them. Taking her fragile hand in his, he led her toward the beach. In silence the two leisurely walked listening to the waves rushing onto the shore. As flashes of the next morning's final good-bye pounded through Luke's minds-eye his face became stressed.

"Well… let me tell you something Claire," Luke interrupted the silence as he tightened the grip he had on her thin hand.

She turned to face him and then slid her feminine hands up and along his muscle bound forearms.

"Never in my wildest dreams did I think that when I stopped to help out at the accident last night, did I ever imagine I'd be sharing such a wonderful evening with a beautiful woman like you the very next day."

Claire's smile widened at the rich compliment.

"It's funny how life works sometimes… isn't it?" she responded softly as she pulled herself in closer toward him.

She felt herself slipping into his spectacular blue eyes as she reached up to touch her moist shimmering lips against his, slipping her arms in tightly around his waist. Lightly she skimmed his mouth feeling as though she were being swept from her feet. He paused for only a second basking in the pleasure of her physical advance as the moon shone down from the clear evening sky. Then hungrily he pulled her in as he passionately kissed her lips and neck. Peaking with desire for the magnificent woman he held, Luke followed her fragile neckline with his powerful fingers, sweeping her fallen locks of hair behind her ear. Kissing her passionately he lightly brushed his callused hand along her cheekbone then slowly reached up to remove the clip that left her cocoa hair to fall down around her shoulders. Luke pulled his lips from hers as he gazed at the beautiful length feeling the silky lace flow between his fingers. Then, overcome by the rhything heat of passion, he pressed his lips into Claire's as the desire shared between them surged wildly. His heart pumping vigorously, desperately craving the woman he held but knowing it could go no further, he then forced himself to slow his outward passion on Claire's lips. Repeatedly running his fingers through her hair he gently pressed her head into the refuge of his chest.

"My God Claire," he whispered into her ear, "You are so beautiful. What… what am I going to do tomorrow after you're gone?"

Wanting to avoid his question she looked up and smiled into his eyes. Taking his hand in hers she slowly walked with him back to the hotel without saying a word.

Both hearts sank despairingly as they approached the door to Claire's suite. Fighting back the untamed desire to plunge into his arms once again, Claire reached up and lightly brushed Luke's lips with her own.

"Thank you for a wonderful evening Luke. In fact, thank you again for everything you've done for me. Without knowing why, you have made me feel alive again for the first time… in a very long time."

Luke stared into her dancing green eyes equally disheartened that the evening was drawing to a close.

"You're a remarkable woman Claire. I've never met anyone like you before," he spoke with tenderness as his sexy grin widened. "I… guess, I guess that's what they call, meeting by accident ay? Believe me when I say," he continued, "It has been my greatest pleasure."

"Good-night Luke," she responded with a smile of embarrassment.

With that, she pushed through the door of her suite and closed it gently behind her. With the incredibly attractive man then out of her sight, Claire felt her body begin to shiver as she physically ached for him. Closing her eyes in the darkness of her room, she leaned against the door.

"Why can't I have anything in this life that I really want?" she questioned under her breath.

With a heavy sigh, Claire undressed and slipped her elegant white lace nightgown down over her head. After sliding into bed she heard the television blare loudly in the room adjoining her own. She yearned for Luke's powerful body as she listened to the pounding water of the shower next door.

Staring blindly into the ceiling of her suite, the minutes, then hours of the darkened night sluggishly dragged past as she thought of nothing but Luke. Wanting him…needing him as she had never needed another man before. The bodily craving overtook her soul as she envisioned his sexy unclothed body sleeping in the forbidden room next door.

The loving attraction she felt for Luke was foreign to her as her husband Jacob had been her first and only sexual encounter. She had always known that her intimate experience with Jacob had been solely for his own personal satisfaction. Claire had never known her body to passionately spill over for a man as she felt it do for Luke.

Claire lay in frustration until the digital clock next to her bed glowed 3:00 a.m. Then she could control her pining for him no longer. Slipping out from beneath the crisp linen sheets, she walked quietly to the door where just beyond Luke lay asleep. Not knowing what his reaction might be, but willing to take the risk, she tapped her knuckles gently against the door. The room remained silent with no response from beyond as she began to have serious doubts about possible rejection and rethink what she was doing. Giving her desire one final chance she knocked a second time. Then still without a response, she stretched her long fingers out against the door.

"Okay then…I guess it's just not meant to be…Goodnight my love," she whispered into the darkness.

Slowly turning to walk back toward her bed the door opened abruptly.

"Claire? Claire, are you okay?" Luke's raspy deep voice questioned.

In surprise she turned back to view the shadow of the man she was longing for. His tall dark, silhouette stood with concern in the doorway wearing only his unbuttoned blue jeans, which gaped wide open in the front. Staring at the masculinity that sleepily called her name, Claire's body surged with burning desire as she craved him.

"No… no I'm not okay Luke," she whispered nervously.

Leaning against the doorframe Luke tipped his puzzled head to the side not comprehending what was wrong with his cherished friend.

Pausing for a moment, not knowing how to proceed, she finally blurted out, "I need you Luke. I need you to hold me… please… please hold me. Please stay with me here tonight."

Stunned by the unexpected invitation for intimacy but without a second of hesitation, Luke walked quickly toward her, his bare feet striding across the rich beige carpeting. With his hair still tasseled from sleep, his sexy muscular body reached out to the beautiful woman that stood in front of him in her short lace gown. Pulling her in close he pressed his hard body into hers.

"I'm here Claire… I'm here…for anything you need."

Instantly they engaged their lips as the fuel simmered between there wanting bodies. Then in silence, Claire took Luke's hand and led him to her bed.

As they slipped beneath the sheets, their obsessions quickly unleashed. Passionately kissing Luke's neck and shoulders, Claire reached down to slip his unbuttoned jeans down his powerful legs. Running her hand back up his thigh and over his enlarged hardened penis, she voraciously fondled his tongue with hers. Holding nothing back, Claire released the yearning she felt for this man whom she knew so little about. It was as if at that moment in the world, everything was right. Luke slid the thin straps of her gown down around her silky white shoulders tenderly kissing her firm breasts. His heart beat wildly with desire to take the woman he lay beneath that night. Needing each other, they shared their bodies openly, arousing their souls to heights neither had ever known. Making passionate love, pressing their nudeness together in a quenching thirst for fulfillment, their souls became one. All apprehension had dissolved as they coiled around each other in the darkness.

The raging fire of their love sizzled endlessly as the dead of night dawned into the hush of the early morning. Both bodies completely spent, soaked in the sweat of their fervor, they lay together in a slumber of immense satisfaction still entangled within the arms of their love.

As the early morning light peered through the curtains, Luke awoke to the sound of his cell phone ringing in the next room. Gazing at the radiant beauty that still lay within his arms he smiled, gently kissed her nose and silently crawled from the bed they had shared. Without movement, Claire remained in the depths of her dreams.

An hour later Claire awoke feeling relaxed and refreshed. Slowly she rolled over to find that her partner of love was no longer by her side. In his place, resting upon the pillow where he had lay his head the night before was a single long stem red rose and a note in which he had inscribed, "Good morning beautiful. I'll be back soon!" Smiling through her sleepy gaze, Claire held the rose to her nostrils breathing in the familiar floral fragrance as she placed her head back down upon the pillow. After reading the note, she closed her eyes and allowed her thoughts to drift back to the previous night of erotic obsession. Smelling Luke's cologne on the pillow beside her head, she was astonished at how much love she felt for him. In only a single day, he had captured her very soul. He had passionately swept her from her feet. His mere presence seemed to instantly make everything "right" again. For the first time in a very long time, she did not feel lost or lonely.

Claire blissfully shoved the linen sheets aside and slipped lightheartedly from her bed only to notice that a silver tray had been placed on the dining table in her suite. Neatly set upon the tray was a pot of hot coffee, a bottle of champagne, two crystal flute glasses, two coffee mugs and a large shimmering bowl of fresh red strawberries.

"You are simply amazing!" Claire whispered as she thought of the man with whom she'd shared so much love.

Contently she sauntered into the washroom and turned the gold plated knobs in the shower as the scorching hot water came rushing down. Lighting the vanilla candles that were placed neatly in a row on the marble vanity, Claire then realized that she had completely forgotten her physical pain from the accident as she stepped into shower, the pounding warm water pouring down over her nude body.

She ran her fingers up over her forehead and then slowly back through her long wet hair as the water relaxed her shoulders. As she thought of her sexy cowboy, she noticed the bathroom light slowly dim. The shower door opened with a rush of cool air and then she felt his two rugged hands run tenderly up her spine as he began massaging her delicate shoulder blades. Feeling his firm body press against her back, she turned her slender nudeness toward the familiar man that had joined her in the shower. Pulling him close into her she hungrily kissed his sensuous wet lips as the blistering water soaked their bodies. Without hesitation she welcomed his enlarged pulsating penis within her, feeling his penetrating tight grasp as he entered. With erotically sweeping kisses down her neck and across her supple breasts he pumped her pelvis, aggressively searching for the satisfaction he had received from her the night before. Tipping her relaxed, wandering head backward in the hot water, Claire smiled as her passionate cowboy took her once again in the shower. She watched as the satisfaction he incessantly searched for swept gradually over his handsome face.

"Oh God…you are so… beautiful," he blurted with a pant of relief as his climax came to a final penetrating height. His lips brushed lightly over hers as he stared into her sensual dark green eyes, tightening his arms around her waist.

"You are so very beautiful," the cowboy repeated with a grin of fulfillment.

Claire smiled serenely then snuggled her face into his strapping well-built chest as the steam overtook the bathroom. Together they stood tightly embraced, wanting to holdfast to the love they shared at that moment. Totally overwhelmed with what they had found in each other…the two lovers declined to let go.

The morning hours passed casually by as the two lay entwined on the massive bed, laughing, drinking champagne, sharing lighthearted stories and indulging in fresh strawberries. The morning was perfect.

As the hour reached high noon, the romantic mood was interrupted as the disturbing ring of Luke's cell phone was heard once again in the adjoining suite. Without answering the call, Luke knew that he would soon have to leave. Planting a playful kiss on her nose, he prepared to break the news to his love.

"Hey there," he whispered gazing into her concerned eyes.

But Claire knew what he was about to tell her placing her fingers over his lips as if to silence him. She knew it was coming but didn't want to hear the words.

"I know… I know it's time," she responded trying to disguise her disappointment.

"Yeah… I'm afraid so," the cowboy agreed. "I'm sure that's my broker calling again to remind me about the hot load I have to run this afternoon. Actually he's probably pretty pissed off that I haven't picked it up yet."

"Well… I guess all good things must come to an end," Claire replied in sadness as she crawled from the bed and started to dress. Feeling her warmth slip from his arms, Luke followed her and pulling the radiant woman back in toward him he tenderly kissed her lips.

Luke held her tenderly for a long moment then whispered, "Lets pack up and I'll drive you over to get your car. It should be ready by now."

Claire turned her eyes from his view as tears of disappointment started to form.

"I'll be ready in a few minutes," she spoke quietly feeling the onset of his upcoming abandonment.

Luke retreated from the room as Claire continued to dress and gather her belongings.

Twenty minutes passed when the handsome cowboy returned to her door. Standing silently in the entranceway with his brown leather bag slung casually over his shoulder, he stared at the woman he had immediately fallen in love with.

"Here, let me help you," he offered stepping forward to pick up her suitcases. She nodded solemnly in his direction.

"Oh by the way," she spoke with anxiousness as she approached the exit, "here is the coat that you lent me the night of the accident."

She handed him the brown canvas coat that he had graciously wrapped around her shoulders as he pulled her from the car in the torrential rain. Forcing a strained smile, he tucked it under his arm and followed her to the door. The two walked silently to the truck. Without words he loaded her cases into the rear bunk and held out an arm of assistance as Claire lifted herself into the front seat of the massive rig. Turning the ignition key, the engine groaned miserably having been awoken from its sleep. Luke sat in stillness staring at the elegant profile of his passenger.

"Hey beautiful," he spoke tenderly reaching to run his coarse fingers through her neatly combed hair, "there's something I want to tell you but I can't seem to find the right words. As a matter of fact, you'll probably think it's kind of silly," he added shyly.

Claire turned to look at the struggling cowboy. Her face was temporarily void of expression.

"What is it?" she probed assuming she was about to be emotionally devastated.

"Well… well it's just this," he fumbled for the words. "I have never experienced the feelings that you brought out in me last night Claire. In fact, I have never known that depth of passion. I've never met anyone like you and never have I felt such an obsessive connection with anyone before," Luke blushed timidly as the words tumbled from his lips. But he knew he had to continue before he lost the nerve. "It's just that… I think… no, I'm fairly sure that…well Claire, I think I'm falling in love with you."

Claire's defensive facial expression vanished as a smile spread across her shimmering lips. Reaching toward him she threw her arms around his neck.

"I know it's strange! I don't understand it either but… I am in love with you as well. I was just so worried that you didn't feel the same way about me!"

Sustaining the embrace, the enchanted pair searched for each other's lips and hungrily joined together once again. Running her hair of silk between his strong fingers, Luke slowly eased himself from her embrace.

Looking deeply into her eyes he reassured her, "Everything is going to be okay Claire. Please trust in me. I don't know where you have come from or what your future plans are, but I can tell you, that if you'll let me into your life and we're together… everything is going to be just fine!"

Claire pulled back further to wipe a crystal tear from her damp eyes with the back of her trembling hand.

"I know it is," she responded with relief. "Now that I have you, I just know everything is going to be okay."

Luke leaned back in his chair and after winking at his gorgeous partner of love, he forcefully pulled at the gearshift and the gigantic rig began to ramble forward.

Swiveling around in her seat, Claire reached backward in search of her safety belt when she became mesmerized with a far off gift seen from the side window.

"Oh my God, Luke look!" she directed his attention through the glass on her right. "There is the most beautiful rainbow!"

Luke smiled as he changed gears and then tipped his hat slightly back on his head in acknowledgement. Staring at the vision in the sky, Claire latched her seatbelt in place then relaxed serenely in her chair. The magnificent rainbow was a gift from above after a light spring shower of rain off in the distance.

"Thank you Amelia...I love you my darling!" she whispered under her breath. Claire knew at that moment that her daughter was with her. She felt her child's love within. She understandably believed that Amelia was guiding her into her future and was no doubt overjoyed to see her mother's heart filled with such love as she smiled down from her home in the heavens.

In spite of Luke's promise for a future together, Claire couldn't help but worry as she tried to disguise her dread of the upcoming separation. The miles of greenery passed all too quickly as it seemed only a few minutes before Luke wheeled his transport into an empty lot across the road from the mechanic's garage where Claire's BMW awaited.

"Well it looks like your car is ready! That's certainly good news," Luke advised noticing the sleek S7 BMW parked outside the garage.

With a sweep of the air breaks he turned in his seat and pulled her suitcases from the bunk.

"It looks like it is," she sadly agreed noticing that the windshield had been replaced but the dent in the back bumper remained.

Luke jumped down from the truck in pursuit of the resident mechanic. The two men stood along side the sparkling beamer discussing the repair work that had been done. Claire climbed from the truck for what she secretly dreaded might be the last time. She wanted to believe in Luke's promise of a life together but she had been disillusioned so many times in her life that she couldn't seem to get past the lurking doubt. Claire joined the men as they chattered about the car.

"It sure is a beauty!" the mechanic gestured toward the BMW.

Claire nodded, void of emotion paying little heed to the vehicle. She then turned to follow the mechanic into the office and paid for the repair work.

"Now you take care of that gorgeous car now Miss, as well as yourself!" the mechanic lectured as he closed the drawer of his cash register.

"Thank you," she responded with dismay as she turned and left his shop.

Pushing her payment receipt into her handbag she then tossed it carelessly into the back seat of the car. Luke stood leaning against the hood of the BMW with his hands warily shoved into the front pockets of his jeans.

"The mechanic said that he only repaired what you needed done in order to get you back on the road. So you can have the body work looked after when you get back home," Luke informed her politely.

But Claire's thoughts had drifted far from the dent in her BMW. At that moment she couldn't have cared less about it. Claire nodded in response as she wrung her hands nervously around each other.

"So," he changed the subject, partially hiding his sorrowful eyes beneath his Stetson. "Where are you going now exactly?" he probed.

Claire shrugged her shoulders in question.

"I honestly don't know Luke," she explained. "I guess I'm just going to do a lap of the country…searching for what? I don't know that either. I guess I won't know… until I get there."

Luke nodded looking intensely into the woman's stunning green eyes. He recognized the same sorrow reappearing that he'd seen on her brow the previous day. Still, that didn't give him any more information about where to find her once his trucking excursion was over.

"Well… I guess this means good-bye," Claire extended her right hand as if to formally shake with his. "Thank you for everything Luke," she addressed him defensively not wanting to bid farewell.

Disguising his emotion at the parting, he looked at Claire in surprise and then brushed her extended hand aside.

"Don't give me that shake-your-hand bullshit," he joked fondly as he pulled her body into his.

Breaking through her defensive shields, Luke embraced Claire as she buried her face into the warmth of his chest. Overcome with the gloom of the separation she wrapped her arms around his waist and held him tightly against her.

"This isn't really good-bye…right Claire? We just talked about that… right?" the concerned cowboy pled in her ear wanting confirmation that they would meet again in the very near future.

Relieved by his statement of hope, Claire looked up and as he brushed a tear from her cheek she replied, "I was really hoping that it doesn't mean good-bye. Right now, I'd even settle for a see-ya-later."

Luke laughed as he released her and pulled a white card from his back pocket.

"Listen…here is my cell number. Now I have to run this load down to Florida but I'll be back home in a couple of weeks. My cell phone may be out of range for a while but please don't give up on me. Why don't you give me your cell number as well and I'll call you as soon as I can?"

Desperate not to lose touch with her rugged cowboy, Claire reached in her car and pulled a navy blue business card from her wallet.

"This card has my old New York office address on it but the cell number is current," she explained.

Luke glanced down briefly at the card then inserted it into the front pocket of his flannel shirt.

"Do you have any idea where you're heading Claire?" he inquired a second time, still wanting more information.

"Quite honestly… no I don't," she responded lowering her eyes to the ground.

"Well then, don't worry my love… I'll find you. Hell…I found you on the side of the road now didn't I?" he joked trying to lighten the mood.

Claire smiled recalling the circumstances of their initial introduction. Then without further probing Luke swept her back into his arms and pressed his warm sensuous lips against hers in a final passionate kiss.

"Now you be careful on the road darling," he whispered as he pulled his lips from hers. "Do you hear me? Be careful now! I don't want to hear on my CB that some other trucker got the opportunity to assist my lovely big city lawyer off the side of the highway…cause then you'll be pulling me out of the ditch," he joked trying to bring a smile to her face.

Claire choked out a laugh as the vision of Luke's rig stuck in the ditch flashed quickly through her mind.

"No…I'm really just kidding. I know you need some time alone Claire. I don't know why…but I can tell from your eyes that you've been hurt deeply. But please be careful darlin'. I'm really gonna miss you," he confessed as emotion cracked his voice.

Then wiping a second tear from her eye, he gently kissed her cheek and turned to assist her into the car. Claire was unable to verbally respond as she fought against her better judgment. She stared at her sensuous cowboy as he pressed his leather hand against the glass and closed the door gently after her. Claire reached up and held her slender fingers against his, separated only by the glass between them. Then swallowing the welling lump in her throat, she started the car engine and slowly wheeled from the parking lot all the while watching Luke in her rearview mirror. He raised a hand and waved good-bye as she rounded the corner of the country road and then…he was gone from her view.

Still worried that she had seen Luke for the last time, she clasp the plain white card he had given her tightly in the palm of her hand as she gripped the steering wheel tensely.

"We'll meet again my love," she reassured herself under her breath. "We will meet again."

Chapter Three

Claire ramped her sparkling hubcaps onto Highway #11 heading north, mindless of a destination. As hundreds of miles wore on her tires, she reflected back to the man she had so recently met and intimately loved. How wonderful he was! How handsome and passionate he was! She had never known anyone like him before and yet she knew so little about him. Claire recalled how secure she felt within his strapping muscular arms. She couldn't explain it to herself. He had asked nothing of her and yet made it blatantly clear that he was as captivated by her as she was with him.

Basking in the recent intimacy, she felt calmly at peace. Never had she so freely given of herself to a man before. One-night stands were definitely not her style. Withered and jaded from the only intimate relationship she'd had with Jacob, Claire was surprised at how willingly she opened up to the gorgeous cowboy. She knew that for a brief period of time he had pulled her from a culvert of bitter misery and carried her emotionally to a far off euphoric place… a place without intruding questions or judgments. It was a place of hope, love and promise. The magnetic attraction she felt was mentally enriching and physically energizing.

Claire drove on through the rolling hills of northern Ontario. The forests and meadows of the far north were bursting with the spring bloom of early May. The world she traveled through was fresh, green and fragrant. She lowered the convertible top of her BMW feeling the sun penetrate against the back of her head, her hair blowing wildly in the wind.

As the afternoon hours turned into evening, Claire drove on refusing to even consider the possibility that she would never see Luke again. She was confident that the bonding love they had shared, even if only for a short time, was the kind of love that was lasting and meant to go on forever. It was the quality of love that a person finds only once in a lifetime. The breathtaking northern scenery blew past as she basked in loving thoughts of Luke.

As the evening poured into the blackness of the Canadian night, Claire realized that exhaustion was creeping over her. With anticipation she checked into a small family run motel and lightheartedly burst through the door of her sparsely furnished room. Tossing her suitcase on a chair, she reached for the white card with Luke's phone number embossed on it. Lying on her bed with expectancy, waiting to hear the sound of his sexy voice once again, she dialed the number he had given her. After three long aggravating rings, she was met with the recorded operator's voice saying, "The cellular caller you are trying to reach is currently unavailable. Please try your call again later." With a sigh of disappointment, Claire disconnected her call as she dangled her legs over the edge of the small bed.

"Well... now... don't over react," she firmly directed her subconscious. "He said he might be out of range for a while."

Claire smiled thinking of Luke's stunning face. She then lifted herself from the bed and began to unpack for the night.

A couple of hours passed as Claire clicked through the limited television channels with boredom. Relaxing on her bed, gawking around the room, she was suddenly swept over by a wave of loneliness. The room fell markedly short in comparison to her suite the night before. But more importantly she felt alone because Luke was not with her.

Claire endeavored to call Luke eight more times that evening but each time she was answered by the same annoying operator. The clock beside her bed read 11:48 p.m. as a tear of agonizing loneliness rolled down her cheek. Falling in defeat of her emotions, Claire turned off the television set, pulled the tacky green comforter up over her body and drifted off to sleep...alone.

As the early morning sun crept over the windowsill, Claire awoke. Without a second of hesitation she reached for the phone and tried to call Luke. She desperately needed to talk with him, to hear his voice, to be reassured that she would see him again. Claire held her breath as the phone rang three times and then predictably connected to the operator's voice, which she had quickly come to detest. Luke was not within her reach. Struggling to remain in control of her whirling sentiment, she quickly showered then packed her bags and left the motel.

As each passing mile took Claire further from Luke, her confused state of emotions consumed her thoughts as the euphoria of her recent encounter became less of a vivid memory. Without stopping, she traveled through the far north of Ontario driving on into the next night. Avoiding the isolation of sleeping in a hotel room alone, she perked herself up on coffee and continued driving through the Canadian wilderness, winding around the massive pine trees and colossal hills of rock.

As midnight approached Claire neared the Manitoba provincial border. Repeatedly she had tried to call Luke that day needing confirmation that he existed and would return to her life again. But each time, she was left increasingly disappointed. As thoughts of doubt swam angrily through her head she realized how little she knew about the man she had become emotionally addicted to. She knew he farmed a bit in western Canada but where in God's name was that? She knew he drove a truck and was running to Florida but that also left her no closer to finding him again. The only shred of evidence she had of his existence was a plain white business card with his name and cell number printed on it.

The night seemed to go on forever as she crossed into Manitoba driving on in flight trying to escape the loneliness she was feeling. Another hundred miles passed beneath her tires and Claire's thoughts grew increasingly more negative. Occasionally pulling her car off the road to try and sleep was of little help. The ghostly memories of her past haunted her more each time she tried to rest. Desperately waiting and wanting for her telephone to ring with her cowboy's deep voice greeting her, she swirled into a state of depression.

"How could I have found someone like Luke and then let him slip through my fingers like that?" she yelled while angrily pounding her fist on the steering wheel.

The tears she knew intimately only a few days before had replenished themselves and ran in a miserable flow down her cheeks. She called herself thoughtless for allowing Luke to disappear from her life without providing her with more information about where he lived.

Her mental head games grew more negative with each passing mile, which in turn lead to harrowing thoughts of Amelia. Her state worsened with each hour as her pessimistic thoughts fed upon themselves. How alone she felt as she ventured on into the changing plains of Manitoba.

Exhausted and bedraggled, Claire drove on without rest for a second full day and night. Then, as she crossed the most western border of Manitoba and ventured into the vastness of Saskatchewan her telephone finally rang.

"Oh my God!" she shrieked with joy as she fumbled around looking for her cell phone.

Clicking the connect button she joyfully sang out, "Luke... Luke?"

A moment of confused silence passed and then, "No baby... it's not Luke," the caller's voice slithered back at her. "It's your husband Jacob! You know, the husband that you ran out on!"

Stunned by the intruding voice, Claire's elation immediately dissolved.

"So how are you doing bitch? But more importantly... how's my baby Amelia? You know how much I miss her now don't you Claire?" Jacob's voice was as blood curdling as ever! "You see sweetheart, I'm getting a little tired of tracking you down all over the fucking country. My level of patience is growing rather thin Claire! Now I'm sure you understand that I'm doing my very best not to get too nasty here, but I want Amelia back and I'm not going to stop until I get her. You can run as far as you want Claire but I'm going to find you very soon."

Paralyzed with the fear she had become so familiar with, Claire froze within the cyclone of his brutally threatening words.

"And you know what else Claire? When I catch up with you this time, which I'm telling you will be very soon, first I'm going to kill you then I'm going to take Amelia back home with me where she belongs. You never should've run out on me Claire. You never should've run!"

Still Claire gave no response holding the receiver to her ear as if entranced by his windstorm of threats.

"Sweetheart, I really thought you were smarter than that. For an overpaid lawyer, you're really quite a stupid bitch! No, your father hasn't exactly been helpful to me but I will tell you that every time you take money out of your bank account I can trace where you are."

Claire said nothing as it finally dawned on her how Jacob kept finding her.

"Enjoy the freedom you have right now darling as soon we will meet again."

Hearing his final malicious threat Claire snapped herself from her daze. Nervously groping the keypad of her phone she hastily disconnected the sound of his slithering voice. She tossed the cell phone to the floor and sped her tires onward in a quest to flee from the influence she despised.

"Jesus Christ!" Claire yelled as she pounded her clenched fist on the console. "That raving lunatic son-of-a-bitch!"

Staring out through the bug-spattered windshield, the lights on the highway reflected beams into her eyes. She fell into a hypnotic trance of old thoughts as she pierced her eyes angrily into tiny slits. Claire had put up with years of Jacob's intrusive telephone calls. Although that was the first time he had actually threatened to kill her, she was growing weary of being afraid all the time, never knowing when or where Jacob would crawl back into her life.

Realizing the speed at which she was traveling, Claire attempted to pull herself together. Then feeling an unexpected rush of courage, she pulled her shoulders erect against the backrest and grinned as she thought of her husband.

"Well now baby! Haven't I got a surprise for you!" she taunted sarcastically as if Jacob could hear her voice. "Amelia is dead! She has left us both! She is gone from this tormenting life of hell on earth! You'll never have her now you bastard! So you can take your malicious, foul-mouthed threats and shove them up your ungrateful selfish ass!"

Claire had been hiding from her husband for years and was tired of living in constant fear. She was fed up with him landing back in her life when she least expected it. She had deliberately avoided seeking a divorce knowing full well that any kind of legal action against him would only aggravate his revengeful tantrums. She was also concerned that divorce proceedings would leave an obvious paper trail to her whereabouts. Perhaps the day would soon come when she would face her estranged partner once again. With Amelia out of harms way, perhaps it was time to finally end it with Jacob for good.

Claire worked to dismiss the battle of emotions raging in her head and refocused her eyes on the road. Snapping herself from her angry state she turned the radio volume up and started to take notice of the sprawling natural beauty that surrounded her. The vastly stretching fields of wheat were breathtaking. Claire drove on admiring the beauty of Mother Nature. Miles of the fresh emerald spring crop were swaying gracefully in the gentle breeze of the May afternoon. Saskatchewan was indeed beautiful, possibly a sample of Mother Nature's finest work, so unhurried, so serene. Miles passed without another car in sight. It was magnificent! With a refreshing, healing sigh of relief Claire felt relaxed and at peace with herself.

"Okay Claire," she spoke aloud to herself, "it's time for you to take care of yourself now! Amelia is gone forever. Luke is gone as well… and Jacob can go to hell!"

Claire laughed to herself thinking about Jacob as she noticed a cluster of massive silver grain elevators standing majestically in the distance of a passing field.

"What a beautiful place this is," she muttered with amazement. "Maybe it's time to find a new home and create a new life. And maybe… just maybe, this is going to be the place!" she continued her self-talk.

Loving what she saw, Claire wheeled her car over the perimeter of the lovely farm community of Yorkton, Saskatchewan.

Claire spent a full hour touring the quaint rural settlement and knew instantly that she could easily make it her new home. The pace of the community was tranquil and welcoming.

"Yes, I could live here quite nicely," she confirmed.

The town noticeably catered to the local farm operators with heavy equipment dealers located on all the major crossroads. Yet it also nurtured the typical business necessities that a big city girl might require. Yorkton undeniably lacked the air of tension, timelines and pressure that Claire had become accustomed to in the massive metropolitan cities she had lived most of her life in.

The golden afternoon ramped its prairie glow down into the early evening dusk as Claire began searching for a hotel to stay the night in. She was fascinated with Yorkton and planned to continue her exploration the next day.

As she journeyed back across the town's perimeter making her way to a motel she had noticed on the way in, a small white weather-beaten sign secured by a wooden post caught her eye on the side of the two-lane highway.

"Cottage for rent," the sign advertised.

"Hey!" Claire stated reading the sign as she quickly passed. "Now just what do we have here?"

Grinding her car to a screeching halt on the gravel shoulder, she jammed her gearshift into reverse and backed up through the cloud of dust. She quickly wrote the telephone number down that had been sloppily painted on the sign in dripping red letters. Noticing that the old wooden board was partially covered by overgrown grass, Claire hoped the cottage was still available.

"This may be my lucky day after all!" she chattered pulling back out onto the country highway.

Curiosity quickly got the better of her and she wanted to catch a glimpse of the cottage immediately. Clutching the tiny paper on which she had scribbled the owner's telephone number, Claire drove down the highway for another mile until she saw a similar sign advertising the cottage with an arrow pointing to the right through a large cluster of trees. Again she slammed her breaks on as her sleek black vehicle was blanketed with a second coating of dust. She swerved from the highway and onto the dirt road in search of the cottage as her interest peeked. After driving down a long winding dirt pathway that was almost completely overgrown with weeds, through a nominal cluster of trees and across a stretching wheat field, Claire finally came upon the little cottage nestled cozily within a huge shelterbelt of magnificent pines. The intrigued woman slowed her vehicle and coasted up to the rear door of the house. She climbed from her car with curiosity as if she was visualizing an old friend for the first time in many years.

The cottage was in dire need of repair as the shutters hung tilted from the windows. The exterior paint was peeling badly and the shrubs were overgrown with sorrowful neglect. The front veranda sighed with exhaustion as the broken railing sagged outward. But Claire could see past the structural repairs of the inviting little nest. She envisioned healing and serenity close within her grasp.

The cottage was snuggled up against a small winding creek that chanted a hushing welcome as she stood staring at the charming homestead with her hands resting upon her hips.

"My search is over! I think I've finally come home," she stated reaching for her phone to call the owner.

Within an hour, an old time farmer had arrived at the cottage and given Claire a tour of the property. Claire was unalarmed at the cosmetic work the house needed. More so, she found herself captivated by the general setting of the modest shack. She loved the entire package.

"I'll take it!" she announced to the quiet old man standing next to her taking long slow draws on his pipe. "Today… right now if possible!" Claire was bursting with excitement.

Knowing very little about his new tenant, the farmer turned and obligingly handed her the key to the disheveled front door. He then reached out his weathered, callused farm hand to welcome her.

"So you say you're from New York City. Now that's very nice…welcome to Saskatchewan Claire. My name is Joe," the man introduced himself shyly avoiding contact with her eyes. "I'm sorry the place needs a bit of fixing up," he continued in his deep unhurried voice. "We use to keep it for our farm hands to live in. But now that I've gotten so damn old, I don't bother with much extra labor anymore. You can fix it up pretty much how ever you want," he confirmed.

"Thank you Joe. You have no idea how much this means to me!"

Joe was amused with the young woman's excitement not fully understanding her joy as he stood staring at the broken down shack.

"So… I guess…the place is yours… as long as you need it. Now as I told you before…my name is Joe…Joe Whitman. My wife Sarah and I farm just down the road apiece. Come by anytime you want."

Claire nodded to the old man as she scribbled out a series of rent checks on the hood of her car.

After handing the accommodating gentleman her money she responded, "Joe… you have no idea how glad I am to be here."

With a nod of his head, he tipped his well-worn baseball hat in her direction and slowly hobbled back to his pickup truck.

"Well…you have a good evening now young lady. Been nice to meet you. I recon we'll be seeing you around in the near future," he shouted back to the woman.

Claire grinned watching the old man load himself into the pick-up truck and drive back down the dirt road and into the small forest.

No sooner was he gone from her sight did she merrily open the trunk of her car and reach in to get her suitcases. But just as she latched the trunk for the night, her cell phone rang once again. Feeling confident that all would soon be well in her life, she picked up the phone, glanced at the display, saw that it was Jacob calling and turned off the phone without answering.

"Good-bye Jacob! Good-bye you miserable cuss!" she chanted in rhyme to herself as she climbed the sagging front stairs and ventured into her new home.

Claire spent her first peaceful night in the little cottage among the cobwebs and dust piles. The place was sparsely furnished and filthy dirty however she had not felt such spiritual harmony in many years. Lying on the slumping double bed, she listened late into the night as the soft hush of the creek synchronized with the sorrowful hymn of the crickets.

The next morning, the early prairie sun woke her from a hypnotic sleep as the melodic sound of the birds sang out in cheerful celebration of the new day. With a renewed inner excitement, Claire sprang from her bed anxious to begin her housekeeping.

After sweeping the dusty remains from the cottage, she drove into Yorkton to shop for her new home. Feeling re-energized, she indulged in a hearty bacon and egg breakfast at a local café then sourced a local contractor willing to repair and paint the cottage. Satisfied that she was well on her way to creating a new life; Claire roamed the city center with her credit card in hand, gleefully purchasing flooring, furniture and groceries. The morning flowered into the afternoon as Yorkton hustled busily. Claire simply couldn't wait to get back to the cottage and begin its maintenance.

Quickly the weeks passed as the grubby little shack was restored from its sorry state of neglect into a charming country dream. Standing knee deep in the cool water of the creek that gently flowed around the protruding rocks, her hands resting on her hips, Claire stared up at her new home. The neglected, shoddy structure had been stripped, repaired and painted in a lush cream color, trimmed in dark green. The spindles on the sprawling front porch had been replaced and the damaged shutters were repaired. Claire had spent numerous lazy afternoons cutting the lawn, trimming the overgrown shrubbery and planting brightly colored flowers. The interior was repaired and lovingly decorated with new furniture and floral curtains. The derelict hovel had been given a new breath of life and murmured a soft "thank you" as it stared back at her.

Several times over the first month, Joe's wife, Sarah Whitman had arrived at the cottage with piping hot dinners and sumptuous home baked goods for Claire to enjoy. Sarah was a sweet old woman who swayed slowly from side to side as she walked. She was a short, slightly round female in her early 70's with a heartwarming smile and protruding rosy cheeks. She adored Claire and was eager to adopt her as the daughter she'd never had.

"I've got four boys Claire!" Sarah would announce proudly as she set her baked goods down on the counter and touched Claire's cheek gently, repeating the same story each time she called on her. "But I was never blessed with a daughter!"

Claire always welcomed Sarah's visits and didn't seem to mind the repetition of the old woman. Each time she simply smiled and acted as if she had never heard the story before. As the summer months passed Claire in turn grew equally fond of Sarah. Though Sarah never realized it, Claire restricted their dialogue to that of light and general conversation never sharing memories of Amelia or any other intimate details of her past.

"Now Claire my dear if you need anything…anything at all, you just ring me up and I'll send one of the boys over to help you."

Joe and Sarah's sons ranged in age from twenty-five to thirty-five. Though they had all left the farm to seek alternative careers in the nearby city, they remained loyal to their parents and helped out on the farm whenever they could.

The weeks turned into months as the searing prairie summer danced across the horizon. The vastly stretching wheat fields turned golden brown and Claire watched on in amazement as the rows of massive combines took the harvest from the fields in late July and August. At long last she had found the serenity and healing that she so desperately needed. Though she missed Amelia dreadfully, wishing that her beautiful child could've shared in the joy of her new cottage life, Claire could feel her own inner healing begin to take place.

Claire had called Luke repeatedly over her first month in Saskatchewan, though she never did reach him. Thus she came to believe that she would never hear his voice again. She realized that Luke had been a gift of the moment. He was a heroic angel that was sent to pull her out of the ditch and give her a direction, a renewed hope in life. Claire continued to pine for Luke as the summer turned over wondering what life would've been like with him by her side. But as time passed without any word from him, she conceded that he was not meant to be a part of her future.

On a lazy afternoon in late August as Claire rocked in her chair on the front porch while having a leisurely visit with Sarah, she heard the urgent ring of her cell phone from the kitchen. Startled by the piercing sound she so seldom heard, Claire excused herself from her jovial guest as she continued to split fresh peas in preparation for dinner. Rushing into the kitchen Claire snatched the telephone from the top of the fridge and read the callers identification number fearing that it might be Jacob. But the number was preceded by the New York City area code, which drew Claire's curiosity.

"Hello?" she spoke into the receiver.

"Hello… yes… I'm looking for Ms. Claire Morgan," the formal voice quizzed her.

"Yes, this is Ms. Morgan, who am I speaking with?" Claire shot back with irritation.

"Yes Ms. Morgan, my name is Conrad Leudshaw. I am the attorney of Mr. James Morgan," he spoke void of emotion.

"Yes, James Morgan is my father. How can I help you?" Claire continued, her curiosity building.

"Well Ms. Morgan, I am sorry to be the bearer of bad news. But I am calling to inform you that your father James Morgan has passed away. He died about six weeks ago here in New York City. Unfortunately I have had an extremely difficult time locating you."

Claire's shoulders drooped as she covered her eyes with her free hand.

"I'm sorry Ms. Morgan."

"How did he die?"

"He had a heart attack Ms. Morgan. He was rushed by ambulance from his office to the hospital but then died shortly thereafter," the man explained in a matter-of-fact tone.

"I see," she sounded vague.

Though Claire had not seen her father often since she fled New York, she had maintained regular contact by telephone. She thought of him regularly and undoubtedly still loved him. James Morgan had stayed true to his word and routinely made sizable monetary deposits into Claire's bank account. He saw to it that his daughter never ran short of money.

Her father had eventually been told the truth about why Claire and her daughter were on the run from Jacob. He remained supportive, yet never advised or voiced his opinion on the matter, perhaps because he viewed Jacob's conduct as a mirror image of himself in earlier years.

James had been made aware that Amelia's health was failing. Not knowing how else to help his beloved granddaughter, he further increased his overly generous bank deposits with the hope that somehow his money would help resolve the illness.

Claire did notify her father about Amelia's passing shortly after she had settled in Yorkton. She wanted to keep him informed on her life yet declined to involve him in her riotous affairs with Jacob. She was of the opinion that the less her father knew the better off he would be when it came to Jacob's harassment.

"Hello? Ms. Morgan are you still there?" Mr. Leudshaw probed rudely into the phone line.

"Yes... yes... I'm still here, I'm sorry... I'm just a bit shocked," Claire confirmed. "What do you need from me?"

"Well, it appears to me that your father has left his entire estate to you. Now from the numbers I have calculated here in front of me Ms. Morgan, it would appear that you are now an extremely wealthy woman," Leudshaw dictated in his monotone voice. "Now what I need you to do Ms. Morgan is to come down to

New York City and sign a few papers so we can tidy up the remaining details of your father's estate."

Claire's eyes widened at the thought of returning to New York. It was something she had hoped she'd never have to do again. There was so much pain for her there.

"The sooner the better," the lawyer urged, insinuating that she was holding up the transfer of his own fee from the estate.

"Okay…okay, I'll come down," Claire responded with annoyance, "I'll fly down on Monday."

"That will be fine. I'll leave my afternoon open for you. My office is in the same building as your fathers was so I'm sure you'll locate me quite easily."

"Thank you for calling Mr. Leudshaw," Claire regressed. "Oh! Mr. Leudshaw!" she yelled into the receiver with an important after thought. "I expect that you will not be telling anyone that I'm coming in to town! I expect that our meeting and the affairs of my father will remain strictly confidential! Do you hear me! Strictly confidential!"

"Naturally Ms. Morgan. That is… how I conduct all of my business!" Leudshaw shot back at her feeling insulted. "I'll see you on Monday." Then he abruptly hung up the telephone.

With a despairing breath of air, Claire disconnected her cell phone and backed up to lean against the kitchen sink pausing to collect her thoughts. She felt absolutely no contempt for her father in spite of all the pain he had bestowed upon her and her mother in the early years of her life. She had healed from the abuse and since realized that he had succumbed to the deadly disease of alcoholism and then done his utmost to rebound from it. Claire also realized just how much she loved her father feeling the familiar blade of death sear its jagged edge through her heart, losing yet another family member within three months of burying Amelia.

"Is everything all right dear? You look rather upset! Can I help you with anything?"

In dire need of a supportive ear Claire responded solemnly, "Well it seems that my father passed away about six weeks ago back in New York City. That was his lawyer calling just now. Sounds like they have had a bit of a tough time finding me up here. They must have found my cell number in my father's rolodex."

Saying nothing, the elderly woman dropped her bowl of peas noisily on the countertop. She then rushed over and hurled her chunky arms around Claire's shoulders.

"I'm sorry my darling. I'm so sorry," she spoke robustly into Claire's ear. Raising a house full of boys, Sarah's voice seemed incapable of whispering. "So I reckon that you'll have to go down to New York City sometime soon? Though I sure do hope you're not going to leave us here without you for long!"

Claire forced out a smile as she pulled herself from the woman's mighty grip.

"Yes, I guess I'll fly down there on Monday and sign the papers. I have no intention of staying in New York for more than one day," Claire responded with intention.

Grasping Claire's shoulders between her rugged farm hands, Sarah planted a hearty kiss on her cheek.

"Well my dear, I'll leave you alone. I'm sure you've got things to think through and arrangements to make. I'm only a phone call away if you need me."

With that, Sarah patted Claire's shoulders in a kind but slightly rough manner, then picked up her bowl of peas and hobbled out to her dusty old truck. Claire watched from the window as the dirt swirled beneath the tires, the cloud of dust following the vehicle down the laneway.

For what seemed to be the first time in several months, Claire felt hollow inside. She felt the old familiar loneliness creep over her as she dialed the phone to book her flight.

Sunday passed by with an eerie sense of quiet and then at 8:00 a.m. on Monday morning Claire boarded her flight in Regina, Saskatchewan bound for New York City. The in-flight hours dragged on endlessly then a wave of nausea washed over her as the plane lined up for its final approach into LaGuardia Airport. Closing her eyes, leaning her head back against her seat, she recalled how bumpy the final approach had always seemed every time she traveled home from the ballet school to visit her parents. With her eyes closed and her hand covering her mouth, she waited for the lingering nausea to pass. The rocketing wheels of the plane bounced along the asphalt as it landed causing Claire to gag as they hit. Upon reaching the arrival gate, she made her way from the plane and through the hectic airport as the nausea churned with nervous anticipation for what she had yet to do that day.

After hailing a cab, she was driven to the posh Manhattan legal office that also once housed the highly prestigious firm owned by her father. The taxi drew to a screeching New York City halt as the busy traffic hustled along the street. After passing the driver her payment, Claire slid across the slimy car seat and stepped out onto the sidewalk. Busy people, mindless of courtesy, bumped her as they rudely scrambled to enter the taxi she had just stepped from.

"My God! How I hate this city!" Claire scowled as she clutched her handbag and stared upward at the huge skyscraper in front of her. After pausing briefly, she pushed herself through the revolving doorway into the monstrous glass office building and made her way toward the elevator. Cramming herself into the steel box with thirty other irritated people, she was once again overcome with nausea. Holding her breath, she closed her eyes and waited until the elevator finally stopped at the twenty-seventh floor.

"Excuse me!" she demanded stridently as she forced herself through the crowd of impatient people and out the elevator. After brushing her crumpled black skirt downward, she entered the legal office of Conrad Leudshaw & Associates.

"You must be Ms. Morgan!" a spurious voice beckoned as she entered the reception area.

"Yes I am," Claire responded with disgust.

"I'll notify Mr. Leudshaw that you're here," the receptionist with a mass of teased blond hair responded as she arose from her desk and wiggled down the hallway in her tightly fitting skirt.

"Christ," she mocked quietly, "what a piece of work she is!"

Claire rolled her eyes in repulsion as she picked through the outdated magazines on the table.

"Ms. Morgan!" Leudshaw's monotone voice called out as he stepped lightly down the hallway. "I see you have made it!"

"Yes," Claire responded without emotion, "I'm here. But I'd also like to get this over with as quickly as possible if you don't mind," she stated in an icy tone.

"Of course, I understand," Leudshaw responded. "Please come this way to my office."

Claire followed the insensitive man all the while wondering how he managed to hold his bifocals on the end of his nose. Sitting down in his luxurious office, she found herself instantly yearning for her simple lifestyle back in Yorkton.

"Well now Ms. Morgan," Leudshaw broke the silence across the desk as he shuffled his paperwork into a neat pile, "your father James was a great man, now wasn't he? Did you see him often Ms. Morgan?"

Claire simmered impatiently as the lawyer in front of her spoke in a patronizing tone.

"Yes, James and I worked together on various legal issues over the years," he continued with pompous tonality.

"Look Mr. Leudshaw," Claire quickly snapped at him feeling her dislike for the stuffy over-rated lawyer nearly explode. "I don't have a whole lot of patience for small talk right now! I am also a lawyer and am quite familiar with the proceedings necessary to close an estate. So if you would just simply hand me the papers that I need to sign, then we can get on with it. And since you will be taking a sizeable chunk of money from the estate under the title of "your fee," I expect that you will be managing all of the remaining housekeeping details; such as the selling of my father's house and the asset liquidation of his law firm. I don't want any part of those headaches! I simply expect that you will do it!"

The unexpected projectile venom spewed at him by Morgan's daughter unmistakably took Leudshaw back. She glared directly into his eyes whipping her right hand out toward him ready to receive the stack of papers. Then after abruptly snatching the gold plated pen that lay in the center of his grand mahogany desk, Claire quickly scanned the documents scribbling her signature at the bottom of each page.

"I believe that should do it!" the assertive woman maintained complete control of the meeting slamming the gold pen back down on Leudshaw's desk. "Now then Mr. Leudshaw, is there anything else that you need to tell me before I leave?" she inquired of the unattractive yet well-dressed lawyer.

"Well Ms. Morgan, I guess I only need to inform you that you are approximately fifty-eight million dollars richer than you were yesterday," the man spoke in a condescending manner unappreciative of Claire's snooty attitude.

"Fifty-eight million dollars?" she repeated in question, shocked at the monetary figure he was giving her.

"Yes Ms. Morgan that is correct. The net sum of fifty-eight million dollars will be transferred over to you by the end of the week."

Claire plunged backward in her seat while fumbling her arm to the right to pick-up her handbag. Attempting to disguise her astonishment, she then pushed herself from the leather chair and stood erectly before the desk.

"Thank you for your assistance," Claire reached out a hand to close the meeting in a cold yet professional manner. "Also, can you please tell me where my father's remains have been buried? I would like to visit the cemetery this afternoon before I leave."

"Yes Ms. Morgan I will have my assistant verify that information for you."

Claire turned toward the door as Leudshaw picked up a small white piece of paper from his desk.

"Oh yes, Ms. Morgan!" he called out to her smiling smugly as if he was about to play his trump card. Claire stopped and spun around to meet with Leudshaw's unfeeling eyes, his bifocals still dangling off the end of his nose. "I have a note here for you from a Mr. Jacob Redkin."

Claire gasped hearing the name of her husband. A chill ran down her spin as she tried to maintain her composure. Terrified of what Conrad Leudshaw was about to say next she listened as he glanced down at the note.

"It seems that this gentleman has called my assistant repeatedly looking for your home address. Now I'm sure that she has not given out any of your personal information Ms. Morgan, however his telephone calls have become quite harassing."

Without hesitation, Claire retraced her steps with aggressive sweeping strides across the office floor. Reaching out and plucking the scrap of paper from where Leudshaw held it between his fingers she responded in anger.

"Yes Mr. Leudshaw! Jacob Redkin is my husband! He is a rotten, threatening, abusive son-of-a-bitch and let me be very clear here Conrad! If you or your blond hairball assistant in the tight mini-skirt give him any information about me what so ever, I will personally sue you for every slimy cent you've got. Am I making myself fairly clear here?" she shouted directly into Leudshaw's face, her tone escalating into rage.

"Yes… perfectly clear Ms. Morgan," the man responded, once again stunned by Claire's strength of character.

"Good then!" she replied as she turned to leave the office. "Good day!" she barked as she pounded her elegant high heels swiftly down the hallway.

Stopping only briefly at the desk of Leudshaw's assistant, Claire attained the whereabouts of her father's grave and then left the office. With nausea creeping up her throat, she forced her way through the crowd in the elevator and out on to the street. Standing on the curbside, Claire waved an arm at an oncoming cab. Quickly the vehicle swerved out of the mainstream traffic halting its screeching front tires within inches of her lustrous black shoes. Claire slid into the soiled vehicle and pulled the creaking door closed behind her. The irritated driver turned his head in Claire's direction waiting for her instructions.

"Lakeview Cemetery on Bay and Seventeenth streets," she rolled her eyes at his rudeness, repulsed by the greasy sheen to his hair.

But before she had gotten the words out of her mouth, the driver snatched up the microphone to his radio and began rudely babbling away to his dispatch office in broken English. Claire was disgusted as she sat back in the seat waiting for the man's attention.

Staring out the side window, Claire watched as the multitude of people rushed passed the stationary cab. She examined the crowd with trance-like expressions on their faces routinely whirling through the rotating door of the office building she had just left.

Scanning the masses, her heart suddenly skipped a beat as she squinted her eyes to focus on a face that she thought she recognized. A man with common dark eyes and slightly hunched shoulders rushed passed her in the awaiting cab as the zipper on his coat clanked against the car door. Their eyes locked momentarily as he hurried by the car then turned in through the rotating glass door of the building

"Jesus Christ… it's Jacob!" she shouted in a panic stricken voice.

But it was too late as Jacob had also recognized Claire. Quickly he rotated around the revolving door and back out onto the street.

"Get going!" she screamed reaching forward and pounding on the driver's shoulder with her scrunched fist. "Get me out of here now!"

Quickly she locked the car door from the inside.

"Alright…alright!" he responded curtly as he dropped the microphone and pulled the gearshift into drive.

Jacob dodged the swarm of people and bolted over to the departing cab. Pressing his face against the gritty glass window he thumped his fist angrily against the doorframe screeching, "I'll get you bitch! I'll get you!"

Their eyes had locked! Claire twisted her torso to watch him through the rear window as he hailed a cab directly behind her.

"Step on it!" Claire demanded. "I'll give you an extra hundred dollars if you lose that cab behind us!"

The eyes of the driver popped open at the financial wager as he stared curiously at Claire through the rear-view mirror. Wildly the cab wound in and out of the afternoon traffic that clogged the busy streets of Manhattan. Honking his horn with annoyance, he swerved around corners and down long narrow alleyways as he dodged the bullet for nearly twenty minutes until finally the trailing cab was nowhere to be seen. Then as if the foreign driver was fed up with such nonsense, he slammed on the brakes at the front gates of Lakeview Cemetery.

"There you go lady! I trust you're satisfied! That'll be one hundred and forty five dollars," the driver demanded as he pivoted his rotund body around in Claire's direction.

With her adrenalin still pumping, Claire pulled the money from her wallet and jammed it into the driver's hand.

"Thank you!" she replied with sarcasm. "And you have a nice day as well!"

Opening the battered door of the cab she stepped out onto the street. Glancing around she felt satisfied that Jacob had been lost in the city street shuffle. Still nervously clutching her handbag she bought a bouquet of white roses from a nearby street vendor and walked back to push open the heavy black gate that guarded the entrance to the cemetery.

Positioning herself in front of the grave index board, Claire ran her finger down the lengthy type written list of names of the people that had been buried there in.

"James H. Morgan," she breathed heavily as her finger stopped at the proverbial name. "Section C-3."

Claire wandered through the divine place of rest recalling the daggers in Jacob's eyes only a short time before.

"What madness!" she stated. "What utter madness!"

Slowing her pace as her heels tapped rhythmically on the cobblestone footpath, she finally entered section "C". As she searched the headstones for her father's recent burial sight, she felt a calming sensation overcome her body with a spiritual sense of presence. Her rapidly beating heart slowed still further and her shoulders began to fall from their tensely inclined position. A peaceful serenity swept over her angry thoughts of the past hour.

Then she found it…her father's gravesite…the burial plot so recent that only a small white wooden cross marked it. The name James Hamilton Morgan was humbly stenciled in plastic across the horizontal bar of the grave marker. The ground was still up-heaved from the committal six weeks prior and the faded dying floral arrangements from the funeral still lay strewn across the freshly piled top-soil.

"Oh daddy," Claire knelt before the grave as she pulled the dead flowers from the site. "Daddy, I'm so sorry for not being here for you. I'm so sorry for abandoning you. I hope you understand that I had to leave. I hope you understand everything now," she mourned. "You are with Amelia daddy. I know you missed her terribly when we left New York. I know you missed us both! But now you understand why we had to run… I hope you understand."

Claire bundled the dead flowers within her arms and stood to dump them in a nearby trashcan. Returning, she knelt a second time and whisked away the desiccated leaves clustered around the base of the cross that had fallen from the massive chestnut tree directly above. With sympathetic thoughts she pulled the string from the fresh bouquet of white roses she had purchased. Separating each perfect flower with care she placed them in a neat row beneath the cross.

"In all your greatness daddy… no one could be bothered to get you a proper headstone," she mumbled in the silence of the cemetery. Then with a smile she added, "I hate to tell you this dad… but your lawyer – you know the guy who should've taken care of everything for you, like ordering a headstone… that Mr. Leudshaw guy, he is a total ass!"

Claire laughed at her comment to the grave. She envisioned her father's image chuckling at the statement as she admired the flowers she had just placed. Then standing, she sauntered over to a nearby bench. Sitting down on the weather-beaten wooden frame Claire continued to reflect.

"You know dad…we've had a lot of tragedy in our lives. Though I was pretty angry with you as a kid, I now realize that you were doing the very best you could with the parenting skills you had at the time. I have since realized that it wasn't that you didn't love me. It was more that you just had trouble showing your love." Claire paused as she wiped a tear from her cheek with the back of her hand. "But do you know what daddy? I love you and I have forgiven you for the past. I guess I've become a much stronger person for surviving it. You've made me a very independent, optimistic person!" Claire smiled to herself. "You're with mom and Amelia now dad and I'm happy for you."

The gentle breeze flowed through the air as Claire paused to meditate over the past.

"Thank you daddy. Thank you for all the money over the years. At least that's one thing that I didn't have to worry about all this time. Hey by the way dad, I was just thinking that I would like to donate part of my inheritance to the cancer foundation in memory of mom and Amelia. I thought you would like it if I did that."

Leaning back on the bench she closed her eyes and allowed the healing power of the White Holy Spirit to embrace her body. Sitting there silently Claire met with serenity.

A full hour passed as Claire reflected upon her father and all that he was. She thought it sad that after working so hard his entire life, James H. Morgan died alone. How pitiful it was! The sun hid behind a billowing fall cloud as her thoughts eventually drifted back to the present.

Glancing at her watch Claire realized that she only had an hour to catch her flight back to Saskatchewan. Amazed that so much time had slipped by, she raised herself from the bench and returned to the humble gravesite. Kissing her hand tenderly, she slid her fingers along the generic twelve-inch cross as if to leave the kiss behind for her father.

"You were a great man daddy! You were a great man and I love you. Please watch over Amelia for me. Enjoy her as she laughs and plays, healthy and whole once again. You are all in heaven now. Everyone is there…except for me. Someday…we'll all be together again." With an empathetic sigh she closed her private eulogy, "But until then, I guess I have a life to live. I have to find a new life. I'm just not sure where or how." Then standing, Claire slowly backed from the grave. "I love you daddy. Oh and by the way, I'll order the gravestone myself. Be happy and be free!"

With that, Claire turned from the gravesite and slowly left the cemetery. After hailing a cab, Claire felt at peace with herself. She felt inner healing begin to take hold from all the pain of the earlier years.

With the exception of seeing Jacob momentarily flail his temper at her, she felt the trip to New York City had been a success. Perhaps it was a trip she should've taken months prior.

On route to the airport Claire instructed the driver to pass by her childhood home. The taxi eventually halted in front of the large stately mansion she had lived in as a child. The house remained relatively unchanged except for the "For Sale" sign that dangled from a post on the front lawn. The grass was left in obvious neglect waving its shaggy green stems in the breeze. Claire stared up into the windows of the mansion with a desperate longing for her mother. How she missed her mother's beautiful face and cheerful smile. But Claire felt no anger. Her childhood of abuse and chaos had been defused.

"The meter is ticking lady!" the impatient cab driver interrupted her private thoughts.

"Yes…yes okay," Claire responded softly. "We can go now."

The taxi pulled from the front of the house as Claire watched the mansion vanish from her sight. Her afternoon of reflection had been therapeutic. She felt that she was finally setting her bitter childhood to rest. Her family was together in heaven. Claire grinned as she imagined Amelia sharing precious time with her grandparents. She felt relieved and at peace that her child was not alone.

Later that same evening Claire arrived back in Canada. Her plane landed in Regina on schedule and although she was emotionally drained, she drove the one-hour journey back to Yorkton. Exhausted, but fulfilled, Claire fell into her warm double bed where she silently reflected upon her life, her family and all the adversities her thirty-two years had presented her with.

Chapter Four

Early in September as Claire's BMW drove slowly out the dirt road heading to town, she was met by a familiar red pickup truck with Sarah propped behind the steering wheel. Claire pulled to the side of the dusty path as her friend dawdled toward her smiling through her rosy cheeks.

Unwinding her dusty window Sarah greeted her, "Good morning' darling. I was just coming to see you."

"Good morning Sarah," Claire smiled in return.

"Now listen here Claire. We're having our annual harvest dinner tonight back at the house and I want you to come join us dear." Claire was grateful for the invitation but before she had a chance to respond Sarah cut her off. "Now darling let me explain. Every year after the grain is hauled in from the fields the family celebrates with a huge dinner together complete with roasted turkey, mashed potatoes and fresh baked rolls. If I get back home in time I'll even make you a home made apple pie. You've just got to come and meet my boys. I've told them all so much about you. You've just got to meet them!"

"Thanks so much Sarah. I'd love to come for dinner but actually I'm not feeling very well this morning. I was up most of the night with the flu and..."

"Well now darling," Sarah cut her off a second time, "You'll feel much better after you've had a proper meal... so we'll see ya up at the house tonight around six tonight!"

With a smile, Sarah jammed the squeaky clutch inward with her left foot and ground the gearshift into reverse. Backing her truck up over the ditch and into the grain stubble, she fluttered her fingers at Claire through the dirty windshield.

"Tootle-lou darling," she called out and then rambled off down the laneway.

"Well," Claire stated, "I guess I'm going out for dinner tonight."

In spite of her ill health, Claire continued on her journey into town to make arrangements for her father's headstone. As the golden prairie morning glowed across the clear blue sky, she painstakingly chose a stately white stone for her father. She dictated the inscription "Until We Meet Again" then discussed the details of having the stone shipped to New York City as soon as it was ready.

Feeling satisfied with her primary mission of the day, she then ventured on to make her next stop where she had her cellular phone number changed for the seventh time hoping once again to avoid calls from Jacob. Then in turn, she moved on to the Cancer Society Office where she made a five million dollar donation to the charity in memory of her mother and Amelia. Needless to say, the women in the office thanked her heartily from their desks where they sat in shock at the sizeable donation.

As evening approached, still feeling nauseous, Claire dressed her thin, tanned body in a peach colored sundress. She knotted her sun-streaked hair up into a loose bun, passed over a light dusting of make-up and set off to join Sarah's family for their annual harvest dinner.

"Evening darling, so glad you came over. Come right in!" Sarah greeted her robustly at the door of the old farmhouse.

Claire had not yet met Sarah's infamous sons as she bashfully entered the expansive kitchen that was filled with the savoring aroma of a golden brown roasted turkey.

"Now you come right into the parlor and sit and relax while I make you a nice cup of tea," Sarah directed her by the shoulders passing the timid woman through the kitchen.

As Claire entered the parlor, silence won over the conversations already in progress as all heads turned in her direction. Enthralled by her natural beauty, the cluster of statuesque men immediately rose from the chairs they were lounging in and nodded in response to Sarah's introductions. Amusedly Claire acknowledged the greetings reaching forward and shaking hands with each of theirs. Sarah indeed had a group of handsome young sons to her credit.

"Now Claire, this is Mike, he is thirty five and he's our eldest boy, then there is Josh, he's 32, then there's Robert who's 27 and then there's Ethan who is our baby at 25. Can you imagine Claire! My baby is 25 years old!" Sarah broadcast in her intruding tone of excitement, patting her youngest child heartily on the back with pride.

"It's very nice to meet you all," Claire relayed as she was guided by Sarah to sit on the antique sofa in the corner of the parlor.

After an awkward moment of silence as the group of men lowered their eyes to the floor, Joe attempted to start the conversation stating that his eldest son, Mike was a high-feluting lawyer in Yorkton.

"Oh that's very nice," Claire assisted with Joe's timid attempt to ease the strain in the room. "I'm also a lawyer…or at least I use to be before I moved to Canada."

Becoming aware of the common ground, Mike swiftly picked up on the exchange as he told Claire about his small legal firm in Yorkton. Leading the discussion among the group gathered in the parlor, Mike and Claire shared common stories of past legal issues while comparing the disparity in laws between Canada and the U.S.A.

The evening progressed from polite discussion on into a delicious home cooked feast. Then burst wide open with hearty laughter roaring across the massive dining table as tales of past harvests were shared between the boys and their parents. Claire laughed hysterically as they spoke of various farming stories and pranks of years gone by. She found the time purely pleasurable and admired the family that seemed so eager to embrace her friendship.

With the dishes stacked several feet high on the counter, Sarah bound from her chair preparing to offer another round of warm apple pie and vanilla ice cream.

"No thank you Sarah. I'm so full I could just burst!" Claire laughed as she ran her hands over her stuffed abdomen.

The harvest meal was superb as the family relaxed sipping on piping hot coffee served in oversized brightly colored mugs. The invited guest felt pleased that she had attended the meal and sat relaxing in her chair enjoying the kinship that was evident among the family members before her.

As the evening drew to a close, Claire was overcome with exhaustion. It was nearly midnight when she finally stood to bid farewell to her new friends.

"Thank you all so much! I had a wonderful evening," Claire relayed to the group who was obviously disappointed that she was about to leave. Planting a loving kiss on Sarah's right cheek, she squeezed the elderly woman's arm.

"Thank you Sarah. You have been very kind."

The old woman smiled at her young friend and while fluttering her fingers in Claire's direction she shouted, "Tootle-Lou Claire. I'll run you over some turkey and stuffing tomorrow dear!"

After nodding graciously, Claire turned to leave the farmhouse. As she prepared for her departure, the eldest son, Mike, dashed from his chair and held the door open then insisted that he walk her out to her car.

The two new friends ambled down the long driveway toward Claire's BMW. Just as they reached the vehicle, Claire realized that Mike had been awkwardly fumbling for words trying to ask her something as they walked.

"Say Claire... I know... I mean I know you're fairly new in town and all, but I just wanted to let you know that I've been looking for a good business associate at the office and if you're ever... well... looking to get back into the legal rat-race, please be sure to keep me in mind," the tall lanky man quickly blurted out as if the window of opportunity was about to close. Then realizing that he may have been a bit too forward with his statement he offered further explanation, "I pretty much deal with farming issues right now, but I've been wanting to expand my services and well... I could use a good expert to help me... if you're ever interested that is."

"Thank you Mike. That's very nice of you to offer. But I've been away from it for quite a while now. I'm sure I'd have to update my credentials for Canada... but...I'll definitely consider it," the exhausted woman replied flattered by his generous offer for employment.

Claire stared back at the intriguing gentleman who was obviously captivated by her beauty. She reached out her hand to shake with his.

"Please thank your mom again for dinner and thank you for the job offer. I'll put some serious thought into it, I promise! I'll see you soon Mike."

With that, Claire climbed into her car and drove out of the sprawling farm estate.

Upon arriving home well after midnight, she gazed contently at her beloved cottage as she approached. The tiny building warmly beckoned to her as the dim glow in the living room welcomed her return. She had a wonderful evening with her friends, leaving them feeling calm and at peace. At long last, Claire felt as though she had established the loving family circle that she had craved as a child.

Collapsing into bed, she pulled the thick comforter over her body. How she cherished the sounds of the country at night. Relaxing with a full stomach, she fell into a sound slumber.

Three hours passed when Claire awoke overcome with nausea.

"I've had the flu before, but this is really awful!" she grumbled miserably as she dragged her weary legs to the toilet. After vomiting repeatedly she dabbed her drenched face with a cool cloth then crawled back into bed.

Over the murky hours of the night, Claire repeatedly rushed to the washroom in failing health. The night seemed endless as her nausea worsened. Finally, after enduring a dreadful night, she awoke late in the morning feeling drained and exhausted.

The following days found Claire increasingly ill. She nursed her sickness with rest and hot tea but established little relief. During her hours of quiet recovery, the disgruntled woman considered Mike's offer to join his legal firm. Then after a full week of self-pity, still overcome with nausea, she felt it was time to stop feeling sorry for herself and move on.

Determined to follow through on her commitment to create a new life for herself, Claire arose early one morning in late September. She dressed in a navy blue business suit and white blouse. She clipped her hair back in a soft roll, took a deep breath to muster up the strength and drove into town to accept Mike's offer.

Elated to see Claire again, Mike immediately welcomed her to his small legal team and without hesitation he led her toward the empty office he had available next to his own.

"When would you like me to start?" she inquired, caught up in Mike's excitement.

"Well...I've got work coming out my ears, so how about today? How about right now!"

Claire laughed as she moved around her new office and sat behind the desk.

"Okay partner...show me the files and give me a pen!" she stated jokingly.

As she had done year's prior, Claire spent the afternoon delving into the stack of case files that Mike had accumulated but not yet attended to. By the end of the first day, she was worn out but entirely fulfilled. She had repeatedly proven herself a valued asset at the various legal firms she had been previously employed by over the years as she moved from state to state with Amelia. Though it always seemed that as soon as she established herself with a firm, Jacob reared his ugly head searching for Amelia. Then the mother and daughter would have to dash off to find another new home in seclusion. Claire had not worked since she had found out about Amelia's Leukemia.

As she closed her first day of work at Mike's firm, she quickly realized that it would take a couple of weeks to build her stamina back up, enabling her to manage the stress level that went with the job.

Claire enjoyed being back in the legal stream. Focusing on other people's problems took her mind off her own. Mike's legal firm in the farming community of Yorkton was a booming, successful little business. With their offices sitting side-by-side, she increasingly enjoyed the bonding friendship that rapidly blossomed between Mike and herself.

Mike was a tall, thin man over six feet in stature. His dark brown, slightly balding hair was typically gelled and combed neatly back from his distantly handsome face. Having been totally absorbed in his career development, he had not yet taken the time to love a woman and marry. He had casually dated friends in the area but had not yet found the love of his life. But as he spent time with Claire, he began to secretly hope that his personal life would begin to evolve as well.

As the little office hummed with minor legal problems submitted by local farmers, Claire educated herself on Canadian Law. She assisted Mike with his manifesting caseload during the office hours and studied Canadian law in the evening preparing to update her credentials. She joyfully dug into her new workload and before long was putting in twelve-hour days as the firm's clientele continued to steadily build.

Weeks passed as Claire aimed to take on more responsibility in the office. However her frustration escalated as her ill health lingered. She couldn't seem to shake the flu-like symptoms that had taken a tight hold of her weakening body. Each evening she left the office feeling nauseous and exhausted.

Late one evening in mid October, Mike and Claire were discussing an in-depth case where a local cattle rancher was being sued. Together they consumed cold Chinese food and argued about the case across the boardroom table. Without explaining why, Claire typically tried to be out of the office and at home by 7:00 p.m. as the on-set of her dreaded nausea hit each evening like clockwork. But due to the pending case, that evening was an exception.

"I'm sorry Mike, I just have to get a glass of water," she cut her boss off in mid-sentence feeling a wave of sickness rush over her.

Claire arose from her chair. Her body was weak and unstable. Trying to conceal her physical state, she clung tightly to the edge of the table feebly making her way to the water cooler. But just as she stepped away from the table she fell lifeless to the floor.

"Oh my God Claire?" Mike shrieked as he dashed from his chair toward her failing body. Gently cradling her head in his hands he yelled into her face. "Claire... Claire what happened? Are you alright?"

A few seconds later, Claire sleepily awoke hearing her name called repeatedly. Prying her eyelids apart, squinting to focus on Mike's concerned face, the limp woman regained consciousness.

"Yeah... yeah... I'm... I think I'm okay," she slurred as she struggled to her knees. "Sorry Mike. I don't know what happened."

"You stay right here. I'll pull my car around. I'm taking you to the hospital right now!"

"No... No... I'm fine Mike. I just need to get some rest."

"Bullshit you do! There's something wrong here!" he responded firmly. "We're going to the hospital right now."

After assisting Claire to a nearby chair he dashed from the room. Then after what seemed like only a few seconds later, the frenzied man returned with her coat and purse in his hand. Gently he assisted the ailing woman to her feet and walked her out to his truck.

Mike drove swiftly to the hospital then led her in through the emergency doors where an awaiting nurse took her information. Standing nearby, he remained worried for the new friend he had quickly come to admire, looking on as the nurse led her down the hallway and out of his sight.

Mike paced back and forth across the sterile hospital corridor for over two hours. Then finally Claire returned to the information desk where he had last seen her.

"Hey there," he spoke in a gentle voice as he swept Claire's coat around her shoulders. It was apparent by the look on her face that she had received some disturbing news from the doctor. But as he had not yet reached out to his new business partner on a personal level, he hesitated to ask too many personal questions.

"Claire, is everything okay?" Mike asked with generality trying to interpret her state of shock. She was clearly bewildered.

"Yes, I'm okay Mike. But I'm also nearly five months pregnant," she blurted out failing to remind herself that she habitually kept all secrets hidden deep within.

"Pregnant?" Mike replied in question.

"Yes pregnant," she confirmed lowering her tone to a whisper.

Mike's expression subsequently evolved from worry to puzzlement. He was utterly confused knowing that Claire had been living alone in the cottage. She had been unaccompanied since she moved in and during all the work hours they had spent together she had never mentioned having a relationship with anyone.

After a long moment of silence as Claire stood in the corridor collecting her thoughts, she raised her eyes to meet with his look of concern.

"Mike, have you got time to talk?" she imposed needing a shoulder to lean on.

"Of course I do," he reassured her without hesitation.

"But first, can you take me home?"

"Sure, let's go," he confirmed as he curved a supportive arm around her shoulders and led the way to his car.

Their voices remained still during the ten-minute ride back to the cottage. The expectant mother was obviously in deep thought. Assisting her up the porch steps and through the front door Mike said nothing. Though he undoubtedly felt a growing attraction for Claire, he had never made any physical advances toward her and clearly felt uncomfortable within the private confines of her home. Aware of his dawdling, Claire openly invited him in to sit down then disappeared into her bedroom.

"Wow!" Mike shouted across the room trying to break the embarrassing silence. "You certainly have done a great job fixing up the place Claire."

"Thanks," she replied returning from her bedroom wearing a pale yellow tracksuit. "I love it too!"

Claire made a pot of tea and after handing a cup of the steaming beverage to Mike she sat down beside him on the overstuffed floral couch.

"First of all Mike... thank you for helping me tonight," she plunged immediately into the ensuing conversation.

Mike responded with a nod, his eyes never departing from hers. Then over the course of three hours, Claire shared her entire life story with the man whom she held prisoner by her words. She told him of her lonely childhood. She advised him of her father's abuse and of her mother's death. She shared collective memories of Amelia and of their ever-changing life in hiding. She explained why they had to run for their lives from Jacob. Saying nothing, but listening attentively, Mike fought back the tears as he learned of Amelia's fatal illness then inevitable death. Claire enlightened her sympathetic friend about the car accident and of the chance encounter with Luke. She searched Mike's face for potential rejection as she concluded her lifelong saga explaining how she arrived in Saskatchewan searching for solitude and then established herself in the cottage. Throughout the three hour tale of astonishing adversity Mike never said a word but only nodded with understanding.

At the end of her story, Claire sat her cold empty teacup gently down upon the glass table in front of her.

"So, here I am, in Yorkton, Saskatchewan," she concluded with a shrug of her shoulders. Claire tipped her head back against the sofa and ran her fingers through her hair further scrutinizing her personal state of affairs. "So now let's see... I've got an exciting new job, a quaint little home and a wonderful doting family. I've finally acquired some peace and solitude for myself and now I'm five months pregnant by a man that I immediately fell in love with but will likely never see again! Oh and just for good measure," she continued with a note of sarcasm. "I'm still hiding from my vicious husband who has threatened to kill me." Claire paused for a moment closing her eyes then added, "When Jacob finds out that Amelia is dead, he'll blame me and that will unquestionably be the end!"

Tears gathered in Claire's eyes as she sat wringing her hands reflecting upon the story she had just shared with Mike. Realizing he was completely unprepared for what he had just been told, he was uncertain how to respond as a deafening hush fell between them.

"Please don't get me wrong Mike," she pressed on as tears plunged down her face. "I'm going to keep this baby and naturally I'll love him or her. I'll be okay." She raised her eyes to meet with his offering him a defeated grin. "Well now...I've got quite a story haven't I?" she tried to joke. "But you know what Mike? I have been issued a lot of tragedy in my life but I have also experienced tremendous joy. I don't harbor any anger toward my father or need for revenge. Why would I? What good would that do?"

Still Mike said nothing, sitting quietly next to her.

"You know, I heard it once said that as adults we can blame our childhoods on our parents but we can blame our adulthood on no one other than ourselves. Yes I've been through the ringer," she lectured on. "But experience… isn't that what life is all about? And yes, we as humans do become stronger from adversity even if we don't feel strong at the time, we do become stronger!"

Wanting to comfort the frail beautiful woman but cautious not to send the wrong message, Mike reached out and took Claire's right hand into his own. Feeling her soft skin against his sent a shudder through his body as he recalled how often he wanted to touch her day after day as they sat together in the office discussing business. He had come to love her aromatic floral perfume as it wafted by his office door each time she passed. But it wasn't until that moment when he actually touched her flesh did he realize how deeply he had fallen in love with her.

With hesitation, fully respecting her personal boundaries, Mike slowly pulled Claire's shoulders in toward his own as he enveloped her upper body within his empathetic arms. He wiped a huge tear from her face as it rolled over her cheek then swept her long hair back from her eyes.

"You know what Claire?" he whispered softly in her ear. "You've had one hell of a life. It sounds to me that with the exception of the love you shared with Amelia, you've been scared and alone most of the time."

Claire nodded in agreement.

"But I want to tell you something," he continued. "I'm not going to leave you Claire. I'll be here for you and I'll be your friend for as long as you need me. I'll be right here for you."

Rocking her gently in his arms Mike waited as Claire evaluated his promise of support and friendship. Then after a weak grin she closed her tired, tear stained eyes feeling glad that she had shared her burden of secrecy with him. Quiet overtook the air as Mike held her closely against his chest for over an hour until she drifted off to sleep.

Loving how it felt with Claire in his arms, but knowing it was time to leave, Mike carefully lifted her thin body from the couch and carried her in to the bedroom. Placing her gently upon the beckoning mattress, he covered her sleeping body with the large, fluffy comforter that had been neatly folded at the foot of the bed. Before turning out the hallway light that dimly lit the cottage, Mike turned to steal one final admiring glance at the sleeping woman he had fallen in love with. With a sigh of acceptance that he would likely never have her for his own, he locked the front door behind him and left for the night.

The next morning Claire awoke feeling bewildered. Lying in bed, she contemplated the news she had received at the hospital the night before. Feeling naïve that she hadn't known she was pregnant, she wondered how she had not seen the signs in her own body. Her thin body had changed very little over the

81

preceding five-month term, however she recalled not gaining much weight when she was pregnant with Amelia. Not menstruating for months at a time was not uncommon for Claire either. She had never had a regular cycle and had simply put it down to the enormous level of stress she had been under since Amelia's passing. The thought of being pregnant with Luke's child was the furthest thing from her mind.

As the moments ticked by on the bedside clock her natural optimism took over. Claire then pushed her worries from her mind replacing them with a warm sensation of happiness as she gently rubbed her hands over her abdomen. Smiling to herself she realized that she was being given a second chance for a child. She knew it was undoubtedly Luke's baby as he had been the only sexual encounter she'd had for years. Claire still ached for him to be a part of her life but had conceded months earlier that it simply was not meant to be.

"Well little one," she lovingly acknowledged her unborn child. "Soon I will welcome you into this world. You will be a survivor little one. We will love each other and build a wonderful life together as no doubt you have been sent to me by God and Amelia." As Claire lay in the stillness of her room, the initial shock rapidly evolved into joy. "We're going to be just fine my little babe. You and I will be just fine!"

Claire arose from her bed as a wave of nausea got the better of her. The morning sickness was severe as it forced the unsettled saliva up her burning throat. Making her way to the shower Claire recalled the evening before. Feeling vulnerable, she remembered telling Mike about her personal tale of sadness. He was the first person she had ever shared the intimate details of her life with.

Claire clothed herself in a tan-colored business suit, taking new notice that her skirt was fitting rather tightly around her expectant abdomen. With a steaming cup of tea in her hand, she loaded herself into the car and drove to the office not knowing what Mike's reaction would be when she arrived.

"Well, if he fires me…then he fires me!" she muttered defensively as she pulled open the heavy glass door of her office building.

"Good morning Claire," Bernice the receptionist greeted her with her usual cheerfulness. "How are we today?"

"I don't really know just yet Bernice. Give me a few minutes and then I'll tell you," she responded with a nauseous chuckle.

Claire walked hesitantly toward Mike's office hoping to avoid eye contact with him. But as she passed she was relieved to find that he wasn't there.

"Oh Claire," Bernice shouted from down the hall. "Mike said to tell you that he was out meeting with a client this morning and he'd see you later this afternoon."

"Thank you," Claire shouted back feeling relieved that Mike was away.

She ventured on past Mike's office and on into her own. Walking swiftly through the door of her chambers she stopped abruptly in her tracks and stared at the massive bouquet of fall flowers that were sitting in the center of her desk in a sparkling crystal vase.

"Oh my... how beautiful!" she stated with surprise feeling Bernice's presence close behind her.

"Aren't they gorgeous Claire?" Bernice's middle-aged voice chirped excitedly from the rear. "They came for you this morning. Now I don't know who they're from and I didn't open the card, because really... as you know... it's none of my business."

The burly receptionist was clearly dying of curiosity with regard to who had sent the exquisite floral arrangement. She was a robust good-hearted woman who meant well but who also enjoyed knowing the intimate details of everyone's personal lives.

"Thank you Bernice," Claire responded politely as she hung her coat up and closed the door leaving the unknowing assistant without an explanation. Claire pulled the small white card from the sealed envelope and read the inscription aloud to herself.

"Thank you for sharing your life with me Claire. I'll always be here for you! Signed, Mike."

Claire smiled as she held the card to her lips, reflecting on the night before. Mike was remarkable! He was the long lost friend she had been searching for. A friend with whom she could unload some of her baggage, share her troubles and occasionally lean on his shoulder. Reading the card a second time Claire felt relieved. She had secured her job and gained a true friend. Bending down to smell the breathtaking floral bouquet, Claire evaluated her feelings. Her platonic relationship with Mike was extraordinary. She felt a close kinship with this man who had been so kind to her. She felt a friendly love but knew she did not feel a physical attraction for him. Little did she realize at that moment that Mike had fallen hopelessly in love with her.

As the months flew by, Mike remained true to his word. He babied and nurtured Claire with each passing day. The nausea eventually subsided and in the third trimester of her pregnancy she developed a radiant healthy glow as her abdomen protruded. Claire tried earnestly to manage her share of the workload but Mike grew increasingly persistent about her taking more time to rest and relax as he retained the bulk of the clients.

As the final two weeks of her pregnancy came and went, Mike instructed her firmly to stay at home. Against her will, Claire finally agreed as her typically petite body had blossomed largely into a healthy round uncomfortable full term pregnancy.

Each morning on his way to work and again in the evening, Mike routinely stopped at the cottage to check in on Claire and bring her a hot meal, which had been lovingly prepared by his mother. Though Sarah did not understand the details of Claire's pregnancy, she was ecstatic about having a new baby to share in and take care of.

Then on a blistering cold morning in late February as Mike paraded through the front door carrying a steaming tray of hot porridge, tea and toast, he found his beloved friend buckled over in pain struggling to make her way through the living room towards the telephone.

Claire looked up through her agonized face, shot Mike a painful smile and screeched, "Okay lawyer… have you ever delivered a baby before?"

Quickly realizing what was about to happen, Mike spun into a state of panic overload. Emotionally unprepared for the child's arrival, he scurried around the main room of the house shouting orders in an alarmed voice.

"Oh God… Okay… Okay Claire… Okay… now try to remain calm!"

Claire burst into laughter as she pointed toward her packed overnight bag sitting next to the front door.

"Yes, Mr. Lawyer…let's try to remain calmmm" she began to say as another shrieking labor pain shot through her groin.

"Okay… okay then… let's get you out to the truck," Mike shrieked loudly in a worried, distracted voice as he ran to grab the bag then rushed back to wrap Claire's coat around her shoulders.

The two shuffled out to the awaiting vehicle as a frigid air stream swirled irately about them. Claire's labor was progressing rapidly leaving her hardly able to catch her breath between pains.

Forcing himself against the glacial current of air while at the same time trying to shield Claire from its gales, Mike carefully loaded the expectant mother into his truck. He slammed the door behind her then ran around and leapt into the driver's seat. The olive green SUV screeched irritably back at him as he thoughtlessly turned the ignition key, only then realizing the engine was already running. Slamming his foot down heavily on the gas pedal, he propelled the snow-covered vehicle around in an impressive three-sixty spin in the driveway. Plowing through the two-foot snowdrifts that had covered the winding lane from the cottage to the main highway, the truck jarred as the front bumper aggressively forced its way through each packed surface.

"Ouucchhhh!" Claire shrieked as another gut wrenching bolt shot through her body.

Mike's anxiety level doubled with each stabbing pain.

"Jesus! This hurts!" Claire hollered into the frosty air as she squirmed uncomfortably in her seat.

Mike's eyes darted nervously back and forth from his passenger to the road as Claire tensed herself in agony.

"Ouucchhhh!" she bellowed again as she grabbed hold of Mike's arm and yanked it to the right in response to the pain.

The unexpected heave on his nervous limb caused him to swerve his new sport utility vehicle fishtailing across the thoroughfare. Spinning wildly out of control, the rugged tires snarled with each attempt to grip the icy laneway. Blinded by the wintry blizzard, the truck whirled forcefully to the right where its back end powerfully earthed itself in a cavernous snow-covered ditch.

"Holy shit! Holy shit!" he screeched hysterically as his rear tires sunk deeply into the snow. "Are you alright Claire? Holy shit! Are you alright?" Mike panicked as he neurotically fumbled between the steering wheel and his passenger.

But just as Claire was about to laugh hysterically at the preposterous situation, another excruciating labor pain yanked harshly at her pelvic bones.

"Yes... I'm okay...Ouuuccchhh... But if you don't get me to the God damn hospital right now, then you're going to be mopping up these haughty leather seats after I have this kid right here!" she hollered at the panic stricken lawyer, knowing that the time was quickly drawing near.

"Jesus Christ!" Mike shrieked as he slammed the vehicle into four-wheel drive. Visibly distressed, he forcefully jarred the gas pedal to the floor. The vehicle moaned as it rocked back and forth trying in earnest to reach the crest of the ditch seemingly aware of the flustered state of its passengers. Then with an almighty roar, the tires sped through the snow packed crevice and merged its' massive body back up onto the drift-covered road.

"Okay! Okay! Claire you hang on now.... cause we're on our way!" Mike forged his bogus instructions trying to reassure and calm the woman beside him as beads of sweat gathered on his forehead. Claire clenched the door handle as she closed her eyes trying to focus on her breathing.

After twenty painful minutes, Mike sped his tires into the hospital grounds and leapt from his seat. In sheer hysteria, he darted over and pounded his fists on the glass doors of the emergency entrance.

"Bring a stretcher out here right now God Damn it!"

Then he rushed back to assist Claire from the truck. Honoring his urgent commands, two nurses and an orderly raced out to the truck as the steam from the sweating woman in full-blown labor escaped from the vehicle with a whoosh. Pushing a gurney to her side, they assisted Claire up onto it. The medical team immediately realized how quickly the birthing process was progressing.

"Where are you taking her? Where are you taking her God damn it?" Mike demanded to know as they directed him to move his vehicle from the emergency area. "I'm not going anywhere until you tell me where you're taking her!"

Lying on the stretcher, in spite of the pain, Claire broke into full-blown laughter at Mike's distressed state. Her friend was irrationally beside himself.

"The second floor sir! She's going up to the second floor maternity ward! Now you go and move your truck and we'll see you up there in a few minutes," the orderly directed him as he rolled his eyes at the attending nurse.

"These first time father's," the nurses chuckled between themselves as they calmly wheeled Claire into the elevator. "You'd think they were the one who was about to give birth!"

Claire joined in on the hilarity thinking about Mike until she was shocked back into her excruciating labor. The medical team swiftly propelled the expectant mother up to the second floor and into an awaiting hospital room. They routinely removed her clothing and bundled her round body into a faded blue hospital gown.

Her labor was progressing rapidly just as it had when she gave birth to Amelia ten years prior. The nurses were kind and supportive as the birth of her second child quickly approached.

As the final fifteen-minute stretch arrived, Mike continued to make an absolute nuisance of himself out in the corridor. Demanding updates on Claire every five minutes he paced nervously up and down the hallway.

Finally, the senior nurse of the department entered Claire's room.

"Please dear," the perturbed woman pleaded, "Can your husband come in and see you? I realize that this is his first child and that he is extremely anxious. But he is driving the staff around here to the brink of frustration!"

As beads of sweat drenched Claire's face she couldn't help but smile.

"Sure, send the anxious first-time father in to see me."

Within a second Mike burst through the door overcome with anxiety.

"Claire! Claire! How are you feeling?" he shouted as his worried eyes fretfully explored the room.

"Actually… actually…oh shit… it hurts like hell if you really must know the truth," Claire groaned as she managed a painful stab at her groin.

Mike's face was pouring with sweat. Instinctively he raced to the nearby table, grabbed a wet face cloth and dabbed his own forehead looking as if he was about to pass out.

"I know… I know I shouldn't be in here! I know you need your privacy and all that, but…"

Mike was interrupted in mid-sentence as a team of nurses burst through the door. With an attendant maneuvering each end of the bed they released the brakes on the wheels and chauffeured the expectant mother from the room.

"You're on your way now Claire!" the nurse interrupted with an understanding smile. "It won't be long and you'll have your little darling in your arms."

86

Shocked by the sudden intrusion, Mike found himself standing alone in the center of the floor with the damp face cloth dangling from his fingertips.

"Let's go lawyer!" Claire yelled as she tilted her head upward searching for the dazed man they'd left behind in a stupor. "You're not going to bail on me now after I've taken care of all that legal crap for you all these months!"

Claire extended her arm searching for Mike's hand as her bed was wheeled from the room.

"If you're coming then let's go," the nurse instructed him in a no-nonsense tone.

Dropping the cloth in the center of the floor, Mike rushed out the door and followed the moving bed down the hall.

"You go in there and get a gown and cap on. Wash your hands thoroughly then come on through into the birthing room," the same nurse pointed to an area across the corridor.

"Oh Christ... I've never had a baby before!" Mike nattered to himself as he clumsily pulled a discolored green gown down over his crumpled business suit. He washed his hands, quickly plopped a matching cap on his disheveled hair and rushed through the swinging doors to where the birth would take place momentarily.

Feeling disoriented with the moment and overwhelmed with what was about to happen, Mike quickly stepped to Claire's bedside where he found her engaged in the final pushing stages of the birth. Feeling self-conscious, seeing his beautiful friend in a state of shear agony and near nudity, his face flushed with embarrassment as he began nervously tapping on Claire's shoulder.

"Claire... Claire...Claire" he repeated softly to her.

Irritated with his interference, her sweat soaked face turned and yelled, "What! What the hell do you want Mike? Can't you see that I'm a little busy here? Can't you see that this hurts like hell? So unless you want to take my place on this bed then please, please shut the hell up for a minute!"

But paying no attention to Claire's angry remarks he nervously continued to seek her attention.

"Uh, Uh, I know you're very busy sweetheart! But, but are you sure... are you sure you want me in here?"

"Yes I want you in here! Now will you shut the hell up and hold my hand!" the woman screeched with irritation as she bore down on nearly the final push of her child's birth.

The doctor then entered the room with a brisk walk clothed in his green gown and rubber boots and instantaneously took over from where the nurse was standing at the foot of the bed.

"Okay now Claire, you're almost there. This baby is ready. So give me one big push," the little man directed through his miniature bifocal glasses.

"Uhhh Chrissst!" Claire shrieked as she bore down heavily on her pelvis.

Then feeling a painful sweeping whoosh in her lower abdomen, the child came sloshing out and into the doctor's arms as Claire fell back exhausted against the bed.

Silence then fell upon the busy staff members as they hustled about the room attending to their routine duties. Straining to see what the doctor held, Claire struggled to lift her torso back up as she heard the shrill whistle of a newborn infant's cry.

"Well Claire! You have a beautiful, healthy baby boy," the doctor announced with joy as he held the crying newborn in the air for her to see. Efficiently the nurse then took the squirming child from the doctor's hands and wrapped him in a soft blue receiving blanket. Blotting at his tiny face and hair with a sterile white cloth she walked slowly around the bed toward Claire and placed the crying infant upon his mother's breast. In a state of shear relief that only a new mother can realize, Claire wrapped her long thin arms around the bundle of innocence that nestled comfortably into her chest.

"Hello my darling," she whispered to her new son as she ran her fingers through his tiny quivering head of wet blond curls. "Hello my little sweetheart."

Her eyes beaming with satisfaction, Claire turned to look at Mike who stood numbly gazing outward at the scene before him in disbelief. With his arms hanging limply by his sides and tears streaming down his anguished face, he looked on at Claire and her new son with absolute wonder.

"Look Mike," Claire spoke in a hushed tone. "Look what I have here. I have a new son. Isn't he beautiful?"

Staring at the child from the side of the bed, Mike broke down into a full-blown cry as he slowly stepped forward and placed a loving kiss upon Claire's cheek.

"He is beautiful Claire," Mike choked out between his tears. "It is a miracle!"

Mike stood motionless at Claire's side not offering to touch the new child, feeling as if he should not infringe on her glorious private moment. Transfixed in a state of awe of what he had just witnessed, he stared at the newborn as tears of joy continued to stream down over his cheekbones.

"Would you like to hold him Mike?" Claire offered as she held the calming child in his direction.

"Uh... Uh... no I don't think so Claire. He's so little. I might hurt him," Mike struggled trying to compose himself.

Claire laughed sweetly at his timid reaction.

"Don't worry Mike! He won't break," she reassured as she held her son out toward him a second time.

Taking note of the hesitant, frightened man backing away from the bed, one of the nurses left her duties at the counter. Smiling at the moment, she pressed her strong hands down on Mike's shoulders encouraging him to sit in the empty waiting chair. Giving Claire a wink of her eye, she then swept the newborn child from his mother's chest and placed him directly into Mike's apprehensive arms. Confidently, as if she had done it a million times before, the nurse positioned Mike's hands properly, showing him how to support the baby. She then gave the nervous man a gentle pat on the back and with a smile she returned to her duties.

Feeling awkward with his own massive clumsiness, yet amazed at the tiny miracle he held, Mike looked up to be met with Claire's gaze as she stared lovingly from the bed.

"Look at me Claire," Mike responded as if he couldn't believe what he was doing.

Claire smiled tenderly at the man she had grown so fond of then watched as he began to gently rock back and forth in the chair.

"Hey there little guy! Hey there! We've been waiting for you to join us! Welcome to the world little one. Welcome to your new life." Oblivious to the fact that Claire was still staring at him adoring the tenderness he shared with her son, Mike continued, "You know what little guy? You're really lucky to have such a beautiful mommy. Yes, you've very lucky indeed."

Taken back by what she was hearing, Claire felt a purge of emotion for the man that was holding her child. At that moment, as the world seemed perfect and still, she saw Mike in a new light. She stared at him with wonder not knowing how to label her feelings for him. Claire watched on for several minutes bathing her self in the extraordinary aura of love that filled the room.

"Mike was right," Claire mentally recalled. "Everything is going to be just fine."

Then slowly raising his eyes from the tiny bundle of blond curls, he shyly inquired, "Well, what are you going to call him?"

"I thought I would name him Michael, Lucas, Morgan. What do you think?"

Mike's eyes filled with glistening tears as he choked over the lump that had welled up in his throat. The child that he had been waiting for but was uncertain of was to be named after him. Unable to respond, he nodded his silent approval as billowing tears of joy streamed down his cheeks and on to the bewildered child.

The moment was perfect. To Claire, all was well. Though Amelia had been called back to heaven and given another purpose and even though losing her had maliciously cut her heart out, Claire was granted the glorious gift of a second child. As she lay in her hospital bed drenched in sweat, she felt whole once again. Claire felt her spirit renewed. She was reborn with new purpose and a direction to stride in. Together she would walk with her son into a brighter future.

After several moments of jubilation the euphoria was interrupted. The attending nurse courteously took the child from Mike's arms announcing that she needed to weigh him, wash him and would return him momentarily. Mike's eyes followed the baby as he was swept from his embrace. He felt the warmth dissipate from his chest as Michael vanished with the nurse. Feeling self-conscious of the sentimental moment, Mike pushed his lanky body up from the chair.

"Hey there lady, great job! And... I'm really sorry about the truck in the ditch thing!" Mike shook his head from side to side feeling responsible for the unscheduled delay on the way to the hospital. "I knew we'd get out but I just didn't know how long it would take. Hell... I've never delivered a screeching pregnant woman to the hospital before!"

Together they laughed at the memory of earlier that morning.

Still feeling awkward about the moment, Mike pulled off his hospital cap and gown and placed them on the chair in the corner of the room. Shoving his hands in the pockets of the badly creased suit he had dressed in early that morning, he shrugged.

"Well, now that everything is settled, I'm going to call my parents and give them the great news. Is that okay Claire... that I tell them that is?"

"That's just fine," Claire replied softly with the satisfied smile of a new mother. "I'm going to try and sleep for a while."

"Okay! Well I'll see you a bit later then," he promised brushing the wet hair from her forehead.

With that, he walked toward the door of the hospital room.

"Hey lawyer!" the new mother shouted with a final thought. Mike turned back to look at her in question. "Thanks for your help! You were just great!"

Mike's face beamed as he winked at the exhausted woman and left the room.

An hour later Claire awoke from a restful sleep to find Sarah, Joe and Mike standing quietly at the foot of her bed gazing down upon the babe that lay resting in the bassinette next to her.

"Good afternoon dear!" Sarah spoke cheerfully as Claire struggled to open her eyes. "My goodness you have a beautiful little boy there," she tried to mask her husky farm voice into a whisper. "May I hold him?"

"Yes of course Sarah," Claire replied pleased to share her new treasure with the people she loved. Sarah handed a large bouquet of fresh cut flowers to Joe and quickly moved around the bed. Tenderly lifting the contented infant who lay staring up through his midnight steel blue eyes at the blurry figures above him, the experienced farmwoman bundled him carefully into her loving arms.

"Oh my little darling," she spoke to Baby Michael as she kissed his tiny forehead. "You are Nana Sarah's little treasure now aren't you?"

Clearly overjoyed to welcome the new child into her life, Sarah moved to sit down in the empty chair while cuddling the contented babe warmly against her chest.

"Now Claire," Sarah started to direct. "Now you will let us help with this little boy, right? He is a precious part of our family too now don't you agree?" the hearty countrywoman inquired wanting confirmation that she would be closely involved in the child's life.

Charmed by the vision of the grandmotherly woman holding her child, Claire warmly agreed, "Thank you Sarah. I'd love that. Little Michael is going need a wonderful set of grandparents."

Joe stood along side Mike with a proud smile saying nothing but clearly enjoying the rapture of the scene before him. Once again with her new loving family surrounding her, Claire felt...all was well. Life seemed perfect!

The next day Claire and Baby Michael were released from the hospital and chauffeured cautiously back to their cottage. Mike remained respectfully in his place of being a friend not a new father but clearly he wanted to be more as the mother and son settled together in the warmth of their little home that afternoon.

Mike hustled about the cottage as Claire comforted her son with the warm natural milk from her breast.

"What a miracle children are," Mike stated as he returned from the kitchen with a hot cup of tea for the new mother.

"Yes Mike! They are indeed. But a person really has to experience the miracle of life as you saw it yesterday in order to appreciate it don't you think?"

Less than an hour after they arrived home, Mike had unpacked Claire's hospital bag, done a load of dirty laundry, replaced the sheets on her bed, double checked the bassinette for safety, made Claire a hot cup of tea and shoveled the snow from the front walkway. Stamping his boots off on the porch, he placed the shovel back in the corner and peered in through the icy window at the wonderful loving sight.

"What a perfect day it has been," he admitted.

The snow was lightly covering the sleeping wheat fields in mammoth fluffy flakes as he watched Claire lying warmly covered on the sofa in front of the blazing fireplace with her precious babe sleeping soundly on her chest.

Opening the door carefully, trying not to disturb the new babe, he slipped his boots off in the entranceway and crept quietly across the floor. After throwing another log on the fire he walked lightly across the room toward the sleeping mother. Admiring the loving scene before his eyes, he bent down and kissed Claire gently on the forehead and then with a warm sigh of satisfaction he silently left the cottage. The day had been perfect indeed and Mike wanted to leave the scene of beauty undisturbed.

Baby Michael Lucas thrived wonderfully as the passing weeks turned into months. With his glorious head of soft blond curls billowing around his tiny skull, his steel blue eyes stared out attentively from beneath the lush warm blankets he nestled into. Joe had lovingly hand carved a gorgeous mahogany bassinette for Michael as he snuggled deeply within it, his innocent gaze puzzling over each approaching voice. Both Sarah and Mike spent endless hours with Claire and her son and their love grew deeper for them both.

As the blistering Saskatchewan winter subsided into spring then followed by summer, the close family bond firmly took hold. Mike had never before experienced the wondrous love of such a beautiful woman and her child and he continued to hope that one day the platonic relationship would blossom into his own family.

A full six months passed when Claire returned to work with the baby in tow. Entirely neglecting her duties as office receptionist, Bernice joyfully bounced Michael on her knee as she cooed and cackled to the happy child. Though often distracted by the sound of her son's laughter in the reception area, Claire did her best to concentrate on her work and eventually assisted in balancing half the caseload backlog.

As the first year turned over, Michael thrived into a curious toddler. Unsurprisingly, Nana Sarah insisted that she be Michael's daytime caregiver as Claire swung back into her work full time. Claire loved seeing Michael and his grandmother together. Though she missed him desperately during her days at the office, she knew he was in the absolute best of care.

Mike spent increasingly more time with his adopted family. Gifts, toys and flowers flowed into the cottage weekly as Mike happily bound through the front door with his arms loaded. The relationship boundaries between Claire and Mike had never been clearly discussed though Claire seemed comfortable with the arrangement and put little thought into anything further. But Mike kept hoping for more. Although he spent countless hours with Claire and Baby Michael at the cottage, he still left each night and returned home to his lonely, dark apartment in the city. Physical advances had never been made between the two that cared so much about each other. The platonic relationship seemed too precious to risk changing.

Chapter Five

The bronze landscape of September presented itself and Sarah's annual harvest feast had arrived. The family gathered together and the magnificent social evening with Mike's parents and brothers was again delightfully shared with Claire and her child of nineteen months.

As the evening came to a close and Claire bundled up her son, Mike readied his SUV for the short journey down the road. The three drove back to the cottage in a merry state after a spectacular dinner and several bottles of wine had been shared. Mike put the sleeping child in his crib, kissed him tenderly on the cheek then stood marveling at the wonder of the baby he had come to love so deeply.

"I love you Michael," he spoke with a hush as he stroked his fingers against the child's silky skin. "But I need to share a secret with you Mikey. I just wish your mommy loved me as much as I've come to love her."

After a pause of quiet admiration, he turned out the small lamp and closed the door gently behind him.

Claire was busying herself in the kitchen serving up a pot of hot tea. Mike stood leaning against the door as she waltzed happily about the kitchen. His heart was overflowing with love for the woman that he spied on but he had never before told her how he felt. Their relationship had stopped at being simply the best of friends. They remained undefeatable business partners. He was the best substitute father a woman could ask for. But that was the boundary on which the relationship ended.

Claire loaded the two steaming teacups onto a tray and then placed it on the coffee table in the living room as she plunged happily into the deep floral sofa. Noticing Mike standing in the doorway she smiled over her shoulder and patted the backrest of the sofa with an unspoken invitation for him to come and join her.

"My gosh! Your mother is the best cook in the world! Her cherry pie is to die for!" Claire blurted out with the total satisfaction of a full stomach.

Mike moved around the couch and sat down as he always did, a respectable safe distance away from Claire. Through curious eyes she studied the unfamiliar strain on his brow wondering what was on his worried mind.

"Are you okay?" she inquired handing him a cup of tea.

Mike politely took the cup from her hand then immediately placed it down on the table in front of him.

"No, I'm afraid I'm not okay Claire," he replied.

"What's wrong then?"

"Well, I'm not really sure how or where to begin."

"Then begin at the beginning silly," she continued to push in a joking manner.

Mike's face blushed as he reached to take Claire's free hand into his own. "You see Claire, when I first met you a year and a half ago, I immediately felt that you were a strikingly beautiful woman. And well…as time has passed I've had the privilege of working with you."

Claire nodded, curious where the conversation leading.

"I have come to admire your sharp business intelligence and I've always enjoyed your witty sense of humor."

Claire smiled at his flattering words feeling slightly awkward as she lowered her gaze to her teacup.

"But there is a problem here I'm afraid," he continued then paused as if he was losing his nerve.

Increasingly aware of the discomfort he was feeling Claire extended her arm along the backrest of the sofa setting her hand gently upon his shoulder.

"Go on Mike," she prodded.

"Well… well… Claire, it's just this…" he blurted awkwardly. "As time has passed I've grown to love Michael like I've never known love before. I feel kind of like a father to him and I always want to be a part of his life."

"Uh-huh…that is what I want as well," she assured him.

"But the other part of the problem is that I've grown to love you more deeply than I could ever possibly put into words."

Mike's honesty shot through Claire's heart like a bullet as she sat riveted on the sofa. Claire had no idea that he felt so deeply about her. Realizing the significance of the discussion Claire reached forward and placed her teacup on the table trying to remain calm and appear unsurprised at Mike's confession. Claire also loved Mike but she had never thought of the love as anything more than that of a brother and sister relationship.

"I think of you constantly," the stammering man continued as if he was on a roll to get the words out before she rejected him. "Night and day, I only think of you! Everyday you sit next to me in the office and I'm overcome with your fragrance. I miss you desperately when you're not there and can't wait for the next time that I'll see you. Now I know Michael is not my child but I feel as though he is. I love him Claire. God, I love that little boy," his pace quickened as the words of truth tumbled rapidly from his lips.

Stunned by his candor Claire searched her heart for an honest response. Mike reached out and touched her chin softly turning her face to look into his.

"And I love you," he confessed from the bottom of his heart looking deeply into her sparkling green eyes. "God, how I love you Claire!"

Time stood still as Claire found herself at a complete loss for words. Then Mike continued as his tone turned to impending defeat. "But I also know, that you'll never feel the same way about me. I know your whole heart was stolen by a truck driver nearly two years ago."

Claire looked away sorrowfully knowing that Mike spoke the truth. She did love the father of her child but she also had surrendered to the fact that she'd never see him again.

Mike was knowingly leaving himself open for his heart to be broken into small pieces. The candle that flickered dimly on the table swept muted waves of light across his desperate face. Claire turned to stare into his pleading eyes as she moved her fingers up to the collar of his neatly pressed shirt.

"Mike, you have surprised me!" she admitted, nervously fingering an empty buttonhole. Pausing momentarily to think over what she had just been told she then continued, "Luke remains a mystery to me. I only spent one very special evening with him and yes I will always love him. He gave me a beautiful child... though he'll never know it. My heart had been trampled on at that time Mike. I had just buried Amelia the day before and Luke somehow found his way to me. I'll always be grateful to him for that... wherever he is."

Mike's eyes showed of the disappointment he had been expecting as Claire reminisced about Luke.

"But..." she continued touching his chin, "you also mean a great deal to me."

Mike noticed that her well-chosen choice of words left out the fact that she would ever love him as a husband.

"I know you love Michael and I always want you to be a part of his life but..." she reassured him weakly as she studied his saddened face. Confused by her own emotions yet equally struck by the vulnerability of the man that sat next to her, Claire cut herself off from speaking further. "Oh never mind all that," she closed the conversation.

Claire reached up and pulled his chin closer towards hers then pressed her shimmering lips gently against his. Surprised by her intimate invitation Mike pulled his mouth away quickly. Seduced by his feelings and honesty Claire slid herself across the sofa pressing her thigh tightly against his. Never losing contact with the sadness in his eyes, she stretched her long slender fingers around his muscular neck and aggressively pressed her lips against his once again. Unable to resist, Mike joined her willingly in the second kiss as she slid the tip of her tongue into his mouth.

The heat of the moment quickly boiled into an inferno as the two passionately kissed. Claire's heart had fallen victim to Mike's loving honesty as she wrapped both her arms around his shoulders pressing her breasts against his broad chest. Hungrily Mike responded as he stretched his arms around the back of her silky white blouse.

In an instant the love starved woman unleashed her physical loneliness as she kissed his face and neck ravenously, fumbling to undo the buttons on his shirt as the passionate heat engulfed them both. The first tender kiss of understanding quickly turned into lustful desire as Mike pulled Claire's blouse down over her shoulders showing her bare breasts and firm nipples welcoming his desire. Slowly pushing the beautiful woman backward on the sofa, Mike stretched himself out on top of her as Claire felt his throbbing penis pulsate through his jeans. Overcome with desire, they hungrily tore at each other's clothing wanting to feel nudity against their skin.

"Oh God Claire," Mike mumbled swallowing Claire's mouth into his own. "You feel... you are... you are so beautiful." Rapaciously struggling for nakedness, they ripped at each other's clothing until it was found. As the heat of passion vigorously throbbed between them, Claire anxiously invited Mike to take her loved starved soul into his own. As the confines of the sofa restricted the two lovers from unleashing their obsessions, Mike arose from the couch. With the candlelight dancing off his tall, muscular nudity he swept Claire into his arms and carried her into the bedroom where he placed her unclothed body on the waiting mattress. Unrestricted, the lustful fixation continued as their hearts pounded together, rolling over each other in a desperate search for passionate fulfillment.

Bringing each other to obsessive heights, they engulfed their naked bodies in the luring seduction of the other. Together they dissipated into each other's souls becoming one. The fervent lovemaking lasted for hours, fulfilling each other time and again until exhaustion overtook them. Then feeling drained and overly satisfied, they drifted off to sleep within the security of each other's arms.

The next morning arrived as the wind blew the copper leaves in a choreographed dance through the air just outside the bedroom window. Claire awoke still entangled in Mike's strapping embrace of love. She lay in silence recalling the previous night of passion as she stared at the leaves that swirled through the atmosphere just beyond the glass. In confusion she tried to sort her feelings for the man who still confined her. Clearly Mike was in love with her. But though she felt a very special bond with him, she knew that she did not feel the same depth of emotion for him.

In the quiet of her thoughts she strived to justify making love with him but discovered herself consumed with guilt. Yes…she did love Mike, but she could not honestly admit that she felt the necessary attraction one needs for an enduring long-term relationship or marriage.

Mike soon awoke and nibbled gently on her ear.

"Good morning beautiful," he began tenderly kissing the back of her neck.

Claire knew she had crossed the sacred line with Mike. She also knew that in her heart she could not offer him the love that he deserved. He was a wonderful man and he was worthy of a woman who could return the same depth of love that he freely offered. Feeling trapped, not wanting to devastate her cherished friend; she turned over and kissed him softly on the cheek. Without question, Claire knew that she would have to be honest with Mike. As she prepared her thoughts for the sensitive discussion to come the telephone rang on the bedside table. Startled by the ring Mike instinctively reached over and grabbed the receiver.

"Hello?" he cheerfully greeted the caller. "Hello?" he repeated, hearing no response on the other end of the line.

Shrugging his nude shoulders in question, he replaced the dead receiver back on the base and slid back under the covers to find that Claire had gotten up. Standing at the foot of the bed she looked at him in question about the caller who had refused to speak. Then tossing her partner a meek grin, she reached for her bathrobe and left the room to check on Michael.

As she changed her toddler into a dry diaper Claire heard the telephone ring a second time. She paused to listen as Mike picked up the receiver. He said hello insistently three times then slammed it back down with annoyance. Claire wondered who was calling and why they were refusing to speak with Mike.

A few minutes later, Mike entered the baby's room fully dressed. Sensing that Claire was uncomfortable with her actions the night before, he greeted Baby Michael running his large fingers through the child's curls.

"How about I make us some breakfast?" Mike suggested.

"No thanks. I'm really not very hungry."

Mike read in Claire's tone that it was not in his best interest to persist and that it was likely best if he left her alone.

"Well hey then, if you're okay I'm going to go home, get changed then take a run into the office okay?"

"Sure that's fine," Claire responded shortly.

Mike leaned over and kissed her lightly on the cheek then left the room. Picking up Michael and cuddling him in her arms, she watched Mike walk around the outside of the cottage, get in his truck and drive off down the dirt road. Feeling confused, she knew she loved him but she also felt a significant vacuum of emptiness in her heart. Mike was truly a sweetheart. He had been so loving and kind since she had arrived. However he was right in that her lost cowboy had stolen her heart completely even though she'd had such a brief encounter with him.

Mike made himself scarce around the cottage for the two weeks that followed. Though Claire went into the office everyday, she felt awkward around him maintaining a polite but professional presence. The workload in the office increased as the fall months rolled on. Mike sensed Claire's distance and respected it not venturing again to cross the line of intimacy as they worked endless hours together late into the night.

Chapter Six

In early November the prairie winter reared its' cold ugly head. At four in the afternoon, Mike peaked around the corner and into Claire's office where she remained buried in a stack of paper.

"Hey there," he interrupted politely. "I've got to run and meet a new client for dinner. Are you okay to close up the shop tonight by yourself?"

Startled by his intrusion she glanced up through her thin steel framed glasses and laughed, "Sure I think I can manage that!"

"I told my mother that you'd probably be home late tonight and she said that was fine. She also said she would get Michael ready for bed and keep him at the farm until you got there."

Claire smiled learning that Mike had made arrangements for her child.

"Okay then, be careful on your way home! It's pretty nasty out there!" he instructed her with care.

"I'll be fine. Have a great dinner!" she shouted after him as he dashed down the hall with his brief case.

Claire returned to her work until another full hour had passed and then heard Bernice packing up her desk for the evening.

"Goodnight Claire. See you tomorrow!"

"Goodnight Bernice! Hey can you please lock the front door for me as you go out?"

But Bernice didn't respond as the heavy wooden door to their office suite clicked shut. She hadn't heard Claire's request as she darted out to catch the elevator. Claire sighed with exhaustion as she returned to studying the details of a new case.

The evening hours progressed and the darkness of the prairie winter swirled with anger outside her frosted office window. The snow was rocketing down from the sky in a bitter skirmish with the howling wind. Mesmerized by the details of her case, Claire fell into a somnolent trance as the antique grandfather clock in the hallway slowly swished back and forth with precise accuracy.

It was nine o'clock in the evening when Claire finally raised her head from her paperwork rubbing her tired eyes. Rolling her head from side to side she tried to relieve the tension that had built up in the back of her neck.

"I sure need a coffee!" she admitted rising from her desk. Feeling the need to stretch her legs, Claire left her office and walked down the darkened hallway to the coffee station. After pouring herself of a cup of dark over-brewed caffeine she stood dazedly in the hallway swirling the cream around watching the stir stick melt in the murky mixture.

Alone in the darkened office, Claire's mind returned to the details of the case she was currently working on involving an elderly widowed farm woman.

"How unfortunate," she stated aloud thinking about the widow who was left with an unproductive farm and an insurmountable amount of debt.

"Actually, I feel quite fortunate," a recognizable voice slithered defiantly from behind her.

At once Claire knew the tone of the voice. Without needing to see the face her heart began palpitating into overdrive.

"Hello Claire. God I've missed you!" the voice continued.

Terrified, Claire spun around on her heels as she spilled her coffee down the front of her white blouse. She wanted to catch a glimpse of the influence that was so near to her. In horror, Claire gasped as she met with the eyes of Jacob sitting in a chair in a dark corner of the entranceway.

"Jesus Christ Jacob! How did you get in here?" she yelled as she struggled with both the coffee burn down her chest and the utter shock of seeing her husband sitting so close to her.

"Well baby, the door was wide open," he responded smugly. "You see… I was walking along on this very nasty night and I saw the light on in this office building. So I said to myself, well hell, I need some legal advice anyway so I might as well go on in."

Jacob reached into the pocket of his beige trench coat and pulled out a cigarette. Claire stared at him frozen with fear as her fingers anxiously clutched the counter top behind her. Calmly he put the cigarette in his mouth and lit it.

"You see Claire my love," his insulting tone continued. "My little legal problem is just this... a long time ago, my deceitful bitch of a wife ran off with my little girl. And well now... I've been looking all over the fucking world for the past eight years trying to find her and get her back. Let's just say that it's taken me a while to get here...but here I am at last." Jacob exhaled a thick billowing cloud of smoke from his cigarette as he collected his thoughts. "Hell... it looks like my luck might just be changing. Wouldn't you say so Claire?"

He smiled callously, reaping great pleasure from the intimidation he was inflicting on his estranged wife. Claire's body began to tremble as she clutched a tighter hold on the counter top crushing her finger nails into the marble surface never taking her eyes off the looming dark figure that sat nearly motionless in the corner.

"So now, let me tell you something. No doubt you have filled my daughter's head with nasty, horrible stories about her father. In fact, I don't doubt that for a second," he slithered. "But that doesn't necessarily concern me because I'm here now to pick her up and take her home. I can set all that spiteful nonsense straight as soon as I get her back home."

Claire closed her eyes tightly, saying nothing.

"It looks to me like you're doing pretty well for yourself here Claire. No doubt getting a tidy chunk of cash from your dead father helped set you up in this office quite nicely. It's funny though...I never took you for a farm girl."

Claire's heart pounded nervously through her chest hearing each degrading syllable. She knew that on such a stormy winter night she was completely alone in the building with no hope of escape from the enraged madman that was then slowly rising from his chair. Leisurely Jacob began to saunter across the reception area toward her as tears of shear terror began to pour down her face.

"Now Jacob, just stay calm and listen to me," she pled to the approaching figure.

"Oh the time I've spent. Oh the money I've wasted," he boorishly cut her off as smoke discharged from his jaws, each anticipated footstep drawing nearer to her.

"You've ruined my career Claire. You've ruined our family. You have destroyed my life," he skulked emerging from the darkness.

Nervously glancing from side to side, the frenzied woman searched for an escape as the infuriated lunatic approached.

"Now Jacob please just wait a minute!" she pled for mercy.

Slowly he rounded the end of the counter then dashed his cigarette out on the marble finished coffee station. Claire understood the depth of rage that simmered within the villain that had come so threatenly close.

As he finished crushing his cigarette into the counter top Claire made a desperate attempt to dash past him heading toward the entrance of the office. But as she tried to hastily pass through the narrow gap between them, Jacob instinctively reached out and snatched her elbow. Fiercely he yanked her thin frame back toward him violently snapping her neck around with his insane grip. Claire winced with pain as his firm hand secured the pinnacle of her spine pulling her face in only a few inches from his own.

"My patience has run out!" he bellowed into her face, his breath reeking of alcohol. "I've had enough Claire!"

Paralyzed by his psychotic grip, Claire's quivering body was held captive within his abusive seizure. Jacob then reefed her right arm up behind her back as she cringed in pain, but still she said nothing.

"You know what Claire?" his tone was vicious. "I have really come to hate you over the years."

Jacob's eyes seethed with the uncontrollable anger Claire had become so familiar with. She knew he would stop at nothing until he got what he wanted… and this time he wanted Amelia. But this time he could not have her.

"I saw you in New York. I saw you bitch!" he screamed as he reefed her arm further up her back. Claire grimaced a second time as her limb was twisted backward.

"Now tell me what I want to hear Claire. Tell me…where is Amelia?" his voice escalated.

Then fearing she had nothing to lose, Claire hoisted her right knee up and slammed it with full force into his groin.

"Ohhh Christ!" Jacob bellowed as he buckled over in agony. "You God Damn bitch!" he screeched in pain as he reached out to seize her. But Claire's second attempt to escape was also a failure as he grabbed a hand full of her hair. Jacob's volcanic fury was erupting as he reefed her body inward then forcefully slammed her into the adjacent wall sending the coffee station crashing to the ground. Violently he belted her across the face as she grunted out an agonizing wail. Shoving his left hand up under her slender chin while pinning her right arm to the wall, he braced her neck firmly cutting off her airway as he repeatedly punched her back and forth across the face. With every stinging blow, Claire's head swung lifelessly to the side until numbness overcame her relieving her consciously from the pain of his beating as it had done so many times in the past.

"God Damn it Claire!" he raved into a crazed irrational state. "This time… I'm really going to fucken lose it if you don't tell me where Amelia is!"

As fury overcame him, Jacob reached down with his right hand and fumbled through the pocket of his coat. Pulling out a switchblade, which he immediately triggered, the demented rogue held the sparkling steel blade mercilessly before Claire's frantic eyes. Barely conscious from the beating, Claire focused on the long razor sharp weapon then closed her eyes with acceptance knowing full well that her life was about to end. After scraping the blade down the pulsating tissue on her delicate neck, he slowly drew the point up and over her left cheekbone. Taunting the terrified woman, he directed the razor sharp tip downward a second time then encircled her neckline pausing briefly where he pressed it firmly against her vocal cords. Claire's heart hammered in her chest as she began to silently pray for mercy.

"Yes, my darling Claire. I've really come to hate you," he whispered pressing his unshaven cheek against hers.

Claire hated the feeling of his skin as he touched her. Then as if amused by the terror he witnessed in her eyes, he added force to the trenchant blade against her neck. Trembling, Claire sealed her eyes closed bracing herself for the sting of the cutting edge, feeling it begin to slice her velvet skin.

"Tell me…where is Amelia?" Jacob questioned as he snatched both her tiny wrists within the grip of his left hand. "Where is she?"

"You'll…you'll never…have her," Claire choked out with defiance for the man that had caused her so much trauma.

Then as she closed her eyes bracing her soul for what would be the final moment of her life, Claire heard the sound of a key unlocking the front door. Startled by the oncoming intrusion, Jacob spun his head around to see the heavy oak door of the office being swung open. Further enraged with the unforeseen intrusion, he withdrew the blade from the threatened woman's throat and belted Claire's face a final blistering blow sending her body crashing into the adjacent corner.

As a hand reached in through the doorway groping for the light switch, Jacob turned from the hysterical woman and ran swiftly down the corridor. Forcefully he shoved the fire exit open and disappeared down the back staircase vanishing into the darkness of the winter night.

The fluorescent office lights started to glow as Claire slid down the wall breaking into uncontrollable sobs of anguish. Mike nervously glanced across the reception area and down the corridor. As his eyes adjusted to the light, he caught a glimpse of his distressed associate dazed and crumpled in the corner.

"Jesus Christ Claire!" he shrieked hurdling the reception desk and darting to her side. "Are you alright? What the hell happened in here tonight?"

Gently placing both hands under her shuddering arms he assisted the broken woman back on to her feet. Claire's body wobbled as he wrapped his arms around her torso and led her to a chair in the reception area. Bending forward, Claire covered her face with her hands and cried mercilessly. For several long moments she wept unable to verbalize what had just happened. With trepidation Mike tried to sooth the frenzied woman still unaware of what had occurred just prior to his return to the office. Pulling her body from Mike's support she reached to tug a tissue from Bernice's desk. Only then did Mike notice the trickle of blood seeping down her neck and onto her blouse.

"Jesus Christ Claire! You're bleeding!" he shouted frantically into her strained face as if she were unaware of the blood seepage.

Claire acknowledged the hemorrhage with a dazed blink. Mike rushed over to the shattered coffee station and rinsed a cloth with warm water. Horrified at the scene, he returned and pressed the cloth gently against her bleeding neckline. Then he swathed her body with his arms once again as black eyeliner streaked down over her swelling cheekbones.

"It's okay darling. It's all over now. I'm here with you."

As Claire slowly began to compose herself, she pulled her body back and looked into his questioning eyes. Pausing for a moment to swallow the lump in her throat she then tried to explain. "It was Jacob! Mike... he has found me again! Somehow that lunatic found me and got in here. Mike he was going to kill me this time! I had asked Bernice to lock the door as she left...but I guess she didn't hear me."

Mentally reliving the unprovoked attack Claire broke down completely. But Mike had heard enough! He assisted Claire to her feet, peeled off his warm knee length overcoat and wrapped it around her quivering shoulders.

"That son-of-a-bitch," he muttered angrily. "Over my dead body will he ever hurt you again!"

Leaving her side for only a moment, Mike darted to the end of the hallway and peered through the frosted picture window. Glancing down several stories to the rear parking lot below, Mike could see the fresh trail of footprints that Jacob had left in the snow as he cowardly dashed off through the back door, across the lot and down the street. Needing to reassure himself that Jacob had left no way back into the building, Mike pushed through the exit and ran down four flights of stairs, leaping two at a time. His rage escalated as he thought of what the madman had done to the woman that he loved but couldn't have for his own. Mike trudged across the parking lot through the blundering snow retracing Jacob's hasty exit. As he investigated the fresh trail of footprints he noticed a black leather glove sitting on top of a nearby snowdrift. Continuing toward the edge of the parking lot, Mike bent down a second time to pick up a cell phone that had also been accidentally dropped. Holding the glove and the cell phone within his frozen grasp, Mike stood at the edge of the road staring down the darkened residential street. He noticed that a car had recently pulled away from the curb about half a block down. The tires had spun bitterly through the snow packed surface leaving black pebbles of asphalt spewed to the rear.

"Son-of-a-bitch coward!" he yelled into the night as his own anger seethed. "I'll kill you myself if you ever show your face again!"

The blustering wind blew wildly as Mike trudged back through the snow to the office building. After making one final check that the rear exit to the building was securely locked, Mike walked the perimeter of the office structure and entered in through the front door.

Returning to the suite, Mike found Claire just coming out of the washroom. She was pressing a fresh tissue across the scrape in her neck as her eyes searched his.

"He's gone! Looks like he was parked about half a block down," he explained.

Claire said nothing as she stared at her friend from across the reception area.

"I did find these items though." Mike held up the glove and cell phone for her to see. "If I didn't think that the police would need this as evidence then I'd smash this God-Damn phone right now!"

Claire momentarily closed her eyes as if wanting the vicious event to vanish from her mind.

Mike reached across Bernice's desk and yanked the telephone receiver into his hand. Without a second thought he dialed 911.

"Yes, I need a police car over here right away! There has been an attempted murder at my office," he assertively informed the dispatch. "Yes, thank you."

Mike completed the call and placed the receiver back down on the base. Claire pulled his large overcoat from her shoulders and left it dangling on the back of a chair.

"You know what Mike?" she started to converse as she yanked another tissue from the box. "Jacob really frightened me this time. I'm not for a second going to deny that. But my God I'm tired of living like this. I've grown so weary of living my life running in fear of him. I never deliberately tried to inflict pain on him. I took Amelia away because he had beaten her tiny body to a pulp!" she continued justifying her actions of years before. Her eyes were filling with tears as Mike waved a hand for her to come and sit beside him.

"When Jacob finds out that Amelia is dead he'll have nothing left to lose next time," she rationalized as she shuffled across the floor and sat down beside him.

Draping his right arm around her shoulders he reached over and placed a kiss on her forehead.

"Then we'll just have to make sure there isn't a next time, won't we!"

The RCMP arrived at the building within moments. With their boots covered in snow, they barged aggressively through the front door of the office. After a quick scan of the reception area, the first officer sat down beside Claire and began taking notes as she described the details of the malicious assault. Two other policemen scoured the area for evidence taking various photographs as they progressed down the hallway. Mike in turn submitted the glove and cell phone that he had found to the interviewing officer.

105

"Well judging by the look of what has happened here, Mr. Redkin must have lost these items as he fled out the back door," the officer stated as he put the two items in a clear plastic bag. "Does your husband, I mean this Jacob Redkin guy have any family around here Ms. Morgan?" the officer probed, wondering where they might start looking for him.

"No he doesn't," Claire replied. "I can only guess that he'll return to New York City right away where he'll wait for another opportunity to corner me."

"Well if he's the sharp shooting lawyer type, I don't imagine that he'll be dumb enough to stay in a local hotel in this town tonight. Though we'll certainly check out that possibility. No offense intended about the lawyer bit Ms. Morgan," the officer apologized realizing that his comment may have insulted the two lawyers sitting before him. Claire couldn't help but smile at the officer's embarrassment.

After thirty minutes, the second and third officers returned to the reception area.

"I believe it's all pretty clear," they discussed the case among themselves. "Ms. Morgan stated that it was without a doubt her husband Jacob Redkin from New York City. Apparently he had come to retrieve his daughter."

Then realizing that he hadn't yet asked the obvious question, the Canadian Mountie turned to Claire and inquired, "Where exactly is your daughter right now Ms. Morgan?"

Claire lowered her eyes to the floor but before she had a moment to think through her reply Mike stated, "Claire's daughter Amelia, passed away a few years ago of Leukemia sir."

The officer's eyes widened as he absorbed Mike's explanation.

Treading carefully, not wanting to upset Claire any further the officer fumbled, "So then, am I right to assume that your husband is not aware that your child is deceased?"

Claire raised her eyes to meet with the constable's kindhearted gaze. "I'm afraid that is correct sir," she replied with remorse.

The questioning officer glanced at the two men observing from behind. "Then we need to remain concerned that Mr. Redkin is going to make a second attempt. He'll likely be back!"

Feeling he had interrogated the frightened young victim enough, he flipped his notepad closed.

"I am going to advise you to go to the hospital Ms. Morgan and get a doctor to take a look at that knife wound on your neck."

"Not a problem! I'm going to take her as soon as we're done here!" Mike immediately replied as he stood from his chair.

The officer nodded then added, "It would be best if the hospital kept a record of the injury."

Without intending to worsen Claire's fears, the three police officers knew they were right to assume that this case was not yet over. Even with the limited information they had, they fully assumed that Jacob Redkin would be returning to Yorkton to pay his wife a second visit.

"Right then Ms. Morgan, judging by the weather outside tonight I can pretty much assure you that your husband will not attempt to contact you again this evening. No doubt the severe blizzard conditions we're experiencing are slightly more than he's used to dealing with back home in New York. So you folks get on down to the hospital. I'm going to radio the details into the office. We'll send a cruiser out to your house in about an hour to keep an eye on things for the night.

"Thank you," Claire replied.

"You're more than welcome Ms. Morgan. We'll be close by if you need anything. You take care of yourself now and don't hesitate to contact us if you recall any other information that might be helpful to the investigation."

Mike and Claire pulled their winter coats on in preparation to leave. The officers waited patiently as Mike locked up the building and then bundled into his SUV.

Plowing through the blinding snow Mike drove to the local hospital. Within a few moments Claire was led to an empty bed in the emergency department and attended to by the doctor on call. After examining the scrape in her neck the physician cleaned and bandaged the wound.

"I assume that you have already notified the police about this incident," the lanky young doctor inquired.

"Yes we have," Mike immediately responded so that Claire didn't have to.

"That's good! Ms. Morgan, fortunately it is only a light flesh wound. It is good that the offender pulled off the knife before he did any significant damage. I'm afraid that cleaning and wrapping it is about all we can do for you tonight. Take some Tylenol when you get home and try to refrain from pivoting your head as much as you can for the next few days."

Claire's eyes portrait her gratitude to the doctor as she slid herself from the bed. Then sweeping her coat back around her shoulders Mike led her from the room and back out into the blustery night.

Through the frigid snowstorm, Mike drove toward the cottage in silence clutching Claire's quivering hand tightly within his own. An RCMP officer followed them down the drift-covered dirt road then parked his cruiser next to the cottage assuring them of a secure night.

After Claire had changed her clothes, she climbed into bed while Mike pulled the comforter up warmly around her traumatized body. Against his better judgment, knowing of Claire's shortfall of intimate feelings for him, he lay down beside her on top of the blankets in the darkness of her bedroom.

"I called my mother and Michael is fine. He's staying with my parents tonight and I'm going to be right here beside you Claire. I'm not going to leave you alone."

Mike snuggled in close and folded his left arm tightly around her waist.

"He will never hurt you again my love. I promise!"

Claire had a restless night being awoken several times after seeing Jacob's threatening face in a recurring nightmare. Each time, she fearfully sprang from her bed and raced to the bedroom window to see if the police officer was still outside her home. With great comfort she peered through the frosted panes of glass to see the patrol car still parked in the driveway puffing exhaust into the crisp air as the officer sat within the lit interior doing paperwork.

Then finally, after what seemed an eternity of cold darkness the morning arrived. With Mike still in a sound slumber curled up in her bed, Claire arose, showered and dressed in blue jeans. Pulling her hair back in a knot, her nervous body shuttered as she heard a firm rapping on the front door. With Mike striding across the floor close behind her, still wearing his crumpled clothing from the day before, Claire hesitantly opened the door. The nearly half frozen police officer tilted his hat as he greeted her.

"Good morning! I'm sorry if I startled you. I'm just checking in to see that you're okay. I've been called back to the office. They'll be sending out a replacement car for surveillance but they can't do so for about an hour. There were so many accidents last night due to the storm that we're a little short handed this morning."

Calming her racing heart Claire smiled nervously.

"Yes I'm okay, but really…you won't need to send a replacement car. Honestly, I'm okay and I'll call you if I ever see Jacob around town again."

"Well…if you're sure now?" the snow covered officer replied with concern.

"I'm just fine but thank you anyway!" she reassured him.

"As you wish then," he replied with a shrug of his frozen shoulders. With that, the Canadian Mountie returned to his cruiser and plowed his way back out to the main road.

Closing the door behind her Claire was met with Mike's angry eyes.

"What the hell are you doing sending those guys away?" he demanded an explanation. "That lunatic could be hiding around the corner for all you know!"

"Mike!" she tried to gain control of the conversation. "What am I going to do have a police escort for the rest of my life? So let's both just try to calm down here. I know Jacob very well. He'll keep me around as long as he doesn't know where Amelia is."

In disgust Mike conceded, shaking his head in disagreement of her rationale as he stomped across the floor.

108

"Mike!" she shouted after him. "Please try to understand!"

Quickly he turned to meet with her eyes from across the room not attempting in the least to hide his aggravation with her.

"Oh don't give me that crap!" he darted back irritably. "I understand everything quite clearly! I understand that there is a little boy in this world named Michael who desperately needs his mother! I also understand that I love you more than you'll ever know! I'll kill the son-of-a-bitch myself if he shows his face around here again!" he yelled slamming the bathroom door behind him.

Plunging her defeated body down into her favorite chair, Claire heaved a sigh from her lungs.

"Jesus Christ!" she grumbled thinking about Mike, Jacob and her precious child. "This craziness has to stop! But how?"

Days passed without any sign of Jacob in the area. But Claire knew him too well. She knew he'd be back. Mike did his best to overshadow the woman he loved wanting to protect every move that she made. But Claire resisted the twenty-four hour shielding coverage, strongly re-staking her independence.

Days turned into weeks as Claire tried to return her life to normal. Even though the workload of the legal firm was steadily increasing, Mike forbade her to work alone at night in the office. He was instinctively terrified for her safety. He struggled with the burden of needing to protect her, wanting to defend her as he increasingly craved to be more of an intimate part of her life. He was frightened for her living on the outskirts of town in the secluded cottage. But he solemnly knew that the door of intimacy between them had been closed and locked months earlier with regard to him becoming a permanent member of their small family. Only then did Mike realize what he had to do. There was a solution! Even if that solution was going to rip his heart out, Mike had to protect Claire and it became abundantly clear what steps he had to take.

Chapter Seven

Two months passed and Christmas had come and gone since Jacob nearly took Claire's life. One frosty morning in January, the busy legal associate entered the office bidding a cheerful greeting to Mike as she swiftly passed his desk on her way to her own. Hanging her coat up on the back of her door she heard Mike shout, "Claire can you spare a second?"

"Sure!" she replied casually sauntering back to his office. "What's up?"

"Well…I know that you're trying to carry as much of the workload around here as you can," his eyes were oddly filled with gloom. "But, I was wondering if you could clear your desk enough for one more case."

Claire smiled teasingly thinking of the mountainous burden she was currently managing.

"You see this is a special case and I want particular attention paid to it but I'm drowning with work and just can't manage it right now," Mike continued to sell her on the need for more assistance. "I have met with this guy a couple of times now. Actually I was having dinner with him the night that Jacob broke into the office. He's a really nice guy and I think you'll do a better job on this one than I will."

Claire stared at Mike in disbelief as he tried earnestly to pass the case over to her. Mike knew that she was already weighed down with work and that his request was unreasonable. But still he persisted.

"Okay…okay! I'll take it!" she conceded as she sat down to hear some brief details of the pending lawsuit.

"This man is a cattle rancher. He has a farm not far from here. Unfortunately it's a farm that has gone completely broke. The bank has committed to take over the estate within the next few weeks. There's not much we can do for him other than hold his hand through it and make it as painless as possible. He is looking to us more for simple advice than for action. He knows his goose is cooked and that he is about to lose everything."

"Okay!" Claire taunted with sarcasm abruptly snatching the white file folder from the center of his desk.

As she stomped playfully out of the office Mike called after her, "Oh and by the way…I have set up a lunch date for you to meet with him today and discuss possible actions or options!"

"Today!" Claire shouted back with irritation. "How the hell am I suppose to have any options for the guy if I haven't even had time to look at the file?"

"Yes! Today!" Mike snapped loudly from the adjoining office. "You'll be fine!"

Claire slammed her office door closed in comical defiance of her boss's unreasonable request.

"He's never bossed me around like that before," she stated with amusement as she plunged into her chair. "What the hell am I suppose to do for this guy, hold his hand while the bank hauls his tractors away!"

The morning hours passed as Claire quickly scanned through the file of the bankrupt cattle rancher. Then raising her eyes to the grandfather clock in the hallway, she realized that it was almost noon. She had only ten minutes to get down the street to the restaurant where she was scheduled to meet the client for lunch.

"Oh cripes I'm late! Alright here goes!" she moaned tossing the file into her briefcase. Bracing her case under her arm, Claire fumbled with the buttons on her long black coat as she stormed past Mike's office.

"I'm off! See you later boss!" she snapped jokingly as she stomped by.

"Hey!" he shouted darting from his desk to the door of his office.

"Yes?" she quickly turned to stare into his saddened drawn face.

"Have a good lunch," he mumbled forlornly. "I hope everything goes okay with this one."

Not understanding his withered look of remorse, Claire returned to him. "Are you okay Mike? What's wrong? You look so sad this morning. You know I was only joking about not wanting to take this case. You know that I really don't mind, don't you?" she badgered him with questions.

"Yeah, I know you were only joking Claire. I'm fine...really! So you'd better get going! And hey Claire..." he chucked her lightly under her chin. "Follow your heart on this one okay?"

Claire laughed, "Sure boss, I'll follow my heart on this one whatever that's suppose to mean."

Spinning on her spiked heels Claire whirled around and swiftly left the office.

The route to the lunch meeting was littered with traffic. The snow had fallen for the thirty-fifth day in a row and cars had spun out all over the road. Quickly wheeling her BMW into the back lot of the restaurant Claire glanced at her watch realizing that she was nearly twenty minutes late. After grabbing her briefcase from the passenger seat, she leapt from the car and dashed across the icy parking lot.

The restaurant was Italian and its exquisite décor captivated Claire immediately upon entering. The hanging grapevines throughout the dining area ensured each table of a quaint private atmosphere.

"Good afternoon," the host beckoned to her in his thick Italian accent. "One person for lunch today?"

"Oh hello," she responded out of breath as she brushed the freshly fallen snow from the shoulders of her coat. "No, actually I'm meeting a gentleman here for lunch. Ah...his name is...oh what the hell is his name?"

Claire fumbled through her thoughts in frustration. Then as she clumsily reached into her briefcase to grab the file the host politely interrupted.

"Well then...please let me help you. What time was your reservation?"

"Twelve noon! I'm late as you can tell!" she confirmed as a chill of winter crept down her spine.

"Yes indeed," he responded after glancing through his reservation book, "there is one gentlemen who has been waiting alone for several minutes. Let me take you over to him," he continued as he pulled two menus from the holding slot in the reception area. Then summoning her to follow him he led the way to a table in the far back corner of the room.

Walking briskly behind the stylish host, Claire caught a first glimpse of the back of her new client's head.

"Oh shit!" she muttered under her breath. "He's a lot younger than I imagined. What a shame for such a young guy to lose his farm."

Swiftly the two walked through the dining area to the back corner.

"Here we are!" the host extended his hand gracefully toward the man sitting alone at the table with his head slightly lowered. "May I get you some wine to start? Our selection is exquisite!"

"No thank you," Claire responded as she slid her briefcase under the table and dropped into the empty chair.

Ready to get into the business of the meeting Claire pulled her coat off the back of her shoulders as her eyes met with her client's surprised expression for the first time.

"Jesus Christ!" she inhaled as her eyes locked securely with his.

Time stopped and a strained silence fell around the couple as they stared at each other in utter shock. Embarrassed by the chance encounter, Claire shook her head as if to wake herself from a dream. Stunned by the image that stared back, her stomach flipped nervously as she quickly pulled her coat back over her shoulders, slid from the chair and reached to grab her briefcase trying to immediately escape the encounter.

"I'm so sorry," she spoke nervously. "I must have the wrong table!"

Claire quickly moved to exit the intimate booth hidden by grapevines. But as she attempted to flee from her new client who was equally astounded, he reached out and grabbed her left hand.

"Claire!" he shouted dashing from his seat and pulling her hand gently back toward him. "Claire, what are you doing here? Claire, I can't believe its you, I've been searching everywhere for…"

"Look! I'm really sorry Luke! There must be some kind of mistake here. I was sent from the office to meet with a new client about a legal issue!" she cut him off.

"Yes! Yes! I know! That's me! I have the legal issue!" he did his best to convince her never removing his eyes from hers.

"It's really you?" she softened her tone dropping her briefcase to the floor in disbelief.

"Yes! Please don't go! Please sit down with me!" he pleaded unwilling to let the woman escape from his view a second time.

Unsure of what to do, Claire crossed her coat defensively in front of her and sat back down at the table.

"But I don't understand what this is all about?" the suspicious woman quizzed.

"Well let me say Claire! Nobody is more surprised about this meeting than I am. But please let me explain what I do know!"

Wanting to keep the dialogue on a strictly professional level, Claire immediately set her boundary as she rudely glanced down at her watch projecting to him that she was on a very tight schedule. As her state of shock thawed her defensive shields were raised into place not interested in discussing anything other than the business issue at hand.

"Then go ahead…explain!" Claire patronized him as angry daggers shot from her eyes.

"Thank you!" he replied gratefully, soaking in the radiant vision of the woman sitting before him. "I was dealing with a lawyer. I guess he was from

114

your firm." Luke began as he slowly reached across the table with an open hand pleading for Claire to put hers within his.

Claire glanced down at the offer of intimacy but refused without acknowledgement as she folded her arms in a distrustful manner across her chest.

"His name was Mike Whitman," he continued feeling the rejection stab at his heart. "We've had several meetings over the past month. I personally thought the meetings were going very well. Then just yesterday I got a call from Mike stating that he felt it would be better if his associate took over the case. He assured me that his partner was better suited to handle my issues and would walk me through the legalities of this mess that I'm in."

Claire said nothing as she mentally blocked the man from explanation. She refused to smile or so much as offer a consoling grin. She found herself stirring with bitterness. For weeks she had called him. For months she believed he would call her. In spite of his legendary promise for a future together he had never bothered at all...or so she thought. Claire felt used and abandoned. Nodding callously as the pleading words flowed from his mouth Claire grew increasingly hostile.

As Luke told his version of how the chance meeting took place, Claire's thoughts drifted back to Mike as she began putting the puzzle pieces together in her mind. Only then did she realize that Mike must have been working with Luke and somehow realized who he was. Knowing that Mike was panic stricken about her safety and considering how she repeatedly refused his constant protection, he must have felt that allowing Luke to be by her side was better than her being alone and in lurking danger of Jacob. Then likely after great deliberation, he arranged for the two lost loves to have a second chance. In spite of how much Mike loved her, he had provided them with the opportunity to be together again.

"How amazing!" Claire thought to herself, oblivious to Luke's words across the table. "Mike is just amazing! So that's why he told me to follow my heart as I left the office. That's why he looked so sad when I said good-bye on my way out the door." Claire quietly mumbled to herself as thoughts whirled through her mind. All the while Luke had grown silent, trying to read what was going on inside her head. Claire leaned forward resting her chin on her hand as her elbow braced the weight on the table. She had moved her eyes to stare out the window as the snow trickled from the sky. Continuing on in her own train of private thought she had not realized that Luke had stopped speaking.

Leaning back in his chair, he sensed the propelling anger that she projected from across the table. He quickly realized how bitter she was and that it was likely because she had never heard from him again. Judging by her defensive body language as well as her sharp attitude, Luke was also betting that he wasn't going to get the chance to explain himself properly.

After a full minute of silence Claire snapped herself from her trance and realized that Luke was quietly staring at her.

"Right!" Claire stated as she gave the attending waiter the brush-off.

Pushing herself back from the table Claire stood and buttoned her coat.

"It was very nice to see you again Luke," she bid him farewell in a formal business tone. "But I'm afraid that I'll not be able to handle this case for you after all. I advised Mike earlier today that my caseload is jammed and I feel there are just be too many details in your case for me to give it the proper attention that it deserves!"

Swinging her left arm under the table Claire reached for her briefcase. Then extending her right hand to shake with Luke's she prepared for a quick exit.

Not missing an opportunity to touch her delicate skin, Luke took her hand within his own. Touching her flesh, the former lovers locked eyes as they both mentally recalled the warmth that pulsated between their connecting palms. Claire felt the electric current flush through her body of ice as the intimacy they once shared came flooding back. But she could not allow herself to back down. She could not leave herself open for his love then face the inevitable abandonment as she had years before. Not allowing herself to weaken, she forced her gaze from his and pulled her slender hand from his calloused grip.

"I'm sure Mike will be in touch with you in the near future. I'm sorry to have wasted your time. Good-bye!"

"Please don't go Claire! Please grant me the courtesy of a proper explanation," he beseeched as she started to leave the table.

But Claire ignored his pleas. Whirling around on the thin heels of her boots she strutted toward the exit. Standing alone watching her leave, Luke felt his initial elation dissipate into utter devastation.

Claire flashed out the front door still clutching her briefcase and ran across the snow-covered parking lot to her car. Fumbling her fingers over the security keypad on the door, it refused to unlock. In a frenzied state she entered the combination a second and then a third time but the security system resisted.

"God Damn it will you unlock!" she hollered, pounding her frozen fist on the window.

"Claire!" Luke's voice barked from the distance as he hurried across the parking lot after her. "Please wait!"

Impatiently slamming her case on the icy roof of her BMW she snapped the lid open and grabbed her car keys. Luke approached in a panicked run just as Claire turned the key and popped the frozen lock open. Rushing to pull the car door open, she felt his masculine body brush up against the back of her coat and shove the door closed in front of her. With both hands he seized her by the elbows and spun her around to face him.

"Wait a minute damn-it! Please just give me chance to explain!"

Pulling her arms from Luke's grip she glared angrily into his eyes. "There is nothing to explain Luke! As a matter of fact, I don't want to hear another word from you! So if you don't mind I have to go!"

Taken back by the anger he witnessed, he slowly backed away from the crazed unreasonable woman. Claire opened the car door a second time, pitched her briefcase into the passenger seat, dropped her quivering body behind the steering wheel and slammed the door shut. Without giving the disconcerted cowboy a second glance, she started the car engine and spun her tires as she drove from the lot.

The fury within her seethed as she thought of what Mike had done.

"He may have thought he was doing me a favor but that son-of-a-bitch did nothing more than screw my life up again!" she grumbled plowing through the snow-covered streets on her way back to the office. Her heart racing, her body still shaking from the unexpected encounter, Claire grew angrier as she drove.

Spinning her tires on the icy driveway, she drove up to the front door of the office. Jamming her foot on the brakes, she jumped from the purring vehicle and slammed the door shut. Her rage intensifying, she bi-passed the elevator and darted up the stairs to their suite. Bounding through the main entranceway she drove her heels into the carpeting with each step then barged forcefully through the closed door of Mike's office.

"Hang up the phone!" she demanded, pointing her index finger at the flabbergasted lawyer sitting behind his desk. "Hang up the phone right now!"

"I'm really sorry but I'll have to call you back," Mike apologized to the caller as he nodded and set the receiver down.

"You rotten son-of-a-bitch!" Claire tore a strip off of him. "What a shitty trick you've pulled!"

She paced back and forth across the front of his desk, her full-length coat swinging on each turn.

"You knew exactly what you were doing didn't you? Bullshit you needed me to take over that case! You knew who he was and you didn't even tell me! You didn't even warn me! You just sent me over there thinking you were doing me a huge favor!"

Mike sat dumbfounded as the woman ranted and raved before him.

"Well let me tell you something Mike!" she continued. "I just got my life back together and I don't need yours or anybody else's help to screw it up again! You had no right to put either Luke or myself in that position! You had no right at all! You made a fool out of both of us!"

During her wrath, Claire stomped about the office waving an angry finger in his astonished pale face.

"If you'll just calm down for a minute and let me explain," Mike tried to break in. "Once I realized or at least I thought I realized who Luke was, I felt

I owed you the chance…in spite of how much I wanted you to be mine. I was worried if I told you who he was then you wouldn't have gone."

"You're damn right I wouldn't have gone! You owe me nothing Mike!" she cut him off from reasoning. Her rage had reached the point of detonation. "So thanks for the job Mike! But you can shove it up your ass!"

Turning around she stormed from his office and into her own. After grabbing an empty cardboard box from the closet, she quickly tossed in the few personal possessions that had decorated her workspace. Then as a final insult, she picked up the stack of twenty-one case files she had been working on, marched back into Mike's office and dumped them in the center of his desk.

"Good luck Mike!" she shouted as she stormed from the business suite.

After throwing the box in the trunk of her car, Claire drove in a frenzied state to the farm. Without announcing her arrival, she stormed through the kitchen where Sarah was doing the lunch dishes.

"I'll be taking Michael home now!" she stated coldly.

Dashing about the kitchen Claire said nothing further as she quickly collected Michael's bits of clothing and toys jamming them in his baby bag as she went. Then pulling the sleeping child from his bed on the second floor she wrapped his coat around him and carried him down the stairs.

"Is everything alright Claire?" Sarah inquired politely, not understanding the break in her child's routine.

"No! Everything is not all right! But I'm sure that Mike will be all too happy to give you the intimate details! Thank you for your assistance Sarah," she snapped rudely as she departed the house with her sleeping child.

Claire drove down the small stretch of highway then signaled her turn into the laneway that lead to the cottage. As she approached, she noticed that a black Chevrolet was pulling out from her private road. Knowing that she was the only occupant who used the dirt path, she instantly had nervous suspicions of Jacob.

"Oh Christ!" she shouted through the windshield. "What's next?"

But without hesitation she made her turn and journeyed down the laneway, noticing that the departing car had left fresh tracks in the snow leading right up to her cottage.

"That better not have been Jacob!" she yelled as her befuddled child started to cry in the back seat. "I'm just in the mood to meet with him!"

By the time she arrived at the cottage, Michael had erupted into a full-blown wail as tears of confusion poured from his tiny eyes. She had angrily interrupted his afternoon nap and his irritation was evident. Still trounced with fury, Claire unbuckled her child's car seat and carried him into the cottage. Placing Michael on a kitchen chair, she removed his winter-wear, flippantly tossed her own coat and boots aside and pulled him tightly against her chest. Wandering into the living room, she grabbed the blanket from the back of the sofa and the two cuddled in the stuffed floral chair.

Trying to calm herself, Claire snuggled against her son. Nuzzling her nose through his blond curly hair she hummed softly, soothing his wailing sobs. Rocking him gently she eventually calmed her son's cries down into a bemused sniffle.

"I'm sorry Michael," she whispered. "I'm sorry to startle you like that sweetheart. That wasn't very fair of mommy was it? Everything is okay my angel. Everything is just fine now that we're together."

Sleepily, Michael closed his eyes and within a few moments he had drifted back to sleep in his mother's arms.

In the silence of the room Claire leaned her head back against the chair.

"My life!" she analyzed. "It has always been wild ride but this one takes the cake!"

Thinking back, she recalled the look of surprise on Luke's face at their meeting. Then she flashed to the astonishment and regret on Mike's as she stormed from his office.

As she unruffled her psyche, Claire realized that Mike was likely trying to help her by setting up the charade. If nothing else, she was aware that he had fallen deeply in love with her and it wasn't in his nature to be maliciously cruel.

"So why would he throw it all away?" she mused. "My gosh! For two years I was desperate to see Luke again! But now everything has changed. I have set my personal feelings for him aside...or at least I think I have."

Claire rested her chin lightly on the top of her son's passive head.

"I have a lovely home now. I have or had a fulfilling job but most importantly I have you my little cherub," she whispered to the sleeping child. "I have you... and no matter what else happens, I won't lose you." Leaning her head back a second time she closed her eyes. "Luke had his chance...and he blew it!"

Two hours passed as Claire and her son remained nestled in the large cozy chair. The telephone rang endlessly throughout the afternoon and each time it clicked into the answering machine. Each time the caller declined to leave a message.

"Mommy...mommy?"

Claire felt her eyes being pried open by her son's tiny fingers. Michael had awoken from his afternoon nap and was ready for his mother to wake up as well. Realizing that her son was standing upright on both of her thighs, Claire suddenly popped her eyes open to stare into Michael's startled face.

"Morning...morning mommy!" he giggled at the game his mother had started. "Morning...morning baby," Claire mocked his childish pronunciation as she began tickling his abdomen. "It's not morning sweetie-pie! It's suppertime! Are you hungry? Are you hungry sweetie-pie?" she cackled in tune with her child's fits of laughter trying to free himself from her devilish fingers. The pair chortled as they rolled about the large oval red carpet. As Michael freed himself he giggled over the victory and went galloping off into his bedroom to seek his favorite Winnie-The-Pooh blanket. With an admiring grin she watched her child's gleeful escape.

Lying on the floor alone, Claire stared up at the plaster ceiling. Reluctantly bathing her mind in thoughts of Luke, she was seduced with emotion for him. She thought of the passionate love they made three years prior. In her heart she knew she still loved him. What she felt for him would never leave her soul. But she also decided at that moment that she would keep Michael a secret for as long as she could. She had already lost one child and she was not willing to risk losing another.

"I will not put Michael through what Amelia went through. I just pray to God that Mike didn't tell Luke about him!" she stated still feeling bitter toward Mike.

"Mommy…mommy…car coming…in snow!" Michael joyfully announced as he watched a vehicle approach from his bedroom window.

"Oh cripes, what now!" Claire moaned as she rolled herself up from the floor.

A heavy rapping was then heard on the front door of the cottage. Claire rolled her eyes in disgust catching a glimpse of Mike's SUV parked just outside the cottage.

"Come here sweetheart," the annoyed woman beckoned to her child that was then standing in the doorway of his bedroom playfully covering his head with his fluffy blanket.

Sweeping him into her arms Claire cuddled the toddler in the living room chair. Sitting silently, she refused to answer the incessant knocking knowing she would then have to speak with Mike. The snow-covered visitor was well aware that Claire and her son were ignoring his presence but still he rapped loudly.

"Come on Claire!" he pleaded through the frosted glass. "Please open the door. Give me a chance to explain."

"Mike?" her child questioned with delight recognizing the familiar voice on the other side of the door.

"Yes Mike," Claire whispered back to the child placing her fingers lightly over his lips.

"Please Claire!" Mike called out a final request.

Claire sat quietly with her child ignoring his request for conversation, the kitchen wall hiding his frozen face from her view. Then after a long pause, she heard his heavy footsteps exit the front porch, get into his truck and drive out the lane.

"You watch cartoons for a while sweetheart and I'll get your dinner ready!" she directed her son who was already mesmerized by the dancing characters on the television screen.

Claire prepared a light meal all the while her mind analyzed the two men she had come to blows with earlier that afternoon.

"I just can't see Luke again!" she muttered as she peeled fresh carrots in the sink. "There is nothing to gain by it! He never called me when he had the chance three years ago. So he can go to hell now! And so can Mike!"

Trying to remain firm with her decision to live without the two men, Claire's emotions swirled. She knew that she loved them both in two very distinct ways. But to re-open her intimate vault of emotion would mean putting both Michael and herself at risk again.

"We're on our own sweetheart!" she spoke in Michael's direction as she peeked around the corner.

Claire returned to her dinner preparation as her son rounded the corner of the kitchen.

"Oh mommy! Mommy...look!" Michael pointed his tiny index finger at the glass as he galloped toward the front door. "Fowers mommy?" he questioned comically pressing his nose against the frosted pane.

Claire turned to see what her child was so intrigued with. Wiping her hands on the sides of her dress pants she approached and saw that a huge, bouquet of flowers had been placed just outside the door.

"Yes...flowers," she replied to her inquisitive child. "Excuse me sweetie," she gently moved him aside and opened the door. Claire picked up the slightly wilted floral arrangement that had been nicked by the frosty air. She brought the crystal vase inside and sat it down on the kitchen table. Pulling the small white card from it's chilled sleeve she read the inscription.

"When you love a woman...you must set her free!" The card was signed, "Love Mike."

Claire analyzed the devoting words while flicking the corner of the card across her chin.

"Nice gesture Mike!" she announced defensively. "But I'm not interested!"

Then with a callus reaction, she picked up the vase and moved it out of sight placing it in the far corner of the living room.

Weeks of unsolicited visits and telephone calls intruded upon their lives as Claire hibernated with her son. The swirling frozen winds of January dragged into February. Then February reluctantly thawed into early March as the vicious Canadian winter subsided.

On a sunlit afternoon as Claire played with her son mischievously tumbling down the dissolving snow banks, Joe's old Chevy truck came meandering down the laneway. Claire stood attentively watching the old man approach feeling the tension build for the upcoming conversation. Joe maneuvered his aged vehicle up to the cottage then backed up preparing to dump a load of firewood for his tenant.

"Afternoon!" the old man tipped his hat greeting her with intimidation as he forced his arthritic body up into the box of his truck.

Claire smiled back at the old friend as she slid Michael's mittens back onto his chilled hands.

"Beautiful day!" Joe shouted making a second attempt at light conversation with the woman he hadn't seen in months.

"Yes it is!" she agreed as she stepped forward to assist the cordial farmer throw the firewood from the box of his truck.

"You keeping well?" he inquired shyly.

"Yes, we're both just fine! Thank you for asking," Claire responded feeling her defenses falter.

"Haven't seen you or your boy for quite a while now," he continued trying to break through the wall of ice he sensed between them.

Claire nodded as she jumped from the truck and began stacking the wood in a neat row against the cottage.

"I guess you've been using the wood I've been bringing over ay Claire? I see the pile has gone down quite a bit. Hope that fireplace is keeping you both warm at night."

"Yes, it's been very kind of you to keep us supplied. The fireplace is lovely in the wintertime Joe. Thank you!"

"Heavy mommy!" Michael boasted to his mother as he tried to haul a log over to the pile.

After struggling his way down from the back of the truck, Joe tipped his winter hat back on his head. Kneeling down on one knee the old man smiled as he watched his dearly loved grandson assist his mother with the wood.

"How is little Michael doing?" he asked the toddler chuckling at his valiant efforts.

"Grandpa Joe!" Michael happily ran over to him spreading his arms wide open ready for an embrace.

With adoring love for the youngster Joe caught him within his burly arms. After swooping him high up into the air he pulled the tiny boy back in against his chest. Michael giggled at the ride then swung his padded little arms around the old man's neck planting a kiss on his weathered face.

"How's my boy doing ay Michael? Oh how Nana Sarah has missed you!" he confirmed into the child's dancing eyes.

"Where is Nana Sarah?" the child inquired lifting his tiny golden eyebrows in question.

"Well now...she is at home making me some supper!"

"We go see Nana Sarah too?" Michael turned and asked his mother with excitement. "We go now mommy?"

"No, I'm afraid not today," his mother responded regretfully, sorry to disappoint him. "We'll see Nana Sarah another day, okay?"

"Okay!" the contented child agreed as Joe placed him down gently on his winter boots.

Claire enjoyed watching Joe and her son together. She found it intriguing how her toddler could instantaneously bring Joe out of his timid shell.

Claire slowly approached the elderly man after she had stacked the last log in place. Joe was an introverted, unobtrusive person that never forced his way into other people's business. But this time, standing by the rear wheels of his truck watching Michael romp blissfully on a snow bank, he was clearly stalling in his departure from the cottage. It was apparent that he wanted to speak further with Claire.

"Sarah and I sure have missed you folks coming around the farm this past while," Joe admitted as he pulled his hat back down upon his balding head. Treading lightly, he took special care not to mention his son's name in his opening statement of sincerity. "We sure do miss spending time with little Michael everyday!" he pressed on warily, trying to read Claire's facial expressions.

Joe was obviously aware of the strained relations between Claire and Mike but in his own simple sense of logic he believed that to be a completely separate issue from Sarah and himself.

Claire smiled at the old timer's honesty. Trying to hide her embarrassment she mentally recalled her harsh offensive action of plucking her sleeping child from his bed at the farm without explanation then abandoning the old couple for nearly two months.

"Yes I'm sure you do miss Michael," Claire acknowledged. "I'm very sorry Joe. I never meant to offend you or Sarah in any way," she apologized guiltily lowering her eyes to the ground.

"You see Mike and I had a significant disagreement a while ago."

"You know Claire, I never much bother with other people's personal affairs," the old man spoke wisely as he pulled a wooden match from the pocket of his coveralls. "But I can tell you," he continued as he struck the match on the back of his boot then held it up to light his pipe in mid sentence. "I can tell you that my family loves you more than we can say. We consider both you and Michael part of our family. We miss you and the little guy an awful lot Claire," he stated shyly as circles of maple smoke puffed from his black pipe. "I just hope… that some day you'll forgive that overgrown boy of mine for whatever he's done…and return to our family again!"

Claire stood listening to the old man speak as rings of smoke encircled his head. Warmed by his words of kindness, Claire shoved her hands in the pockets of her jacket and shrugged her shoulders.

"Thank you Joe. I understand what you're saying and you're entirely right. The issues that I have with Mike have no bearing on either you and Sarah. I do apologize for my harshness. We'll be sure to swing over and visit you both sometime very soon. I promise!" she committed to the old man as his eyes pleaded for her to return.

"Well that'll be just fine then! Sarah will be awfully glad to hear it!" the farmer conceded with satisfaction as he turned and loaded himself into his truck.

"You be a good boy for your mama now Michael," Joe instructed the curious toddler as he climbed down from the neatly stacked woodpile.

"I will grandpa!"

Michael's rosy little face beamed out from under his woolen hat as he reached a mitten covered hand up to his mouth and blew his grandfather a kiss. Claire watched the old man's jovial laughter through the window as he ground his gearshift into reverse. With an amiable wave of his leather hand, his well-used vehicle rambled off down the laneway. Claire stood watching as the old pick-up truck bounced through the winter potholes on the road. She had truly come to love Joe and Sarah as her own parents and she did indeed miss them both.

For the first time in over six weeks, Claire felt ashamed of her harsh judgments and irrational actions. But after surviving such a vast range of agonizing adversities in her life, she had come to instinctively flee when faced with painful situations. Running and hiding had become the mode of survival she was most comfortable with. The shock of seeing Luke that day seemingly had a profound effort on her. She had run from pain and threats her entire life and her instinctive reaction at that moment was to run from what might hurt her. It was the method of defense she had created as a child and it seemed to have worked up until that point. But now she found herself running from people who loved her and who meant her no harm. Claire heaved a sigh as the steam spewed from her mouth. Her shoulders sank deeply in her jacket of shame.

"Come on Michael! It's time for your nap sweetheart," she beckoned to her child glancing at the pile of wood that had since fallen askew onto the slushy thawing ground.

Michael giggled with delight as she swung him over her head and up onto her shoulders. Together they headed inside for the balance of the afternoon.

During the evening hours Claire reflected upon Sarah and Joe. Staring at her handsome son as he played on the floor with his collection of toy tractors, she felt guilty for punishing the two elderly people who had been so kind to her in the past. Because she had issues with Mike, she had deprived his parents of seeing the child they adored. Dropping herself onto the sofa, Claire gestured for her son to join her holding her arms out toward him.

"Michael sweetheart," she spoke softly.

"Yes mommy?" the child responded as he abandoned his fleet of vehicles and galloped over to her.

Claire wound a tight embrace around his shoulders then ran her fingers through his blond curls.

"Do you miss Nana Sarah and grandpa?"

"Yep!"

"Do you want to go and visit them tomorrow?" she probed further as he dashed from her arms and returned to his toys.

"Yep!" he responded not having to consider her question.

Claire laughed at the spontaneity of her child. "Okay then, tomorrow afternoon you can have an early nap and then we'll go visit them okay?"

"Yep!" the child agreed. "Yippee!" Michael sprang to his feet and danced in a circle around his tractors.

Not removing her gaze as he settled back down on the floor, Claire recalled how much he looked like his father. The teardrop contour of his eyes, the natural tan of his skin, his miniature angel wing lips were all tiny replicas of Luke's. He was a strikingly beautiful child with a cheerful disposition. As a nervous tension flipped within Claire's stomach, she nodded to herself as she arose from the sofa.

"Okay then! Tomorrow we go!" she stated boldly as if trying to muster up the courage to face the outside world again.

The following afternoon, as the snow melted and leisurely dribbled down the eaves troughs, Claire dressed her son in his striped overalls and a red turtleneck sweater. She pulled on his navy blue winter coat then loaded him into the car.

Though she was willing to let Sarah and Joe back into their lives, she was not yet ready to meet with Mike. Feeling a bit of unease, Claire drove to Mike's office wanting confirmation that he was at work and not at the farm. Seeing his SUV parked in its usual spot in the back lot, Claire returned to the highway on the outskirts of Yorkton and headed for the farm.

Cautiously bumping her BMW along the slush covered driveway, the welcoming committee of dogs sounded their proverbial alarm as they escorted the car with regal importance toward the house. Joe was in a nearby shed repairing a tractor in preparation for spring planting. Reacting to the entourage of barking dogs, the old man sauntered from the menial wooden structure to see who was intruding. Immediately his face was overcome with delight as he saw Claire lifting Michael from his car seat.

"Well hello there!" he bid a cheerful welcome from the doorway lifting the welding shield from his eyes. After extinguishing the torch, he set the tool down on the bench, pulled the heavy welding gloves from his hands and ambled out to greet the special visitors.

"Hello little guy!" he shouted at the child he adored taking him from his mother's arms. "Boy oh boy, is Nana Sarah going to be happy to see you!" Turning to Claire he then inquired, "I hope you've got time to come in for a coffee."

"Yes, thank you Joe. That would be very nice."

"Then follow me right this way!" the old man instructed with pleasure overtaking his tone.

But Joe had not reached the front stairway when the boisterous sound of Sarah's voice could be heard.

"Hello! Hello! You both come in here right now!" she was bursting with delight at the unexpected visit.

Overjoyed to see the long lost guests, she anxiously waved a dishtowel through the air in their direction. Claire couldn't help but smile feeling her initial apprehensiveness diminish. Snatching Michael from her husband's arms, Sarah covered his giggling face with large wet kisses.

"My darling! My sweet little darling! Oh how Nana has missed you!"

Claire placed the baby bag on the counter, removed her coat and sat down at the massive wooden table. Sitting back in her chair she grinned watching the burly old woman fuss over her child. Unwilling to put the youngster down, she balanced him on her hip as she fluttered about the kitchen filling three mugs with steaming black coffee. After placing one cup in front of Claire she reached to set the other on the table for Joe.

"Your coffee is here for you Joe!"

The old man nodded as he washed his hands in the utility sink at the back of the kitchen.

Michael belly laughed with delight as Sarah sped about the kitchen. Slowing her pace only slightly, she placed uniform slices of lemon cake on a decorative plate then barged into conversation in her typical controlling fashion.

"So now Claire, how has my boy Mike been treating you? Now I told him that he had absolutely no right to put you in such a vulnerable position!"

"Sarah!" Joe commanded firmly from the back sink. "I told you to stay out of other people's business now didn't I!"

Claire chuckled at the unusual boldness of the diffident man. She had never known such opposites as Joe and Sarah. Joe was an intelligent old-timer, mild mannered and unassuming. His seventy-five years of wisdom and experience were ruggedly evident on his tanned, furrowed brow.

Sarah on the other hand was a jovial, optimistic woman. She had a heart of gold though she thrived on gossip and unmistakably controlled the management of the household.

An embarrassed grimace crept over Sarah's face as she glanced back at Joe who was meticulously replacing the towel back on the wooden rack.

"I'm sorry Claire dear! I know I'm just an outspoken overbearing old woman! It's just that I've come to love you and Michael so much and I fear that son of mine has hurt you deeply," Sarah bantered on idly as she placed the cake plate in the center of the table.

"Did Mike tell you what happened back in January?" Claire inquired, wondering exactly how much she knew.

"Oh you know that boy!" she responded with sarcasm nodding her head to the side as if Mike was sitting with them at the table. "He only ever gives me half the story. But I know my boy well enough to know when he's stirred up trouble."

Claire smiled as she placed both her chilled hands around her coffee mug.

"Well Sarah, enough time has passed now that I realize Mike wasn't intentionally trying to hurt me. I do give him credit for that. But I also feel that he used some pretty poor judgment. He left me in quite a precarious situation you know! You see I just can't risk losing Michael. I'm also unwilling to churn up old feelings again. I was quite content with my life before all this happened."

Joe joined the two women at the table and quickly sensed the conversation heading in a direction that he felt it was best to steer clear of.

"So now… how is the cottage holding up for you these days? That place is pretty old you know!"

Claire laughed at the drastic change in conversation however she appreciated the old man's efforts.

"The cottage has been very kind to us," she replied. "We just love living there!"

From that point on, under Joe's watchful eye, the dialogue remained general and light as Claire, her son and his adopted grandparents laughed jovially for over two hours.

As five o'clock approached Claire started showing signs of her departure.

"You both must stay for dinner!" Sarah declared as she leapt from her chair ready to start with the preparations.

Clearly she did not want the visit to end, as she knew not when she would see her loved ones again.

"No we can't stay but thank you anyway," Claire politely resisted. "I should be getting this little guy home and into the bathtub. I'll make a light supper for us a bit later."

Clearly disappointed, Sarah started to wrap up the remainder of lemon cake for Claire to take home.

Then after three rounds of hugs and kisses for his grandparents, Claire bundled up little Michael. With a promise that she would return to visit them again soon, she carried her son from the farmhouse and loaded him into her car.

"Good-bye! Good-bye!" they shouted from the open window of the car watching the elderly folks waving from the front doorway.

Claire dodged the potholes as she journeyed along the slush-covered driveway. Gripping the steering wheel she slowed her vehicle near the edge of the property readying to merge onto the country highway. Reaching to latch her seat belt, she raised her eyes in time to see an olive green SUV nearly carve the nose off her BMW as it wheeled unexpectedly around her idle vehicle. Claire's eyes locked with Mike's as he jammed his foot on the brakes and stopped suddenly along side her. Mike was both surprised and elated to see her sitting there as he hastily unrolled his window

"Hey there!" he hollered from the truck.

But Claire simply raised her left hand to acknowledge his presence then turned and accelerated onto the highway. She was still angry. She was confused and unwilling to let her guard down just yet. Glancing at Mike in the review mirror she watched as he tipped his head back against the seat and pounded the steering wheel with obvious frustration.

Seeing Mike yanked at her heartstrings as she did truly miss him. She enjoyed working with him. She adored his friendship and she loved watching him with Michael. Saddened by her own impulsive rudeness, she regretted her actions immediately but declined to turn around and go back.

Dusk was settling in as Claire reached the cottage. Though spring was in the air, the evenings were still bitterly cold reminding her that winter was in the not so distant past. Michael yawned sleepily as Claire carried him into the cottage and undressed him from his coat and boots.

"Nana…fun mommy!" Michael pulled at the leg of her pants as he looked upward smiling broadly.

Her beautiful child had enjoyed his visit to the farm. "Did you have fun with Nana and grandpa?"

"Yes!" her toddler responded with the clarity of a five-year-old.

"I'm so glad," she replied as she turned to begin her dinner preparations.

Feeling content, the mother and son indulged in a warm meal of chicken and oven roasted potatoes. As their dinner together drew to a close, Claire lightheartedly swooped her child from his booster seat and slipped him into a warm bath. Together they played as Claire sat on the edge of the tub dropping shiny round bubbles down onto his mass of wet curls. After drying and clothing her son in warm flannel pajamas, she plunged down on his single bed and read her weary cherub a bedtime story. After closing the book she watched as Michael's teardrop eyes drooped sleepily closed. Leaning over, she kissed him tenderly on the forehead, pulled the covers up under his chin and crept from the bedroom. Admiring her child from the doorway, she recalled the same image of Amelia as a toddler. With a serene grin, she turned off the light and closed the door.

Chapter Eight

After pouring herself a glass of white wine, Claire returned to the living room. Switching the stereo on, she paused to hear the tranquil sound echo through the speakers. Then reaching for the box of wooden matches on her mantle, she lit the fireplace and nurtured it to a warm glow. How peaceful she felt. How satisfied she was. She hadn't asked for much in her lifetime. She just simply wanted to be able to keep what she had been given…for a short time at least. Reflecting on her life of trial she felt modestly proud that she had never given up. Her undying spirit refused to quit. Life had beaten Claire with a cruel stick over the years. And now after everything she had been through, all she wanted was to live in her quaint little cottage and watch her handsome child thrive and grow.

Lazily sipping her wine in her favorite chair, Claire lost herself in the music and serenity of the evening. Her mind was at ease enjoying the tranquility she found in her own company. As the first glass of wine turned into a second and then third, Claire continued to reflect. She knew she had so much to be proud of. She had followed everything through to its end. Closing her eyes she drifted off, meditating before the warmth of the fireplace. For two hours of passive relaxation Claire enjoyed the peace of the evening.

Abruptly she sat up in her chair as she heard someone pounding on the front door. Startled by the imposition, she flew from her chair, turned the stereo off and rushed to the front door where the urgent thumping persistently continued.

It was Mike and judging by the look on his face through the glass, this time he was not going to take no for an answer. Troubled by the look in his eyes, Claire unlocked the door and opened it slightly.

"Hi," she greeted.

"Hi!" he replied irritably as he shoved the door open and intrusively brushed past her shoulder. "Now look Claire!" the agitated man started to lecture. "I've given you enough time to think things through. I've given you more than enough time to be angry with me! But after the day I've had and after seeing you at the farm, I felt it was finally my turn to talk!" Mike spoke with a firm tone that caught Claire by surprise. "It's my turn!" he demanded. "And out of nothing more than shear courtesy, you're going to listen to me for a few minutes. Then you can do what ever the hell you want!"

Walking aggressively across the floor he then turned and glared into her eyes. Making no attempt to remove his coat, he stood doggedly in front of the woman he loved with the slush on his boots melting in a puddle on the clean linoleum floor. Realizing that she had no other option, Claire walked to the kitchen sink. She turned around and leaned back, crossing her arms defensively over her chest as she had seen her father do repeatedly prior to one of his degrading lectures. She raised her eyes to meet with Mike's deadlock and then waited through a tense moment of silence.

"Okay then superman," she mocked sarcastically, "say your piece!"

"You know what Claire? It's not always all about you! I know you've been hurt in the past. I am aware that people have let you down and yes people have frightened you and been nothing short of cruel. But I have not!" Mike was furious. "I have not only opened my life and heart up to you but I have loved your child and treated him as if he was my own. My parents adore him! And well…I have…well in spite of you not liking it…I have fallen so deeply in love with you that it hurts sometimes. All I ever wanted was to love you and Michael and be a part of your lives somehow, even a small part, I didn't care! I just wanted to be around," Mike continued barely stopping to take a breath. "Then about three months ago as I sat at my desk feeling sorry for myself thinking about how much I love you, smelling your perfume in the office next to me, my telephone rang. The caller was a gentleman I had never met before. He was a sad, lonely, defeated cattle rancher who was about to lose his entire estate because he had gone completely broke. So I met with this guy a few days later and I listened to his story. At that point, I was sure that he was the only man in the world who was further down the path of defeat and depression than I was myself. Then he told me how years before he had found a beautiful woman but he had only shared one short night with her. Quickly he fell in love with this woman and he knew instantly that he wanted to spend the rest of his life with her. But at that time he had a job to finish. He left this woman only because he had previously committed to run a trip down to Florida with his truck.

So he promised to contact her as soon as he returned. Then, half way down to Florida, his truck broke down in the middle of nowhere. It took him over a week to get the rig fixed and then nearly three weeks to deliver the load he was hauling and get back home. All the while, he continued to telephone the mystery woman that he had so quickly fallen in love with. He told me that she was all he could think about. He told me that he had never felt so good as when she was in his arms. When he returned to Saskatchewan he continued with his attempts to reach her but said it was as if she had fallen off the face of the earth. But knowing how he felt about her, he just couldn't walk away from it. He said that regrettably all he knew about her was that she was a lawyer from New York City. The man's eyes welled up with tears as he told me his story Claire! Do you have any idea how that made me feel, watching a disheartened grown man cry as he sat across the table from me? But the really sad part was that he wasn't crying because he was about to lose his farm, his truck and everything he had earned over the years. He was crying because his heart was broken."

Claire's eyes widened and her chin drooped with disbelief as she listened to Mike's words with increasing interest. "But I thought…" Claire broke in to defend herself.

"I know what the hell you thought lady!" Mike raged back at her, belittling her selfishness. "Then this guy tells me that finding the woman he loved became nothing short of an obsession! An absolute fixation Claire! Do you believe it?"

Claire's eyes filled with tears overcome with shame.

"Then this guy…or lets just clear up the facts here Claire shall we? How about we call this man Luke Johnston." Mike taunted her with sarcasm. "Luke spent the next two years searching for the woman he had let slip away from him. Driven by the obsession to find her, he searched throughout Canada and the U.S. His cattle ranching business was set aside and his truck sat idle at his sadly neglected farm. For over two years Luke didn't work! Claire do you hear me? For over two years this man had no income! Then after years of searching but never finding his lost love, the bank finally foreclosed on his estate. He could no longer afford the mortgage! He had used up every bit of his savings. Then in turn, the bank sold off what little cattle he had left. They repossessed his transport truck! They have taken everything from him Claire!" Mike had grown so enraged that the color of his face evolved into a glowing tone of red. The veins in his neck were bulging obtrusively.

"Then just to put the last nail in this guy's coffin, by chance, after two and a half years of heartache, he sat down in a restaurant directly across from the woman he had searched tirelessly for. Then do you know what happened Claire?" Mike's voice had escalated into a full-blown shout as he watched the tears pour down her face. "Oh you're not going to believe this one! After losing everything for her, this woman actually rejected him! The woman that he loved so deeply and

133

had lost everything for…she actually rejected him!" Mike yelled as he waved his arms angrily in the air. His voice started to crack and then he laughed mockingly in disbelief of her behavior.

Shaking his head as he attempted to compose himself, Mike leaned forward and placed both hands on the backrest of the kitchen chair.

So!" Mike paused to catch his breath and regroup his thoughts. "After several meetings with Luke over pending legal issues, I put all the clues together. So much of what he told me I had already heard from you the night you found out you were pregnant with his child. I then realized that I personally knew the woman that he had combed the continent for. I myself had fallen in love with the very same woman! Can you imagine Claire!" he bellowed not waiting for her to respond. "Can you imagine my surprise when I figured out who this guy had been searching for!" Mike's frustration with the female that stood blankly in front of him escalated loudly a second time. Waving his right arm through the air with aggravation he continued. "Can you imagine, that I sat in silence across the table from Luke knowing full well that he has a three year old child living within a few miles of him! He has a beautiful baby boy that I have grown to love as my own! And yet I said nothing about it! I just listened and said nothing! He has lost everything for you Claire! Luke has lost everything!"

Catching himself from completely over-boiling, the unnerved man tried to calm his raw emotions. Shaking his head in disgust, he bit his top lip and shoved his hands angrily into the front pockets of his winter coat.

"For two months I wrestled over this! For sixty days I said nothing to either one of you! For all that time I tossed and turned at night wondering what I should do!" Mike shook his head in complete frustration as he mentally recalled those nights filled with anguish. "Because Claire…" he tried to soften his tone, noticing that tears of shameful emotion were still pouring down her face. "Because I knew," he softened his voice even further. "I knew that by allowing you two to meet, I would be cutting myself out of the deal altogether and that was something I didn't think I could live with. But then again…" he paused to recall his own rational. "But then I also knew that I couldn't live with myself and look you in the eye if I withheld that secret any longer. I love you too much to be distrustful to you Claire."

The stunned woman stood in disbelief. She was at a complete loss for words as Mike paused briefly and then continued, "So I arranged for you both to meet for lunch in a public place. I figured it was the right thing to do. Then I figured I would back off and let the cards fall where they may."

Claire nodded in astonishment at the man standing before.

"I did it because I love you Claire…and for no other reason," Mike concluded his informative lecture in emotional defeat.

Silence overtook the pair as Mike dropped his saddened gaze to the floor. After several deep therapeutic breaths he calmed his rushing heartbeat. Then with his face still flushed he walked with purpose to the door. Turning back he longingly gazed at the woman he loved.

"And now…neither one of us can have you," he choked as the lump in his throat tried to block his voice.

Claire watched him swing the door open as his rage quickly melted into despair.

"But at least…I can live with myself now," he concluded with a shrug of his shoulders. With that, Mike left the cottage allowing the screen door to slam shut behind him.

Still leaning against the kitchen sink Claire pondered over what she had just been told. Realizing that she had been bitter with Luke for not trying to reach her when in fact he had. Her lost cowboy had paid a severe price on her behalf and the realization of it was deeply disturbing.

Claire walked to the side window in the kitchen and watched the trail of exhaust steam from the back of Mike's truck as he spun his tires down the laneway. After wiping the tears from her face she trudged to the bathroom with thoughts swirling madly through her confused psyche. Filling the tub with warm soothing water, she stared at her own reflection in the steamy mirror.

"Mike's right!" she nodded to the reflection in the glass. "I have been entirely self-absorbed. He made a tough decision from his heart and then I stomped all over it!"

Claire felt bitterly ashamed. She loved Mike and indeed he had been very good to her and her son.

"What an awful decision he had to make," she muttered as she slipped her nude body into the warm tub.

Claire leaned her head back against the porcelain as the steam rose in a fog toward the ceiling. She was mortified as she recalled how she had treated Luke at their lunch meeting.

"I just didn't give anyone a chance to explain," she whispered as she filled her slender hand with bubbles and then crushed them within her palm. "My God Luke! You've lost your farm…all because of me! I'm so sorry my love. I'm so very sorry," she spoke with remorse as if he could actually hear her apology.

After twenty minutes of shameful reflection Claire ascended from the bathroom wrapped in a towel.

Opening the washroom door, she glanced across the living room noticing that the light on the stereo was beaming brightly through the darkness.

"That's funny," she quizzed her memory. "I was sure I turned that off!"

Claire shrugged her shoulders unknowingly then turned into her bedroom. After slipping a white silk nightgown over her head she ventured in to check on her sleeping child. Leaning over his bed, she brushed his curls from his eyes and planted a soft kiss on his cheek.

"I love you little one," she whispered admiring his innocence. With a smile, she left the child's room.

"We meet again!" a voice summoned her from across the room.

"Oh my God Jacob! What are you doing here? How did you find me?" she screeched at the figure that stood smugly grinning in the kitchen doorway.

"So full of questions aren't we Claire!" his voice curdled her freshened skin. "Now I am clearly done with your playful games, though this is quite a nice little shack you've got here I must say," Jacob spoke in his degrading tone as his eyes darted around the cottage, his head nodding with approval.

Instantly Claire backed up, nervously clawing her nails into the wallpaper behind her.

"Now I don't have much time so go and get Amelia now! Tell her that her father is here to pick her up," Jacob directed her in a no-nonsense tone.

It was clear that he was in no mood for stalling tactics. Paralyzed with fear, Claire knew that she had no choice but to tell him the truth.

"Jacob I can't...go and get Amelia."

"Go and get her now!" he yelled impatiently, his eyes blazing with fire.

Her body tensed as she stared back at her husband dreading what she was about to tell him. "I can't get her...I can't because...Jacob... Amelia is dead!" Claire spit out the agonizing words as she burst into tears.

"She's dead?" Jacob laughed as he started to close in on her position. "You are creative Claire. That's a really good one," he shot angrily as he stalked across the floor toward her.

Standing in front of the quivering woman, he grabbed the back of her hair and yanked her shying eyes around to meet with his.

"Maybe you didn't hear me the first time," he threatened smashing her across the face with his free hand. The harsh blow to her head sent Claire crashing against the adjoining wall. "Now go and get her!"

Holding her right hand against the sting of her cheekbone Claire tried to stand. "Jacob, please listen to me! Amelia is not here!"

Having zero tolerance for her belligerence he viciously lunged toward her swinging a second lashing backhand across her skull. Claire's head swung backward and hit the wall with a forceful blow. Then just as Jacob went to strike the battered woman a third time, a tiny voice was heard from the nearby bedroom.

"Mommy! I scared mommy! I scared!" Little Michael stood in the shadowed doorway of his bedroom clutching his blanket up under his chin.

"Go back to bed sweetheart," Claire directed the frightened child while trying to straighten her body. "Mommy is okay, now go back to bed right now," she encouraged the toddler not wanting him to see her being beaten.

With one hand twisting a handful of lace on the front of Claire's nightgown and the other fist raised in preparation for the next offensive wallop, Jacob turned his face to stare blankly at the distressed child. In curious disbelief he lowered his clenched fist as he watched him disappear back into the bedroom and close the door.

"That's not Amelia!" he shouted angrily into Claire's scarred face. "Where's Amelia?"

Closing her eyes defensively she waited to be struck a third time.

"I told you before Jacob... Amelia is dead."

Jacob turned his confused unshaven face back to look into her eyes searching for confirmation

"She's dead?" the madman repeated with disbelief.

"Yes," she confirmed with remorse. "She passed away three years ago when we were still back in the states. Jacob... she had Leukemia."

Jacob paused as if mummified by the news of his daughter's demise. Seconds passed as she waited for his untamed fury to volcanically erupt.

"Noooooo!" he squealed as he whirled himself around, stomping wildly across the floor. "Nooooo it can't be! It can't be fucking true!"

Jacob reeled into a psychotic state as Claire watched him hastily pace about the floor with his eyes closed and his hands covering both ears. Wanting to vanish, she stood motionless as Jacob spewed an unprecedented string of vulgarity from his lips cursing God Almighty himself. Then after pounding his fist against the stone fireplace, he set his forehead down on the mantle as if in a state of complete mental break down.

Jacob mumbled nonsense to himself as he tried to absorb the news of his deceased daughter. And then... stillness overtook him. Claire waited anxiously, feeling time pass in slow motion. Then as if he had completely lost his sense of reason, the crazed madman slowly turned to face her. She watched as he pulled a silver handgun from the lower pocket of his overcoat. Slowly he trudged toward her. Crying hysterically, Claire's body shook as she watched him draw near to her. She saw the end of her life quickly approaching.

"You did this to me, you bitch!" Jacob accused as his searing eyes cut through her. "You did this! You killed my baby girl!"

Defenseless to the approaching gunman, Claire began to plead for her life as she backed up along the wall and into the corner like a caged animal. Jacob had completely lost his mind! He had turned into a cold-blooded killer and his swelling rage was soon to be the death of Claire.

Gradually he approached the whimpering female. Rage seethed from his eyes as he forcefully pressed the front of his body into hers. Murderous intent was spewing from every vein. His powerful left hand grabbed Claire under the chin forcing her head upward. Jamming the handgun into her throat the crazed tyrant raged on.

"You killed Amelia…you killed her so… now you must die!"

Jacob has lost all sense of control as his melted eyes of steel seared through her flesh. Realizing she was about to be murdered, Claire pierced her eyes tightly closed and held her breath.

"You bitch," he slithered as he moved his index finger onto the trigger of the gun. "How I hate your fucking guts!"

Claire heard the trigger of the gun begin to slide back as a final gasp of air escaped from her lungs. Then abruptly, the front door of the cottage came crashing open! Heavy pounding feet came tearing across the floor as Claire threw eyes open. In the darkness, a powerful arm swung around Jacob's neck sending his enraged body flying over the sofa and crashing to the ground as the loaded gun slid across the hard wood floor.

"Oh my God!" Claire gasped reaching for her throat as if she couldn't breath.

Her weakened knees buckled beneath her as she fell limply to the floor. "Oh my God please help me!" she screeched.

The two men wrestled on the floorboards as fists flew forcefully between them. Claire squinted through the darkness as the simmering embers in the fireplace cast a haunting glow upon the violent brawl. The brutal struggle continued as chairs were smashed and lamps fell crashing to the ground. The stranger's body structure was larger and stronger than Jacob's as he pinned her crazed husband to the ground pounding his face and neck with his rugged fist.

Then with an almighty roar of insane strength and fury, Jacob forced his opponent off his body sending him flying backward. The stranger was propelled to the rear where he struck his head harshly against the solid stone fireplace. Instantly he fell unconscious.

Realizing that Claire had only one chance for survival, she dove across the floor and seized the gun that lay beside the sofa. Shaking his head as if to regain his balance, Jacob pulled himself to his feet noticing that Claire was numbly standing before him dangling the gun at her side on a limp fingertip.

"You haven't got the fucking guts!" he taunted his bedraggled wife as she slowly raised the gun in his direction, her eyes in a deadlock with his. "And since you killed my Amelia, your son must also die now!"

Unwavering, he lurched toward her with his hands reaching for her throat… then the deafening sound of a single gunshot echoed throughout the dwelling.

Claire's body jolted backward with the drilling force of the blast. Snapping her head back she saw the deadly bullet send Jacob's traumatized corpse flailing into the massive wall unit. Standing before him with smoke trickling out the hollow narrow cavity of the handgun, the heavy entertainment center that had caught his body then came crashing down upon him.

There in the living room of her beloved cottage, Jacob lay motionless, covered in pieces of broken wood as Claire dropped the handgun to the floor. With her body drenched in sweat and her hair strewn across her mystified face she dazedly stared at her husband's lifeless body. She was confused and disoriented, her ears still ringing from the raucous gunfire. She felt nothing...she was completely numb.

The woman stood silent until she was alerted to the shrill whistle of her child's cry in the next room. She instinctively turned and pushed through the bedroom door where she found Michael cowering in the far corner. His little body quivered as he covered his face with his blanket. Quickly she swept him into her arms holding him tightly against her chest. She burst into tears as the raw realization of the shooting set in. Clutching her son tightly within her shuddering arms, she slowly sat down on his disheveled bed. Trying to sooth her terrified child she rocked him back and forth.

"It's okay darling. It's over now. It's all over!"

As the fog cleared from her head she came to vividly recall the tragic altercation of only a moment before. Quickly she placed her distressed child back in his bed and rushed from the room. Snapping the lights on in the living room, Claire gasped as she saw Luke lying unconscious against the fireplace. Blood was seeping down his face from a wicked gash on his forehead.

"Luke!" she shrieked as she ran to dial 911. "Send an ambulance!" Claire yelled into the receiver as hysteria overtook her. "Send the police and an ambulance immediately!"

Without waiting for the woman to respond Claire dropped the telephone receiver to dangle lifeless in the air as she darted back to Luke's side.

"Hello...Hello?" the woman from the 911-dispatch office repeatedly questioned into the dead air.

"Luke! Luke!" she cried leaning over his unresponsive presence. Blood gushed from the gaping wound in his flesh as she pulled at his body searching for signs of life. Claire knew she had to stop the bleeding immediately. Trying to set her panic aside, she yanked the tieback from the window curtain overhead. She wound the floral strip of material tightly around his skull as the bleeding began to slow. Then raising his head slightly, she slipped a cushion gently beneath his neck. Agitated by the movement, Luke stirred momentarily then lost consciousness a second time. Covering his limp body with a blanket, Claire sobbed aloud praying to God that he would survive.

"My God Luke," she wept as she ran her fingers over his dampened face. "Look what I've done to you! Look what I've done to your life!"

"Mommy!" Michael shrieked from his bedroom. The child was terrified to open his door and come out.

"It's going to be alright Luke," she assured him as she bent down and kissed his cheek.

Rising to her feet she rushed back into her child's bedroom. Wrapping a blanket around Michael, shielding his eyes from the sight of what lay before him in the living room she walked quickly through the murder scene. Holding her son in her quivering arms, pressing his tiny face against her breast, she stood in the kitchen doorway wanting to keep Luke within her sight.

Reassured by the approaching sirens, Claire permitted her eyes to glance over into the far corner of the room. The cold, malicious body of her husband lay surrounded by haunting stillness with his eyes open and head tilted backward. His final frozen glimpse of this world was locked gazing upward at the ceiling. Claire winced at the horrific gory sight burying her eyes in her child's hair.

The approaching sirens could be heard from the main highway echoing through the prairie darkness. The blazing red emergency lights quickly came into sight then slid to an abrupt halt just outside the cottage. Clothed by only her torn nightgown, Claire rushed to the front entrance. Only then did she notice that the door had been nearly broken down as Luke had barged forcefully through it nearly pulling the wooden plank from its hinges.

The emergency entourage rushed boldly through the splintered entryway as Claire stood nearby clinging to her terrified child. The ambulance attendants glanced at the disheveled woman as they strode across the kitchen floor. At a loss for words, Claire pointed nervously toward the living room. Hastily, the medical team proceeded to the next room where they immediately checked the pulses of the two men. Quickly realizing that Jacob was dead, they attended to Luke.

Through the chilled kitchen window, Claire watched as a police car came speeding down the laneway with its lights and siren blazing. The cruiser slid forward on the soft ground as the driver slammed on the breaks just outside the cottage. Two uniformed men leapt from the car and darted up the front stairs. Bounding through the broken door with their hands positioned on their gun holsters, they walked hastily through the cottage mentally summing up the murder scene. Then as one officer remained with the ambulance attendants, the second returned to the kitchen carrying a blanket, which he had pulled from Claire's bed. After wrapping the cover around her nude shoulders he escorted the mother and son from the cottage and down into the warmth of his cruiser.

"I'm so sorry about what happened here tonight Ms. Morgan," the officer expressed his heartfelt concern.

Only then did Claire realize by the tone of his voice that he was the same officer who had attended to her after the attack in the office a few months prior. Claire sniveled from the back seat of the car unable to vocalize a response.

"It looks like your troubles with your husband are now over," he continued trying comfort the traumatized woman.

"Yes... I guess you're right," Claire whispered in reply, preoccupied by the voices on the police radio in the front seat.

"We're going to need a coroner here," she heard the officer inside the cottage communicate with the dispatch.

"Roger!" the dispatch responded immediately.

With wide eyes, Claire watched restlessly as a second and third police cruiser pulled in behind the growing line-up of emergency vehicles. Wiping the steam from the window she noticed an officer walk up the front steps and enter her cottage carrying a camera.

"It's pretty obvious what happened here tonight," the sympathetic man addressed her through the rear view mirror. "I'm assuming that the deceased man was your husband Ms. Morgan, but who is the second male?"

"He is a very good friend of mine," Claire responded through her vibrating lips as she thought of Luke bleeding on the floor. "He saved my life tonight! Jacob...Jacob...was about to kill me...and then...and then...Luke came crashing in! Oh my God! I have no idea how Luke even knew where I lived," the distraught woman broke down as she recalled how close she came to the end of her life.

Quickly understanding the confrontational sequence, the officer turned around to face her. With a mannerly smile and a nod of understanding he handed the distressed woman a tissue.

"I'll be right back Ms. Morgan, then I'm going to get you out of here," the officer informed her placing his right hand on her quivering shoulder.

Claire nodded through her murky gaze and wiped her dripping nose on the tissue. The constable then got out of the patrol car and re-entered the cottage.

Cuddling her child she watched intently as the screen door of the house opened and the ambulance gurney wheeled Luke out onto the front porch. Carrying his motionless body down the stairs, the emergency attendants wheeled the stretcher toward the back of the awaiting ambulance. Carrying his intravenous bag high in the air, they lifted the bed in through the rear door of the vehicle and locked the stretcher in place as a paramedic stepped in behind him. After closing the rear door firmly, the second attendant rushed around the vehicle and got in behind the steering wheel. The vehicle beeped a rhythmic warning as it reversed and turned around. Claire watched on as she pulled Michael in tighter to her chest rewrapping his sleeping body within the thick blanket. Unable to pull her eyes from the departing vehicle she stared, blinded by tears, as the emergency lights swirled through the night air and the ambulance bumped its way out along the dirt roadway. Entranced by the lights, she was startled as the officer opened the front door of the car and got back in.

"Well…" the official started to explain. "They said you're friend is likely going to be okay. He is still in shock but his vital signs are stable. They stopped the bleeding and wanted to get him to the hospital as quickly as possible."

Claire sniffled in the back seat, wiping her nose on the damp tissue she still clenched in her hand.

"I'm going to get you out of here now until they finish the investigation and clean up. Is there some place I can take you?" the officer inquired.

Claire nodded meekly as she removed her trembling hand from her nose. She didn't want to involve Sarah and Joe in her night of trauma but she also knew that it would be the best place for her son to settle.

"Yes," she acknowledged as the officer turned the car around in the driveway, "Joe Whitman's farm."

"Okay!" the officer confirmed. "I know where it is. I've known farmer Joe for years," he stated trying to lighten the air of distress in the cruiser.

He drove down the laneway and turned right onto the highway. Silence fell between the occupants as the police radio jabbered on communicating details of Claire's near death incident. Sensitive to her heightened level of distress, the officer lowered the volume on the radio as he turned into Joe's farm.

Darkness overshadowed the familiar homestead as the patrol car pulled up close to the house.

"You stay here Ms. Morgan," the constable directed. "I'll go and wake the old folks up!"

Claire watched him leave the cruiser and stride up the cracked concrete steps at the front of the house. Repeatedly he knocked on the front door waiting for someone to answer. Within a few moments a light started to glow in the upstairs bedroom and shortly thereafter Joe opened the front door dressed in his plaid bathrobe and slippers. With a look of concern, the old farmer's eyes repeatedly glanced from the officer to the car and then back again. The patrolman issued Joe a brief recap of the fatal incident. He advised him that Claire and Michael were waiting in the car and that they needed a place to settle for the night. Hearing only a small part of the conversation, Sarah aggressively bumped her protruding hips past the two men conversing at the door. Quickly wrapping her faded pink robe around her thick waist, she rushed down the steps in her floppy slippers and out to the car. Pulling the cruiser door open, she flung her arms inward reaching for her sleeping grandson. Cuddling Michael against her breast, she reached in a second time to assist Claire from the car.

"I'm alright Sarah," Claire confirmed as black streaks of mascara stained her bedraggled face. "Please…just take Michael in and lay him down."

Without argument Sarah nodded agreeing to rush the child out of the chilled night air. Consumed with worry, Sarah mumbled under her breath as she hurried back up the steps and into the house with Michael in her arms.

Slowly Claire pulled herself to her feet and followed the old woman into the house. Stepping past the two men who were still engrossed in the details of the shooting, Claire cast the officer a tired smile.

"Thank you for everything sir."

The constable nodded in reply touching the tip of his police hat as she passed.

"You try to get some rest Ms. Morgan. Someone will be out here in the morning to talk to you," the officer confirmed.

Claire's dark eyes glanced back in response as she continued on into the warm kitchen.

Soon after, Claire heard the officer bid farewell to Joe and return to his car. After closing the front door, Joe hesitantly shuffled to the kitchen where Claire was sitting with her forehead down on the table. Rarely did Joe display affection, but under the circumstances he placed his rugged callused hands on her shoulders from behind and held them there until he could find the words he was searching for. Claire didn't move from her position as the old man began to speak softly.

"Thank God you and Michael are okay. That's all that matters here."

Slowly encircling her arms around her head on the table, Claire said nothing as she silently disagreed. That wasn't all that mattered! Luke also mattered and he was in the hospital likely still in shock from the vicious attack.

"There now," Sarah announced her entrance to the kitchen snapping the kitchen light on as she arrived. "Michael is just fine dear! He's in his little bed and already off to sleep," the concerned woman stated as she moved about the kitchen preparing to boil the kettle for a pot of tea.

With a worried crease across his brow, Joe disappeared into the parlor as Sarah re-entered. In the silence of the kitchen Sarah said nothing further as she prepared the tea, hoping it would sooth the dazed woman who still sat slumped over the table.

She placed a cup of the steaming beverage in front of Claire, then sat down across from her and waited in question.

After a lengthy motionless pause, Claire lifted her head from the table to be met with Sarah's worried eyes staring back at her. At that moment, in spite of her shattered emotional state, Claire knew the time had come to be fair and tell her everything.

Hesitantly, Claire started to share her story with Sarah. After making the opening statement of her catastrophic tale, Joe returned to the kitchen carrying a pale blue bathrobe, which he in turn handed to Claire. Dropping the blanket she had wrapped around her traumatized body she slid her arms through the enlarged sleeves of the robe and crossed it tightly over her tiny waist.

For twenty minutes Sarah and Joe sat at the table horrified as they learned the gory details of Claire's childhood and then of her marriage to Jacob. Claire told them of his abuse and of her reasons for running. Sarah remained unobtrusive becoming increasingly engulfed in the heartbreaking fable.

As Claire shared her painful memories of Amelia's death, then of how she met Luke and found the cottage in Yorkton, a set of headlights beamed through the kitchen window as a vehicle fast approached the dwelling. The car door slammed and feet were heard running up the front stairs. Completely out of breath Mike barged through the doorway, his eyes frantically searching the room for Claire and Michael. Hurrying across the tile floor he reached for the exhausted unkempt woman then pulled her to her feet and into his arms. Having been swept into the familiar embrace, Claire's remaining barrier of strength faltered as she cried hysterically in the comfort of his arms.

"Oh my God Claire! Are you all right? My father just called me! Where is Michael?" Mike anxiously pelted her with questions.

Claire was incapable of responding as she sank into a sea of disbelief and self-pity.

Mike held her for a long moment as she calmed her distressed nerves. Then taking her face into his hands he kissed her black streaked cheekbones and pulled her in close to him a second time.

"I'm so sorry," Mike whimpered as he started to cry. "I should've stayed with you and Michael. But no! I got pissed off and left you alone! I should've stayed with you! You were nearly killed!"

Opening her weary eyes, she pulled back from the refuge of his arms.

"It's not your fault Mike. It's my fault," she softly affirmed running her fingers over the tears streaming down his distressed face.

"Now then!" Sarah hastily interrupted the unproductive session of self-blame. "Talking like that isn't going to help anyone here now is it!"

Mike assisted Claire back into her seat. He pulled his coat off and tossed it carelessly onto an empty chair. Sarah then rose from the table and poured another round of hot tea as Claire continued her narrative. Though Mike had heard it all before in a different light, he remained spellbound as the devastated woman volunteered her story a second time to his unknowing parents.

It was four o'clock in the morning when the discussion at the table finally slowed.

"What you need to do now," Sarah dictated, "is try and get yourself some sleep!"

Claire yawned sleepily feeling drained of strength.

"Mom is right!" Mike agreed as he assisted Claire's aching body from her chair. Wrapping his right arm around her shoulders he aided the exhausted woman across the kitchen floor.

"Goodnight folks," Claire whispered.

"Goodnight darling," Sarah responded tenderly as she watched Claire leave the room.

"Claire!" Joe shouted unexpectedly.

"Yes?"

"I just...I just wanted to say...that no matter what you decide to do here... I mean with your friend Luke and all...we're here for you. We will always be your family and we always want to be a part of Michael's life...that is...if you'll let us," Joe confessed shyly as he lowered his dark eyes to the floor embarrassed by his emotional confession.

"Thank you Joe," Claire responded, moved by the tenderness of the diffident man who stood before her in his bedclothes. "I hope you'll always be a part of our lives as well."

Claire thought it unusual how a man like Joe, who verbalized so little, could at the same time be so wise and full of sentiment. She took great comfort in what Joe had just said and felt the burden of choice begin to lift. Then turning back, Mike continued to support her weakened body as she climbed the steep back staircase to the second floor.

"Here Claire...you can sleep in here tonight," Mike motioned toward his childhood bedroom.

"Okay. But first I want to check on Michael."

Claire turned to the room across the hall and opened the door slightly as the light cast a dim glow on her child's face. Quietly she approached the bed admiring her son more with every step. Standing behind, Mike watched as she placed a gentle kiss on her child's forehead. Then after wiping a tear from her eye she turned and left the room.

Still fraught with concern, Mike pulled Claire into his arms and held her securely. Nestling his lips through her hair and close to her ear he then whispered, "What my father said...also goes for me."

Claire remained quiet, securely bound in the embrace of comfort. She said nothing as tears gathered in the curves of her eyes.

"I know Luke is the man that you love. I know he fills a void in your heart that no other man could. But I need you to know that whatever you decide to do, I'll always love you and Michael...so please...please don't shut me out completely. Please let me enjoy that little boy as he grows up. I'm willingly to take a back seat to his father but please don't push me away again Claire. I just love you both too much and I don't think I could live with that."

Claire waited a long quiet moment before pulling away.

"Why am I so fortunate to have a friend like you?" she spoke into his beseeching eyes.

Mike had a huge crystal tear trickling slowly down his right cheek as he stared back at her. Shrugging his shoulders, Mike said nothing. Claire felt a mounting debt of gratitude to the man standing before her. Sliding her hands down his muscular arms she laced her fingers with his and pulled him close to her once again. Softly, Claire placed a kiss on Mike's cheek as if to endeavor to kiss his sadness away.

"No matter what happens Mike," she reassured him, "you'll always be a part of our lives. I promise you that. Goodnight my friend."

Then giving his hand a final squeeze, she slid her delicate grip from his and disappeared into the awaiting bedroom.

Chapter Nine

Later that same morning as the early spring sun beamed through her bedroom window Claire sleepily awoke. Groggily she arose from the bed rubbing her eyes then maneuvered her exhausted body into the shower. As the hot water poured down around her delicate bones, Claire's mind weighed heavily on what the new day would bring and the choices she would have to make. For fifteen minutes she stood beneath the soothing water. Wrapping herself in the terry cloth robe, she left the misty bathroom to be startled by Mike who was hastily exiting the bedroom in which she had slept. They were both surprised at the meeting as Mike had hoped to depart the upper floor prior to Claire noticing.

"Hi?" she greeted her friend inquisitively.

"Good morning," Mike replied slightly embarrassed at the intrusion of her privacy. "I stopped by your cottage this morning to get you some clean clothes."

"Oh thank you so much!" Claire reacted with surprise, seeing the folded pile of clothing neatly placed on her bed.

Claire stood centered in the hallway waiting for more information from Mike.

"And?"

"And…there was a team of cleaners there when I arrived. I guess the police must have arranged for the clean up crew. They had just begun their work but I imagine you'll be able to return home later this evening if you choose to. It's really best that you don't go over there right now. Take my word for it!" Mike advised.

"Thanks for the warning. I get chills just thinking about going back there right now. I'm quite content to wait for a while."

With that, Mike smiled amiably at his friend careful to keep his emotional distance from her. Claire watched him descend the stairs and disappear into the kitchen where she could smell the welcome aroma of fresh brewed coffee. Claire quickly dressed herself grateful for the clean clothes. After checking on her sleeping son, she joined the group that was forming at the kitchen table each partaking in hot coffee and home baked bread.

"Good morning dear!" Sarah chirped cheerfully as Claire entered the kitchen. "Take a seat and I'll slice you some bread."

"No thank you Sarah. I should really get going," Claire replied with intent in her manner.

Mike glanced up from the rim of his coffee mug already certain of where Claire had to go.

"Now where are you off to this morning dear?" Sarah inquired with concern.

Claire's eyes immediately filled with indecisive misery as she stared at Mike from across the room.

"Just let her go mom!" Mike mumbled as he dejectedly swallowed a mouth full of coffee.

Still clutching the pot, Sarah paused as she glanced nervously from her son to Claire who was then reaching for her coat.

"Sarah," Claire started to explain. "I really need to go to the hospital to see how Luke is doing."

Sarah nodded sympathetically as she replaced the coffee pot back down on the stove and returned to her chair at the table.

"Would you be so kind as to watch Michael until I get back?" she inquired of the child's grandmother.

"I'd be happy to watch him for you!" Mike committed intercepting his mother's answer.

Rising from his chair Mike walked over to Claire as she awkwardly struggled to find the armhole of her coat. Straightening the shoulders of the jacket, he then held it upright from behind allowing her to slide her arms in with ease.

"You go and see Luke. Take as long as you need. Michael will be just fine here for the day. I promise!" Mike hastened the fretful woman toward the front door. "Here!" he called after her as she pushed herself into the fresh air.

Claire turned back as Mike tossed the keys to his SUV through the air.

"Take my truck!" he offered with a grin. "Sorry…I couldn't manage to get your clothes and your car over here this morning!"

Playfully rolling her eyes at his witty remark she closed the door behind her and crossed the soggy front lawn heading toward Mike's rugged automobile. As Claire slid her petite body in behind the steering wheel of the oversized SUV, she was amused at the comical sight of her own image, distending her neck upward just to be able to see beyond the steering column.

A thick coating of haze was just beginning to lift from the ground as the morning sun started to burn it from the earth's crust. Pulling the truck out onto the highway Claire felt a surge of emotions.

"It is all over now," she blurted audibly. "Jacob is gone and there is no more need to be afraid or hide. There have been enough games Claire!" she spoke firmly to herself as she caught a glimpse of her own eyes in the mirror. "It's time to put things in order."

Claire's stomach fluttered nervously as she thought of the upcoming meeting with Luke and then recalled the sorrowful look of defeat she had just witnessed in Mike's eyes.

"I love you both so much!" she continued in private conversation.

Claire's whirlwind of thoughts then turned back to the tragic event of the previous night. Though she had fled from Jacob for years and lived in constant fear of his unprovoked tantrums, she realized that she could not bring herself to truly hate him. She rationalized that he was a mentally disturbed individual. Perhaps she could not hate him and find solace in his death because he was Amelia's father. Consequently, out of that nightmare of a marriage he had given her the greatest gift of all...a beautiful daughter. As she analyzed Jacob's psychotic mental state, Claire felt a wave of relief plunge upon her shoulders. She could feel Amelia's presence as she ramped off the highway and down toward the hospital.

"It is over now mommy! You are free! Now you are truly free!" she could hear her child's spiritual voice echo through her mind. "I love you mommy and I'll always be your rainbow!"

A serene grin crept over Claire's lips as she reached to wipe a tear from her eye.

"Yes...I am free at last Amelia! Thank you my darling. Thank you for staying so close to me," Claire stammered in response to her daughter's encouraging acknowledgement.

"Daddy is gone from your life forever. You never have to run again! Now, live the life you were meant to mommy. Be happy and be free!" Amelia's voice telepathically reassured her.

Claire could feel the inspiring warmth of her child's divine presence as she proceeded to unroll the window and pull a ticket from the hospital parking meter. Wiping a second tear from her eye, she waited for the barricade to lift and then drove in. After parking the truck, she paused for a moment to compose herself.

Having no idea what she would say to Luke or how he would react, she took a deep breath in search of the courage then got out of the vehicle.

Claire rounded the corner of the information desk and inquired about Luke's room number. Nervously she waited as the elevator slowed and the heavy steel doors swept gracefully open in front of her. Forcing herself forward she shuffled humbly to the nurse's station and confirmed Luke's room number with the attending nurse.

"Yes dear, he is in room seven, straight down the hall, last room on your right," the distracted nurse advised.

"Thank you," Claire responded modestly as she turned and carried herself toward the man she had yearned to reunite with for nearly three years.

"What do I say to him?" she quizzed herself as her eyes unconsciously scanned each open doorway. Then finally she arrived at room seven. Pausing for a moment just outside the doorway, Claire closed her eyes as if praying for the courage to step inside. Just as she opened her eyes and coaxed her feet to move, a hurried nurse who was exiting the room accidentally bumped her shoulder as she passed carrying a tray overflowing with medical utensils and bandages.

"Oh…I'm so sorry," the attendant paused to apologize. "Are you a friend of Mr. Johnston's?"

"Yes…yes I am…I think," Claire muttered confusedly. "How is he doing?"

Claire needed to know more.

"Well Mr. Johnston had quite a nasty bump on the head last night. The ambulance brought him in and within a couple of hours he did regain consciousness. I believe they did some tests and took a series of x-rays earlier this morning. The results came back and it seems there is nothing to be overly concerned about. The doctor has been quite pleased with his progress since then. I changed the dressing on his head about an hour ago," the nurse continued her report barely pausing to take a breath, "but Mr. Johnston was still complaining about a violent headache. So I gave him something to help ease the pain and sleep."

Claire nodded feeling relieved by what she was being told.

"You can go in and visit for a few minutes if you like. But please don't wake him. He needs to rest. He'll be just fine and should be able to go home in a couple of days. The doctor would like to keep him here a while longer for observation."

"Thank you," she replied struggling to keep her eyes from peering into his room.

Claire felt slightly relieved knowing that Luke was asleep, feeling the overwhelming need to take her next steps very slowly.

Leaning against the metal doorframe she instantly sensed the feeling that she been in that exact same situation before…and indeed she had, only it was her that was sleeping in the hospital bed and Luke who approached from the dimly lit doorway.

Quietly, Claire approached the bed where the keeper of her heart lay in a drug induced slumber. Bathing her eyes in the sight of her beloved cowboy, Claire was instantly reminded of how stunningly handsome he was. Though his tanned face looked tired and slightly more worn, he was still a striking individual.

The heart monitor beeped a steady tone as she reached to touch the face that she had fallen so deeply in love with. Luke lay peacefully adrift with an oxygen tube running through his nose and his hand taped to an intravenous needle. His forehead was tightly bound and a small trickle of blood had seeped to the outer lay of the gauze. Claire stood by his side trying to differentiate her feelings of love from her feelings of guilt. Then as the same attending nurse hurried back into the room with a new intravenous bag, Claire's confusion suddenly dissipated. As if being sent the answer from somewhere above…from someone she knew well… Claire instantly knew what she had to do. She could no longer unfairly keep people's lives on hold for the sake of not wanting to hurt them. It all became very clear to her. After taking one final admiring glimpse of her injured soul mate, she lovingly placed a single long stem red rose on the night table beside Luke's bed. After a deep relieving sigh, she turned and left the hospital.

Claire returned to the farm to find Sarah and Michael joyously stacking up wooden blocks as they sat in the middle of the parlor floor. Happily the child giggled as the tower of blocks came tumbling down around them. Claire stood in the doorway smiling at the scene before her realizing how fortunate she was to have Sarah and Joe in her life.

Momentarily Mike appeared from the back stairwell with a look of knowing in his eyes.

"Well? How is Luke this morning?" he inquired politely.

"I didn't actually get a chance to speak with him though the nurses say he's doing fine and should be released from the hospital in a couple of days. How are you Mike?" she questioned in return concerned about his emotional state.

"I'm okay. But more importantly I'm really glad that you're okay. I keep going over what happened last night in my mind and I still can't believe it. The only thing I can figure is that Jacob followed me from the office to your house and then waited until I left before he snuck in," Mike tried to justify, obvious that he was feeling tremendous guilt over Jacob's obtrusive entry.

"It doesn't really matter how he found me Mike. He was a clever man. He has found me many times before and he would've kept searching until he got what he wanted. That's the way his mind worked."

Claire did her best to relieve her friend of the burdening guilt. Turning back to notice that her little boy was smiling broadly at her as he jumped from his position on the floor and began tugging on her pant leg.

"Mommy. We go outside? We go outside Mommy?" the joyful child pleaded.

"Yes darling," she agreed with pleasure. "It's a beautiful day to go outside. How about we go for a walk?"

Before she finished her sentence Michael had pushed his way past her and was in the kitchen trying to pull his rubber boots on.

Together Claire and her son leisurely explored the perimeter of Joe's farm. Jointly they chatted, laughed and discussed each unique object the child picked up from the land. Clearly Michael had dismissed the terror of the night before. Claire only wished that she could forget it all as easily as the innocent mind of her son could. As Michael marched happily along the property edge in front of his mother Claire continued to soul search. Trying to put her own feelings aside, she knew most importantly that she needed to do what was best for Michael.

It was over two hours before they returned to the farm. As Claire leisurely approached the house she noticed that a police cruiser was parked in the driveway.

"Okay...I guess the time has come!"

Claire hesitantly pushed the back door of the house open and entered the kitchen carrying her exhausted child in her arms. Pulling the muddy boots from his feet, she nodded at the officers who were patiently waiting at the kitchen table with their notepads open and pencils poised.

"Good afternoon Ms. Morgan," the same officer from the night before greeted her as he stood from his chair.

"Good afternoon," Claire nodded trying to force a smile in his direction as she transferred her son into Sarah's arms.

"It's time for your nap now, don't you think so darling?" Sarah rubbed her wide nose affectionately against Michael's as he giggled with delight.

"Ni-Night mommy!" the child exclaimed waving his right hand over Sarah's shoulder as she carried him up the stairwell.

"Night night sweetheart," Claire responded waving her fingers in the air.

"We'd like to talk with you for a few minutes Ms. Morgan, if you don't mind," the officer extended his hand to formally shake with Claire's. "I am constable Jeff McGuinnis."

Claire nodded and took her place in an empty chair at the table.

"Where has my husband's body been taken?" she immediately inquired, needing to know Jacob's whereabouts for the sake of her own personal closure.

"Well...last night," Constable McGuinnis explained. "Your husband was taken to the hospital in Yorkton. An autopsy should've been conducted this morning. Once the examiners are satisfied with what they find, his remains will be flown back to his family in New York City. He does have family...does he not?" the officer questioned as he flipped through the pages of his notepad trying confirm what he had said as being true.

"Yes," Claire confirmed as her voice cracked. "Both of his parents are dead. But he does have a sister still in New York. I guess she will take care of his burial."

"Yes that's correct!" McGinnis agreed as he found the notes he had been looking for. "Mr. Redkin's sister Isabel was called this morning and notified of his passing."

"Now then," the second officer took over the conversation. "We have pulled the file from a previous incident in...I believe your office suite here in Yorkton. Is that correct?"

"Yes," Claire agreed lowering her eyes to the table as she recalled the painful memory.

"Now...I realize this is very difficult for you Ms. Morgan, but we will need you to start at the beginning and give us all the details of how this incident came about last night."

Pivoting in her chair to grab the box of tissues from the counter top, Claire started at the beginning of the sordid tale of tragedy. She spoke of her marriage. She told them of Jacob's alcoholism and vicious beatings. She informed the attentive officers of how she ran from New York and hid for years, shielding her daughter from Jacob's rage.

After a ninety-minute period of questions and answers, Claire concluded her story with all the horrific details of the night before. Feeling emotionally drained, she pushed her empty coffee mug into the center of the table and began gathering up the pile of tear-drenched tissues she had strewn in front of her.

"Right!" Constable McGinnis stated as he flipped his note pad closed. "You obviously won't have to worry about Mr. Redkin bothering you anymore. By the sounds of what you have just shared with us, you and your daughter endured more than a decade of fear and torment from that man."

Claire nodded in agreement.

"Well then, we may be in touch with you again if we have any further questions Ms. Morgan. But I believe we have enough information to work with at the present time," the officer confirmed reaching out to shake Claire's hand as he rose from the chair.

"Thank you for all of your help," Claire said as the policemen made their way to the front door.

"You're very welcome Miss. I'm just sorry we couldn't have spared you from the incident last night. Oh also...we checked in with the clean up crew on our way over here and they were just finishing up at your cottage. So it should be okay for you to return home anytime now Ms. Morgan. Good day Miss," the officers tipped their hats and moved to return to their vehicle.

"Return home?" Claire thought to herself as she watched the cruiser pull from the yard. Her stomach churned at the thought. She knew she had to go back and put her life together once again but first she had to find a way to erase from her mind, the searing image of Jacob's bleeding dead body lying in the center of her floor.

The cottage had brought her security and warmth over the past three years. She knew it was the right place for Michael and she knew she'd have to go back sooner or later. As she closed the front door, she noticed that Mike's SUV was also gone from the driveway.

"Now then... Mike said he had a few things to do this afternoon and that he'd see you and Michael later tonight dear," Sarah announced as she appeared from the back stairwell.

Claire felt exhausted as she cleared the coffee cups from the table.

"I'll do that dear. Why don't you go up and get some rest now. I'll not see you go back to the cottage tonight. It's nearly dinnertime! You can go home tomorrow maybe, but definitely not tonight!" Sarah directed the fatigued woman as she pointed her chubby index finger in Claire's direction.

"That's fine with me," Claire agreed heading for the back stairwell. "Thank you for everything Sarah."

After peeking in on her slumbering child, Claire crawled into bed. Seemingly without a moment of hesitation she drifted into a sleep that saw her weary body through until the dawn of the next day.

Chapter Ten

The next morning, Claire awoke feeling as though she had slept for an eternity. Lying in the soft warm bed, she stretched her arms into the air recalling that she had several disturbing nightmares involving Jacob. Closing her eyes tightly as if trying to expunge the frightening images from her mind, she verbally committed that it would be the day that she set things right.

After showering and dressing in the same clothes she had worn the day prior, Claire ventured down to the kitchen to be met with the familiar aroma of Sarah's fresh coffee.

"Here you are dear! Sit down and I'll take care of you right away!"

Claire laughed at the controlling woman who insisted upon directing her every move as though she was a small child.

Hearing the back door swing open, Claire watched as Joe entered the kitchen through the rear entrance where the tired old wallpaper was beginning to peel in several noticeable places.

"Morning!" Joe bid her as he set down a plastic bag on the table full of Claire's clothing. "That's me just coming back from the cottage. I figured you might want to take Michael home with you sometime later today. So Sarah suggested that I go over there and have a look first," the old man admitted. "Mike also told me to get you some more clothes while I was there," he added, embarrassed that he had entered the private realm of Claire's bedroom.

Claire laughed, thinking of how genuine Joe was.

"Don't know if I got the right stuff or not," the farmer confessed as he hung his coat and hat on the wall rack. "Don't know if it all matches or not, but I figured...hell...at least it was clean."

Amused by the old man's ambition, Claire reached into the bag to see that Joe had picked out a striped woolen sweater and three t-shirts.

"These will do very nicely," she replied smiling with gratitude.

Clearly Joe was uncomfortable with the task and had evidently done his best. Claire swept the bag from the table and entered the downstairs washroom to change into the striped sweater.

"Now Claire dear, I'll be happy to watch Michael today if you have anything else you need to do!" Sarah offered as she returned from the lower washroom.

"Thank you so much Sarah. Actually I do have a few things I'd like to get done today if you don't mind," she responded with relief.

But she also knew that Sarah loved spending every available minute with her son Michael.

After taking a lasting sip of coffee from her oversized mug, Claire set the cup in the sparkling clean sink and headed toward the door.

"Oh my goodness!" she exclaimed as she peered out the kitchen window. "Who brought my car over here?"

"Mike and Joe went over and picked it up for you last night while you were sleeping dear. They thought you might like to have your own wheels back," Sarah replied as she hustled about the kitchen. "Now it's almost eleven o'clock dear, so you get on your way and get your errands done. Michael will be just fine here with me. I'll give him his bath and we'll have a lovely day together. I'll keep him as long as you need me to," the elderly woman offered half pleading to have the entire day with the beloved little boy.

Claire smiled as she slung her arms through the sleeves of her coat. "Okay then, I'll see you later on."

Sarah rushed across the floor and started up the stairs after fluttering her pudgy fingers in Claire's direction.

The first thing on Claire's list was to go to Mike's office. She knew she had to talk with him and get it all settled in her mind. Arriving at the familiar office, Claire parked her car in the front and ran up the stairs until she reached the door she was looking for. Her adrenalin pumped as she gained momentum. With a refreshing clarity and a new determination to set things right, Claire bounced through the entranceway of the firm.

"Morning Bernice," she stridently announced her presence to the woman who was startled by the intrusion.

Bernice was at a complete loss for words as she instinctively waved at the woman she hadn't seen for several months. Slowing her pace as she reached Mike's office she excitedly poked her head out from around the corner.

"Good Morning!"

Mike raised his eyes from the stack of papers in front of him and smiled. "The file folder is on your desk Claire," he confirmed without having been asked.

Amused by the fact that he knew exactly what she had come for, she tapped her left hand anxiously on his doorframe and disappeared into her former office. Snatching up the single white folder that sat in the center of the vacant desk, Claire quickly peeled the front cover back as her eyes searched for the information she required. While scanning the pages she walked slowly back to Mike's office ready to have the long awaited talk with him. But this time Mike was expecting her. She returned to the doorway as her eyes searched his, not wanting to hurt him in anyway.

"It's okay Claire. I mean it! I'm really okay with this," he stated convincingly as he rounded the corner of his desk and approached her in the doorway. "I know what you need to do. I think I've known it all along."

Claire stared deeply into his eyes feeling more relief as each understanding word fell from his lips.

"I know you belong with Luke. I know Luke is Michael's father and I know that is where he belongs as well. I only ask you," Mike's tone turned to a plea, "please allow my parents and I to stay a part of Michael's life. We love that little boy and we can't lose him now."

Claire's eyes danced with happiness as she stepped forward and flung her arms around his neck.

"I'm so sorry if I've hurt you in anyway Mike. I'll always love you and your parents and you'll always be a part of our lives. I promise!"

Mike pulled back from Claire's embrace after she planted an affectionate kiss on his right cheek.

"Go on now," he urged her. "Go and do…whatever it is that you have to do!"

Mike smiled adoringly at the elated woman in front of him. Claire turned to rush out the door as Mike called after her.

"Hey Claire!"

Catching her attention she spun around on the carpet and nodded in question.

"Luke is now living at 673 Oakwood Street here in Yorkton. He moved from the farm about a month ago!"

"Thanks!" she hollered back at him as a feeling of sadness overcame her realizing that the bank had indeed foreclosed on his farm.

Regaining her momentum, Claire rushed from the office and darted to her car. Feeling as if she had to catch Luke from disappearing from her life again she drove quickly to the hospital.

Without missing a beat, she leapt from her car, ran into the medical center and impatiently pounded on the button outside the elevator. After making several stops at other floors, the elevator finally drew it's mighty doors open and Claire rushed out. Needing to see Luke immediately, she walked briskly down the hallway and pounced through the door of his room. In horror she saw that the bed was empty. She noticed that the room had been cleaned and prepared for the next patient. Panic stricken, Claire dashed back to the nurse's station and snapped at the first nurse she could find.

"Mr. Johnston...Luke Johnston...where is he?"

Clearly irritated with Claire's abrasive approach, the nurse lifted her head from her paperwork. "He's gone home!" the nurse lipped back with sarcasm. "He insisted upon leaving earlier this morning!"

"Thank you!" Claire replied out of breath.

Quickly she turned and rushed down the stairs.

After returning to her car she forced herself to sit and calm her thrashing emotions before taking the next step. Within a few moments her motives became clear. Claire drove directly to the city bank. Using her aggressive legal skills she arrived at the reception area and insisted upon meeting with the branch manager immediately.

After impatiently pacing back and forth across the front desk Claire was eventually escorted to the office of Mr. William Goldman.

"Good Morning! I need to move some of my money around!" Claire stated boldly as the bank manager waved his arm toward the empty chair across from his desk.

"Well certainly! How exactly can I help you?" the polished financial expert cordially agreed. Claire swung the office door closed behind her wanting her dealings with the bank to remain strictly confidential. Given Claire's wealthy status, her requests were tended to immediately. Within thirty minutes, still clutching the white file folder under her arm she scurried back to her car.

"Now Luke...we shall finally meet again," she proclaimed as she maneuvered the city streets searching for Oakwood.

As she drove to the outskirts of the lovely farm community, Claire's rapidly beating heart began to slow as she followed the banker's directions to Luke's new address. Eventually she brought her car to a graceful halt stopping just outside 673 Oakwood Street. Dropping the white folder onto the passenger seat, Claire despairingly stepped from the vehicle and into a pothole.

Entranced by the state of the dilapidated apartment building, she noticed that several of the windows had large cracks across the glass. The exterior paint was peeling badly and garbage had been sorrowfully piled up around the entranceway. Hesitantly she climbed the five stairs of cracked concrete and stepped through the doorframe, noticing that the door was missing altogether. Running her index finger down the occupant's board she stopped at Luke Johnston's name.

"Apartment #3."

Nervously glancing over her shoulder she walked with uncertainty down the damp, cold corridor. She noticed that all but one light bulb had burnt out in the hallway ceiling as she squinted through the darkness to read the hand painted numbers on the doors.

Then finally, Claire approached apartment number three. First, pressing her right ear to the door, she listened for activity inside the rundown dwelling. Then taking a deep sigh, pulling the courage she required from the depths of her soul, Claire knocked three times on the flimsy door. With anxious anticipation, she heard no response from beyond. Aggressively she knocked loudly a second time and with the final rap of her knuckles the door opened slightly. Still there was no sound from within. Realizing that the lock was broken, Claire passed hesitantly through the shabby entranceway.

"Luke?" she whispered timidly as she peered into the meager apartment. Taking another step inward she called out a second time, "Luke?"

But still there was no answer. Her initial apprehension evolved into fear as she quietly wandered through the sparsely furnished apartment. It was a pitiful sight. Unmistakably, it was the residence of a defeated individual. With a torn sofa in one corner of the small living room and an ancient floor model television in the other, Claire was overcome with shame. She felt responsible that Luke had been sentenced to live in such conditions. The atmosphere reeked of someone who had lost all hope. The only evident sign of life in the small dark apartment was that of a wilted long stem red rose propped in a short glass, half-filled with murky gray water.

Unwilling to relent, Claire ventured on toward the closed door to what she assumed was a bedroom and again she knocked.

"Luke," she whispered through the crack in the door.

Then holding her breath, terrified of what she would find in the next room, she clasp the wobbly door handle in the palm of her hand and turned it slowly to the right. Pushing the door open only inches, Claire peered in and saw that a dark figure was lying in the center of a sagging double bed.

"Luke?"

Alerted to her voice, the man painstakingly rolled over onto his back and tried to focus through the darkness on the approaching face.

"Claire?" he responded sleepily.

"Yes," she replied with relief recognizing the familiar tone of his voice.

While attempting to push himself up from his back he probed weakly, "How did you get here? How did you find me?"

Losing his balance Luke fell backward as a lightening bolt of pain stabbed through his throbbing head. Seeing the unstable man struggle, Claire shoved the bedroom door open wide and rushed to his side.

"I'm so sorry," she began to weep as she pressed her face tenderly into his neck. "I'm so sorry for putting you through all of this."

Luke said nothing as he placed his head back down on the pillow and closed his eyes. Gently he swept his left hand over the bandage on his forehead as if to verify that he was not hallucinating. Reaching out with his right hand he ran his massive fingers through the length of Claire's cocoa brown hair. Overcome by her presence, his eyes formed huge gushing tears that soon began to spill down his face as he bathed himself in the sweet scent of her hair.

"Are you okay Claire? I was so scared for you that night," he attempted to speak. "I had searched for you for nearly three years. I looked everywhere. I tried everything. I went to New York City seven times. I couldn't get through on your cell phone. The more time passed, the more obsessed I became with finding you. It was like you were only a dream."

Claire lifted her face from where it was hidden and with tears of anguish pouring down her cheeks, she listened attentively as Luke stumbled weakly over his words.

"I stopped driving my truck. I stopped tending my farm. I just needed to find you! I had to find you!" Luke wiped his drenched face with the back of his hand then continued, needing to tell her everything before she vanished again. "Then just as the bank was about to take everything, you sat down in front of me. I was blown away Claire. I was in shock! I couldn't believe it was really you! And then…and then you got so angry with me and disappeared again. I went back to your office but Mike wouldn't give me any personal information about you. He told me that he couldn't! So I started to follow him at night. Night after night I followed him in my old pick-up truck. The truck was the only thing that the bank didn't take from me," he added with a weak chuckle. "Then about a month ago, I followed him to your house. I saw Mike turn in to what looked like an overgrown field. So I parked my truck on the highway and walked in during the night. Finally, I found out where you lived…but knowing how angry you were with me, I just couldn't get myself to walk up to the door. So night after night I sat in my truck at the end of your road."

Claire stared in disbelief listening intently to every word.

"Then the other night, I was sitting there just off to the side of the highway. I saw Mike enter your property and then leave again shortly after. I was just about to drive away when I saw some other guy pull in. He was driving a black Chevrolet. I think he was waiting for Mike to leave before he went in. I needed

160

to know who he was. I had to find out! So I left my truck and walked the rest of the way up to the house. It took me a few minutes to get there and when I looked through the window I saw him holding a gun to your head. I lost it Claire! I didn't care who the fuck he was! I just wanted to kill him! When I saw what he was doing to you, I wanted to crush him with my bare hands." Luke paused, getting increasingly more upset as he told his story. "So I broke through your door and well...well...I guess you know the rest!" he conceded as he mopped the river of tears from his face a second time.

"I just don't know what else to say Luke other than I'm sorry. I'm so sorry for hurting you. I'm sorry that your lifestyle changed so drastically because of me. But most of all I'm sorry that you were hurt the other night on my account."

"They told me yesterday at the hospital that asshole is dead! Were they right Claire? Is he dead?" he probed anxiously still running his fingers through her locks of silky hair.

"Yes...Jacob is gone. He was intent on killing me that night. You saved my life Luke."

"Good then," he stated with satisfaction still not knowing who Jacob was.

"Hey there listen," Claire felt it was time to repay her insurmountable debt to him. "We can talk about all of that later, but right now..." Luke turned his head in her direction as she knelt on the floor beside the bed. "Right now I would just love to show you a couple of things if you'll let me." Claire's toned melted as she shyly withdrew into awkwardness.

Luke smiled listening to her sweet voice. "Lady...I'll go with you anywhere you want. Take me...I'm all yours," he joked as he pushed himself up from the bed.

Claire pulled Luke's brown leather jacket from the back of a chair and slid it up onto his shoulders. Wrapping her left arm tightly around his waist, the two walked along the dimly lit hallway and down the front steps.

"Ah yes...the infamous black BMW," he mocked noticing Claire's vehicle parked at the side of the road. "That is where it all began!"

Smiling into each other's eyes, Claire opened the passenger door and Luke slid his lean muscular body onto the black leather seat. Closing the door, she darted exuberantly around the vehicle and plunged herself in behind the steering wheel. Bounding with excitement she could barely contain herself.

Claire allowed silence to fall between them as she smiled to herself. Without a word she drove back through the city center of Yorkton and out the other side of town. Sensing that Luke was staring at her profile she turned to meet with his gaze.

"You are so beautiful," he confessed as he reached out and took her right hand into his own. Raising her hand upward, he pressed his lips longingly against the silken skin on the back of her hand. Then turning it over, he placed her fingers gently against his dark unshaven cheek craving the feel of her flesh. Darting her eyes from Luke to the road and back again, she tilted her head as if wondering what he was thinking.

"I just want to make sure that I'm not dreaming again," he explained. "I want to be sure you're really here sitting beside me."

Claire could contain herself no longer. Swiftly she geared her vehicle down and pulled off to the side of the road all the while Luke wondered what had caused her to stop. Equally needing the reassurance she turned to him. Leaning over the console, she slid both hands up and along his gaunt cheekbones noticing how much weight he had lost since she last touched his face. Gently she pulled him toward her and pressed her shimmering lips against his. Passionately they kissed as the loneliness they had both endured dissolved around them.

"It's really me," the aroused woman mumbled as his lips hungrily consumed hers. "We'll never be apart again, I promise!"

Luke pulled back to stare lovingly into her eyes. Acknowledging his gaze Claire wheeled her car back out onto the road. Refusing to let go of her right hand, he caressed it tenderly needing to feel her delicate skin against his own. Driving on for over ten minutes it appeared to Luke that Claire wasn't exactly sure where she was going.

"So! Where are you taking me?" he joked with his beautiful driver.

With a secretive grin widening across her lips Claire turned to look at Luke. She winked a sparkling green eye in his direction and then drove on in silence. Several moments passed as they journeyed together admiring the lush prairie countryside that would soon bloom into a sea of spring wheat.

"I think I turn here," she muttered quietly trying to recall the directions by memory.

Glancing at Luke a second time she noticed his facial expression change to a sorrowful frown as his farm property came into sight. Saying nothing, Claire drove on until she noticed the *"For Sale"* sign flapping in the gentle breeze at the side of the road. Luke's body slunk deeper into the leather seat as Claire maneuvered the vehicle onto the familiar property. Lowering his eyes to the floorboards, his face was smeared with gloom as she drove up the long stretching driveway of his former estate. Luke stared out the window of the car in misery as the BMW came to a halt at the front of the house,

"Come on, let's go!" Claire invited him with excitement, her face beaming happily as she stepped from the vehicle.

"Go where?" he inquired in a crushed tone as he watched her walk around the car and out onto the front lawn. Prying his long body from the plush interior, he stretched his voice to meet with Claire's ears as she stomped off toward the real estate sign that protruded from the grass.

"Did you know that this use to be my farm Claire?"

"Yes, as a matter of fact I was aware of that!" she shouted back nonchalantly. Pausing for only a moment she stopped to admire the red brick structure of the century farmhouse. "But do you know what Luke?" she stated to the defeated individual who stood gawking around the property with his hands jammed into the front pockets of his jeans. Claire pulled at the sign with all of her might, grunting and groaning until she yanked the post from the soft ground. "It still is your farm!" she continued to speak from thirty feet away.

"What?" Luke's voice puzzled as he turned and walked hastily toward her.

"I said…it still is your farm!" she confirmed brushing the dirt from her hands.

Together they met on the front lawn and only after she had embraced his waist with her arms did she attentively listen to his questions.

"What's this all about? I don't understand."

"Well," Claire ventured to explain, "let me put it this way…I'm only giving back to you…what I took away."

Shaking his head in disbelief, he turned to look at the house a second time. "But I still don't understand…where did you…how did you get the money?"

"I'll explain it all later. But for now, let's get you moved back in where you belong," she cut him off in mid sentence.

Then playfully taking Luke by the hand, she pulled the key to the front door from the pocket of her coat. After unlatching the deadbolt she led him into the grand mahogany entrance.

"Oh my goodness! This is so beautiful Luke!" she exclaimed with delight, her eyes quickly scanning the sensational old home.

The house and all the furnishings had been left untouched since the day Luke had been ordered to vacate the premises. The bewildered cowboy stared at the woman he loved as he leaned against the doorframe in the entranceway. His royal blue eyes penetrated deeply into her soul warming her body all over causing her to turn around and lock with his vision.

"Now there's something I would like to show you!" he stated mischievously as he took her by the hand and led her up the massive antique staircase.

Luke's leather boots pounded heavily upon each step as he retained his tender grip on Claire's fragile hand. Slowly he led her to the master bedroom in which he had spent so many lonely sleepless nights during his search for her. Pulling his coat from his shoulders, he instinctively cast his stabbing headache aside. Without a moment of hesitation he pulled Claire into his arms and began kissing her sensuous lips as he unleashed three years of wanting upon the woman he yearned for. Never removing her lips from his, Claire's body surged with the love she had denied as she pulled her coat from her torso and eagerly tore at Luke's clothing.

In an all-consuming fire of passion, the couple undressed each other as their bodies tumbled into the massive king sized bed. Rolling and turning beneath the sheets with nothing but sweat between their nudity, the love they had experienced together almost three years prior returned with a vengeance. Passionately they pressed their skin against each other searching wildly for the satisfaction they both craved.

Ferverently they entwined, winding their limbs around the other. Drowning in a sea of pleasure, they lust hungrily for satisfaction as their thighs pressed anxiously together. Their souls became one…a reunification above and beyond their previous encounter of intimacy.

After two hours they both lay spent and exhausted within each other's arms. Neither drifted off to sleep, terrified to lose sight of the love they had once lost.

The late afternoon sun warmed the window glass as time snuck past. Still lazily snuggled together, they each shared their experiences of the previous three years and the events that led up to that moment. Claire enlightened Luke on her miserable childhood and of Amelia's death. She spoke of her father's passing and the sizable inheritance he left behind for her. She could feel Luke's body tense within her arms as she spoke of how she struggled through the years of Jacob's abuse. As the sun started its decent from the sky, Claire had finally shared her entire story with the man who wanted to know everything about her.

Once all the words had been spoken, Claire knew it was time for the next step.

"Will you come with me somewhere Luke?"

His eyes widened nervously as he pulled his embrace tighter around Claire's torso, fearing to ever let her go again.

Then as his lips widened into a playful grin, he kissed her nose and whispered, "My love…I'll go anywhere you want. As a matter of fact, I plan on following you for the rest of my life."

Claire laughed at his childish implication and then pulling herself from his embrace she slid from beneath the cotton sheets and began getting dressed.

"So," Luke hurried to follow her lead as he pulled his jeans up over his muscular thighs. "Where are you taking me this time?"

"Well… there are some people I'd like you to meet," she responded nervously without raising her eyes.

"Okay! Sounds good," he replied with an incurable lack of curiosity.

He had undoubtedly found the missing link in his life. Nothing else mattered nearly as much…or so he thought. Then without question, he buttoned his shirt, reached for his coat and followed Claire as she lightheartedly descended the stairs. The two lovers got into the car and drove from the property heading toward Joe's farm.

Claire said nothing as she sped through the countryside. She wasn't exactly sure what to tell Luke about where she was taking him. But she did know the time had come to be brutally honest. It was time to tell him everything.

Unsure of where he was been driven, Luke gazed lovingly at Claire's profile still partially in denial that they were together at last. Leaning over and placing an adoring kiss on her delicate earlobe he finally probed. "So beautiful... where are you taking me now? I simply loved your first surprise!"

"Well...first thing tomorrow morning we're going to buy you a new pick-up truck," she tried to distract him. "But right now...right now I'm taking you to meet someone very special."

Satisfied for the moment, Luke smiled to himself feeling whole once again within the company of the woman he loved.

"Money...doesn't mean anything to me Claire. I hope you realize that," he assured her thinking about her fortune.

"I expected that Luke. Believe me when I say...I know first hand that money doesn't solve all your problems. I've always had plenty of money, but all the riches in the world couldn't stop Amelia from dying or my father from beating me or Jacob from making my life a living hell."

Claire turned left into Joe's farm as she geared down from the highway. Nervously she drove her shimmering black convertible up to the farmhouse. After taking a deep breath she yanked the emergency brake into place and turned off the engine.

"Come on in," Claire invited him as they both unlatched their doors at the same time.

Claire hesitantly approached the front door unsure of what Luke's reaction might be. He followed the petite woman only a few feet behind as he admired the mature farm estate. Before Claire reached the concrete steps, the door burst wide open and little Michael screeched excitedly as he saw his mother approaching.

"Mommy! Mommy! Nana, mommy's here!" the jubilant child darted through the screen door in a mission to seek his mother's attention. Dressed adoringly in striped overalls and a navy blue turtleneck, Michael paused only briefly to carefully maneuver the stairs then ran full tilt to be swept up into his mother's arms. Claire was equally pleased to see her child as she flung him happily in the air, catching and swirling him around in a full spin.

"Hello my darling!" she greeted her toddler as she playfully covered his face with sloppy wet kisses. Sarah stood in the doorway of the house smiling as she watched the happy reunion from the distance. Then as Claire turned to meet with a paralyzing stare from Luke, Sarah disappeared from view allowing them the privacy they needed at that very special moment.

"Luke…" Claire spoke softly to the man that was visually captivated by the young boy she held. "I'd like you to meet my son Michael."

Mesmerized by the child, Luke stared deeply into his teardrop, royal blue eyes as if he was looking into his own mirror image. Stepping closer he gently touched Michael's tiny arm.

"But Claire…you didn't tell me that you had a second child."

Claire watched as Luke seemed mystified by the child she held in her arms.

"How…how old is he?" the bewildered cowboy stumbled over his own words trying to prioritize the multitude of questions that were bashing through his confused brain.

"Michael is two years old," she confirmed as the child wiggled playfully within her arms. Pulling his hand back from the toddler Luke said nothing, standing in question but never removing his trance from the eyes of the glorious child.

"Luke?" Claire continued in a soft voice. "My son's name is Michael, Lucas Morgan."

Hearing the child's full name Luke's face went drawn and pale as if he was about to lose consciousness. Taking a step backward, he shook his head realizing exactly whom he was staring at.

"Luke?" Claire advanced toward the man who had massive tears welling up in the corners of his eyes. "I'd like to introduce you to your son."

Hearing her confirmation of the truth, Luke instantly covered his mouth with his hand in disbelief. Tears streamed down his weather beaten face as his pleading eyes met with Claire's.

"Do you mean?" he fumbled for the words overcome by emotion.

"Yes," Claire responded to the astounded cowboy. "Yes Luke! Michael is your son."

Michael's eyes darted in question between his parents trying to understand the nature of their dialogue.

"Michael sweetheart," Claire whispered to her unknowing toddler. "I'd like you to meet your daddy."

Luke reached his arms out pleading to hold his son as he stared at the wonder of him for a long silent moment. Claire placed the boy down on the grass allowing him to approach his father at his own pace. Luke bent down on one knee and lovingly extended his arms a second time. Instantly Michael rushed to his father where he was pulled into a giant bear hug, his father pressing his unshaven cheek into the mass of blond curls. Holding the tiny boy, Luke wept with shear joy.

"Oh my God Claire! Thank you! How do I ever thank you for completing my life?" Kneeling on the grass, Luke rocked back and forth as his son happily flung his arms around his father's neck enchanted with the introduction. Then after a long endearing moment, slightly bothered by the tight embrace, Michael started to squirm. Releasing himself from his father's hold, the boy turned and playfully looked into his weeping blue eyes.

"Let's play daddy! Let's play!"

Michael rushed across the lawn to seek a ball that sat in a puddle of lasting slush on the grass. Claire stood back watching as Luke broke into a beaming smile of pride. The child fumbled over his little feet, kicking the ball in small strides in his father's direction. Luke laughed through his sodden eyes as the child headed for him with the soccer ball.

"Play daddy! Let's play!"

Claire leaned back against the car and watched the joyous scene feeling her heart nearly explode with happiness. Her life was complete as she watched the two special men kick the soccer ball around the lawn then teasingly wrestle on the slushy wet grass.

Michael quickly accepted his birth father.   The bond of love was immediately formed. Finally their struggle was over! Finally their broken lives were made whole. They were a family!

Laughing as the father and son jokingly tumbled about the front lawn, Claire glanced up to see Sarah, Joe and Mike peaking through the blinds in the kitchen window though trying to stay unnoticed.

"Hey guys," she extended her hand out toward them as she headed for the front door of the farmhouse, "let's go inside for a minute."

Luke swept his son up into his arms and jetted toward the front door as Michael giggled feverishly. Tucking the boy's tiny legs in against his torso Luke followed Claire up the front steps.

Scurrying to make themselves busy, Mike and his parents quickly grabbed their coffee cups from the counter and sat down abruptly at the kitchen table. Beaming with contentment Claire swung the front door open and the new family ventured into the kitchen for further introductions.

"Hello dear!" Sarah greeted, her heart overcome with bittersweet happiness for what she had just witnessed through the window.

"Luke! I'd like you to meet Mike's parents, Sarah and Joe. They have been wonderful to Michael and I. We have adopted them as Michael's full time grandparents," Claire spoke happily unable to contain the pleasure she was feeling.

Luke stretched a hand out to greet the old farm couple.

"Nice to meet you both," he responded as they stood from their chairs and shook his hand.

"And of course you know Mike," Claire added as Mike raised his eyes to meet with Luke's.

Mike stood from the table and forced out a smile, fighting back his own tears.

"Mike has been everything to us!" Claire proclaimed aware of the sadness behind his eyes. "I don't know where I'd be right now if it weren't for Mike," she continued, passing along the credit that her very special friend deserved.

Claire reached up and placed a loving kiss on Mike's cheek as he fought back his surging emotion. After passing Michael back to his mother, Luke stepped toward the man that he knew had reunited him with his lost love. His eyes flooded with huge crystal tears as Luke struggled to speak.

"Man…I know I will never be able to thank you enough for what you've done for me Mike!"

Luke swung his massive arms around Mike's shoulders as his emotions caved. "Thank you Mike!" he wept. "I just don't know how to thank you!"

With tears streaming down both of their faces the two men gave each other a hearty pat on the back.

"Well let me just remind you of how lucky you are Luke…because I sure wanted to keep them both for myself!" Mike joked as he sat back down at the table.

Luke nodded with total understanding realizing instantly how much Mike loved Claire and her son. Wiping the tears from his cheeks Luke turned and took Michael back into his arms.

"Thank you all!" the grateful cowboy repeated. "Thank you for everything you've done! It's a debt I don't think I'll ever be able to repay."

Claire winked at Mike fully aware of the emotion he was suppressing. Then after picking up Michael's coat and baby bag, she directed her new family toward the front door.

"Thanks for everything folks!" she regressed. "We'll see you all again very soon!"

With a nod of gratitude, Luke carried his son out of the house and over to the car. While at the same time Claire strode over to Mike and swung her arms around his neck once again.

"I'll always love you Mike! Thank you for not giving up on me!"

Mike clutched Claire warmly against his body not wanting to let her go but knowing he had to.

"I love you too and don't you ever forget it," he whispered in her ear. "But it's good to see you all together at last," he choked on his words. "It's good to see you truly happy!"

Mike released the slender woman from his embrace as his parent's watched on. They knew how much their son had grown to love Claire and Michael but they also knew that all was now as it should be.

Claire walked to the front door and after pushing herself half through it she turned around unexpectedly.

"Hey lawyer! I'll be at work on Monday! Is that okay with you?"

Mike raised his eyes from the table and smiled at her comment. "Okay! But this time you get the small office and I get the big one!" he joked back at her.

"Can you take Michael on Monday Sarah…business as usual? Luke will likely have some spring planting to attend to," Claire inquired still laughing at Mike's comment about the offices.

"I'd love to," the jovial woman responded with relief knowing that her beloved grandchild would be with her once again on a regular basis.

With a wink and an obliging smile, Claire left the house.

Luke stood at the car door holding Michael as Claire approached them, her heart full of admiration and happiness.

Swinging her arms around them both she stated, "Let's go home!"

The new family ventured home to the cottage. Without a thought for what had happened there a few nights earlier, they lit a roaring fire and enjoyed their first evening meal together as a family. Then beaming with pride, Luke tucked his son securely into bed and read a story to the sleepy child.

After an hour had passed Claire arose from the sofa and pushed the bedroom door slightly open. Her life was complete as she peered into the dimly lit bedroom. She saw Luke sound asleep, lying beside his child with his arm placed securely over his son's waist. Claire felt at peace. Her spirit soared. She had found the inner serenity she had long searched for. She found it asleep in her child's bedroom.

A month passed as the new family bonded together in the little cottage. Then she appeared… with her slender fingers wrapped around Joe's quivering arm, the suited old man escorted her across the front porch and down the stairs. Her thin shapely body was draped in an elegant antique gown that naturally followed the trim contour of her hips. Her hair was loosely swept up at the back of her neck held by a single ivory clip, accented with tiny clusters of baby's breath. In stunning contrast to her purity, she held a flowing bouquet of red roses within her grasp. Michael stood smiling at his mother as he waited by the creek with Sarah at his side. He was handsomely dressed in a miniature black tuxedo.

The rippling whisper of the creek hushed its contribution of nature at the simple April wedding. The minister before them invited the couple to join hands. Luke could not pull his gaze from Claire's breathtaking presence. His magnificent stature carried a midnight black tuxedo adorned with a single red rose pinned to his lapel.

With Mike standing by his side, Luke reached out and took Claire's hand within his own as they were spiritually joined together in holy matrimony. The day of love was perfect as the warm spring sun beamed down upon the harmonious scene of splendor.

Several weeks after the wedding, the well-acquainted family moved into the century home on Luke's farm.

Then after the following summer and season of fall harvest passed by, then Christmas and on into the next year of spring planting, a beautiful rainbow shone down from the heavens. The magnificent band of color hovered over the hospital in Yorkton as Claire gave birth to a baby girl…a precious gift sent from the glory above as Amelia kept her spiritual watch over them. The angelic babe was christened Sarah, Elizabeth Johnston.

About The Author

An eternal optimist, Judy MacPherson serves as an inspirational speaker and author for those who have been inundated with adversity. Having overcome a lifetime of tragedy, she has achieved personal healing and now lives with serenity and fulfillment, remaining fully committed to her dreams and quest for opportunity.

In Ontario, Canada, she lives with passion. Her writing leaves the reader spellbound, riveted to the pages and emotionally enthralled as she strives to touch upon every sentiment of the soul.

Printed in the United States
17590LVS00007B/1-81